1

DARKEST DECEPTION

AKWAAH K

DARKEST DECEPTION
Editing: Kaye Polishing

For those who want a villain with an extreme obsession.
Helia's waiting for you on the dark side.

DECEPTION ORDER

SWEETEST DECEPTION
BITTER DECEPTION
DARKEST DECEPTION

AUTHOR'S NOTE

This is not a dark romance but has a few elements that could be under this sector. This book is book 3 in the Deception series. However, it can be read as a standalone though some questions about side characters may be left unasnwered. This is not a Mafia series. For better understanding of the characters, it is reccomended to read the series in order.

SOCIAL MEDIA:

Instagram: _akwaah_
Twitter: akwaah1
Amazon: Akwaah K
Goodreads: Akwaah K

TRIGGER WARNINGS:

Descriptive scenes of stalking, light dub non con, mentions of suicidal thoughts, use of gun, blood, torture, gore, blackmail, domestic violence, bullying, assault, violence, death and profanity.

This book contains sexual content not intended for minors.

Your mental health matters so if any of these triggers may affect you, please skip this book. You should take care of yourself first before diving into a book that could trigger bad memories or affect you negatively in any way.

DARKEST DECEPTION

Emerald green eyes and ink black hair.

He's become the very thing that I am.

A tormentor. My nightmare personified. My very own hell on earth.

He took from me until there was nothing left, he took what was rightfully mine and yet in this world of deception, in this world where the villains take reign, there is no right or wrong.

There is no peace or justice.

No matter if I see myself change, the very man with serpent eyes and the scar running down his eye that are brimming with hate for me, is set on bringing me to my knees to pay for what I had done.

We both hide secrets, we both fight back but can we really move past this deception we put in front of us and see that something more powerful is on the rise between us?

That the most unlikely two people to deserve love have been given a chance?

PROLOGUE

No one should be happy that their parents are dead. And yet, here I am, standing with a masked smile at my father's funeral.

Rain pours in sheets from heavy, dark clouds, an appropriate accompaniment for the crowd's sombre expressions and attire. The black suits and modest dresses scattered in front of the church fit in, but the melancholy atmosphere never quite settles properly. The paparazzi are pressed against the metal gate of the church just a couple of feet away from the burial site. Their cameras keep flashing in bright starbursts, shattering the shroud of solemn observance, a news bomb ready to detonate and change everyone's lives.

My head is bowed, my face partially shielded. My mouth is pinched in sorrow, eyebrows furrowed and shoulders held tight, but all I feel is freedom.

From his clutches, from his ruthlessness, and from the vise grip he had around my throat.

I am breathing.

I am alive.

And I will conquer his empire.

My empire. My rightful empire.

All everyone sees is a daughter mourning her loving father's death. But my soul is ascending to the highest heavens. I will soar, but then I'll plummet into the darkest pits of hell right after.

Lying is a sin.

Deception is a sin.

And, in my world, happiness is also a sin.

And I will be committing every single one.

The death of a monster should always be celebrated.

1
AMBROSE

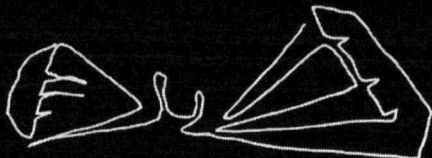

Apparently, I have been fired.

I am about to find out exactly why I have been let go when this whole company is supposed to be mine. No one has as much power as me within Glamorous, so the letter in my hand is meaningless.

My footsteps echo down the hallway with each heel-strike against the marble floor as I pass by managers' offices on the thirtieth floor of the Glamorous building. The faint murmurs of hushed conversations and the shuffling of feet and papers pierce my ears as I pass. My heart pounds, and I brace myself for something big as I stride past everyone to the end of the hallway.

This tall building will be under my name. This is all mine.

All that is left is the announcement.

My younger sister has no interest in Glamorous, too busy

with her own fashion line. But these two towers? They are mine. I am about to inherit the empire my father has built, and nothing will stop me.

Not even this piece of paper.

I reach the brown oak door decorated with a golden plate.

Chief Executive Officer.

Under it will be engraved *Ambrose Torre*. That thought alone has me jittery with happy nerves.

Opening the door to the office, I walk inside, ready to set in place whoever sent me this letter, but I come to a screeching stop.

It's not the temporary CEO the company assigned, obvious from the lack of grey hair and the missing beer belly.

Rather, a man I have never seen before is in his place. He's tall and dressed in a midnight-black suit. The double-breasted suit highlights his lean figure and long legs. My gaze catches on his polished shoe, which is casually crossed over his other knee. My eyes glide up his body, and I suck in a sharp breath at the intensity rolling off him.

It feels as if the whole office is holding a breath as our eyes collide.

He has the deepest emerald-green eyes I have ever seen. A faint scar runs down his left eyebrow to his eyelid, and the sharpness around his features gives him a distinct serpentine aspect.

Something about the darkness within the office and his ability to stop me in my tracks, to have my heart thumping loud enough to be drumming in my ears, has me in a chokehold. His jet-black locks of hair fall into his eyes and yet it looks neat, intentional, enhancing his predatory look.

There is a twisted smirk on his lips, lips that taunt.

"Who are you?" My voice is steady, despite how I feel under the attention of those snake eyes.

Nothing about him seems normal. Not his wicked smirk, his dark eyes, and certainly not the fluid way he moves as he walks around the table. His intense gaze has me captivated, unable to escape the trap he has put me in, no matter how hard I force myself to look away from his eyes. The wicked look in them almost has me stepping back in fear he may pounce on me to destroy me, to eat me alive.

My fingers tighten around the piece of paper in my hand. The crinkle sounds too loud in the quiet office.

"Miss Ambrose Torre."

My name drips like poison from his lips. A sweet poison that makes me swallow hard. It jerks at my stomach, like he is holding my heart and twisting the organ until pain pierces my chest at just the mention of my name.

"I have been waiting for you. Did you receive my gift?"

Crossing my arms, I keep my eyes levelled with his. I won't let him intimidate me, no matter the intensity with which he looks at me. I have a feeling that few people can look him in the eyes.

"So you sent me this joke? Do you know *who* you sent this letter to?" I scrunch the paper into a ball and throw it at his face.

He closes his eyes, inhales, then slowly opens them, fixing his cold gaze on me.

The atmosphere shifts in the room. Those calm, dark emerald eyes turn cruel, and within an instant, his face is right in front of mine. My heart leaps.

I almost take a step back. Almost.

The smell of gardenia and dark musk wafts across my face, then curls around me like a snake suffocating its prey. I can only focus on his green eyes. That scar around his left eye taking my focus for a second. He looks the epitome of a venomous serpent.

His eyes drag over me, analysing me, searching for something, a predator studying the vulnerabilities of its prey.

I truly believe there is something sinful and immoral under that cold smirk. I also know he is one of those people who could easily walk someone to their own demise.

"Keep your attitude in check, Ms Torre. Especially since I'm the person who has the ability to blacklist you from every and any company in not only London but the whole of the United goddamn Kingdom."

My spine straightens.

"How dare you threaten me like this? This office you are standing in? It's mine. This whole building is mine, and I will be damned if I let someone like you talk to me like this," I grit out, taking a step away from him, keeping my distance.

The audacity of this man to think he can control and command me like this…

"You have no idea what territory you are walking into,"

I bite out, barely clinging to the calm tone I need.

The man lets out a humourless laugh, and it feels wrong. Like I shouldn't be the one talking to him like this. I don't know him, and I sure as hell don't know what he wants from me or why he's here. Why is he so hell-bent on getting me to leave?

"Oh, this is going to be fun. I'm going to love watching you come crawling back to beg me to grant you a position within your own company. Go do your homework before you come barging in like this with such a disgusting, entitled attitude, little girl."

My mouth drops open with an inaudible gasp.

I take a step back from him as I look around the office, but nothing is out of place. Everything is as it always has been. So what changed?

What is he implying?

Papers fly in my direction. About ten of them land at my feet, covering my heels. The man turns, then strides around the desk. He sinks into the large leather chair and leans back, his watchful eyes on me. Hate slowly fills those cold, dark green eyes, like water poisoned by black ink.

"How dare you throw—"

"Are you raising your voice at me?" He lifts a mocking brow.

Unease and a sick need to throttle him fill me. Rage burns through my veins. Power oozes from him; though he doesn't look like he should be here in this office. He's not refined enough, and there is something deadly about him. I feel certain that if I were to ever cross him, the consequences would be me losing everything.

"Watch that attitude of yours. The mercy I am showing you could easily be retracted. You wouldn't want to displease your employer now, would you?"

Everything around me stops as I try to wrap my head around this information. Everything is slowly slipping out of my grasp.

"Pick up the papers, and you will realise what you just lost." he continues.

The office starts to spin, and a faint headache flares to life behind my eyes.

"As of two days ago, I am the new Chief Executive Officer of Glamorous Magazine, and you have been fired. Effective immediately."

My eyes flick to the papers at my feet. There's a picture and a headline on one of them. I bend down to grab that one. The man before me stands next to my sister's husband at a press conference I wasn't invited to. The headline announces him as the new CEO, placed in that position by Remo Cainn.

Helia Nashwood. The new face of Glamorous.

A line of text catches my attention. The stock price of the magazine is now expected to rise.

In the picture, he actually looks part of this charade he is putting on. He looks like he fits in, with his black suit and eyes that showcase dreams of making this company reach new heights.

Red fills my vision. This whole thing was done by Remo Cainn and this man, Helia Nashwood, behind my back. I don't know what their agenda is, but I will figure it out. How dare he steal what is rightfully mine?

I take a deep breath.

"Is this some sick joke?" I walk over to the desk and slam the papers with his face on it on the shining surface.

When my eyes connect with his, it's a declaration of war. A war of leaders fighting with their full power, trying to kill each other.

"I do like to think I am funny, but in this case, I haven't thrown out a joke yet."

I grit my teeth. He wants me to fight, and he wants to decimate me. He wants to see me lose. I can see it in the fierceness behind those eyes.

"I don't even know you, but you think I will succumb to your little threats?" I grit out, my hands turning clammy.

He clicks his tongue as he looks to the side, the tendons in his neck throbbing. My eyes trace the line of this throat, then catch on a tattoo that peeks out from under his black dress shirt. I clench my jaw and force myself to ignore any hint of curiosity about the tattoo. I need to focus on the task at hand. I will not back away from him.

"You will quickly realise just how much of a mistake you are making by not walking away. I know how to bring people like you to their breaking point, and I've just happened to find myself a new little target. A fierce one with a pretty face and an ugly personality."

My hands tighten into fists. I want to scream in his face, but I am not that stupid. I can admit just how easily he snatched all my power from me.

I am intelligent enough to know just how hard it will be to fight Helia Nashwood.

The devil with emerald eyes.

2

AMBROSE

"I'm sorry, but the legal papers have been signed by both parties. There is nothing we can do."

My lawyer looks down at his hands, trying to avoid eye contact with me. That is what everyone does. They never look me in the eye, but soon I will lose even that power I have over people.

"Fuck!" I swipe my arm across the table, grab the pencil holder, and throw it across the room. Papers fly everywhere. I really am losing everything.

It's been close to a week, and I have been in meeting after meeting. Not a single person is ready or willing to help me get back what is rightfully mine. I wish I could say owning a significant number of shares in my company means something, but the reality is that the contract my father signed to hand the company over to Helia Nashwood is real. He actually signed it. The lawyer showed me the document just now, and it's not a forged document. And that means Helia is now the owner of the shares my father once held. His shares are greater than mine.

Helia has shaken the very ground I stood on. The one thing that I was hoping could keep me sane, the one thing that belonged to me, has been snatched out of my hands and given to a devil whose eyes I am starting to hate.

Sharp eyes filled with poison. He looks like he wants to consume my world, leaving me standing in nothing but ashes of what I had. The scar running down his eye only lends credence to his look. He evokes fear in me, but I will never admit that out loud.

I was the finance manager before Dad died, before the announcement of the new CEO, but now I am uncertain about everything. It's not that I missed going to such an important meeting; it's that I was never told, not invited, when all active board members should have been there.

What will I do?

What do I have left?

I have spent the whole day in my room staring at my laptop screen, scrolling for hours, trying to decide whether I should barge into Helia's office and demand for him to give me back my company or if I should build a case against him that he won't win and take him to court.

I should have made Dad sign the company over to me when he was alive, but he had to go make deals with the wrong people, getting himself killed in the process and leaving absolutely nothing to his family. My mum, Leysa

Torre, left for Glasgow after my father died just two months ago. Since then, I had been preparing myself to take over Glamorous, but as I stood in front of Helia in that office, watching his eyes rake over me in undisguised disgust, it made me reel back and ask myself exactly why he thought so little of me when he didn't even know me.

I have been labelled as rude, spoiled even, and I admit I was privileged, but my work is not something I lack skills in. I am good at what I do. That is undeniable. The success of my father's business is because of me. My decisions. My plans. I have worked for this moment my whole life, waiting for the day my father handed the company over to me.

Only to have some stranger waltz in my life, insult me, and snatch it out of my hands before I can taste the success I was working towards.

I want to know what he knows about me, not because I care about anyone's opinion, but because I need to know who I am fighting against and what he has on me.

I get up, stretch the kinks out of my back, and change into my yoga clothes as the night falls outside. I block everything from the day and the past few months so I can focus on calming my mind.

My curtains flap against the harsh wind outside as I place a yoga mat on the floor in front of the balcony.

I stretch my legs and arms before sitting down in a lotus position. Closing my eyes, I take deep breaths in and out.

Doing yoga at the end of the day helps me keep my mind in check and helps me organise my thoughts.

And then they start.

The voices and screams.

The pained cries.

My body twitches with the reminder of everything from my past.

I force myself to stay still as I try not to move and not recall what happened.

My body starts to strain, my muscles tightening as the screams get louder and louder. My heart clenches inside my chest, and my lip trembles before the pounding in my head starts to take over.

Thump.

Thump.

Thump.

Louder and louder.

My eyes snap open, and I gasp.

My hold on my body fails, and I fall forward. Sweat covers my back and chest. I take deep breaths to level my breathing, but the screams and cries in my mind don't dim.

They never will.

Pressing into my hands and feet, I push up into a downward-facing dog pose, taking deep breaths as I will my body to relax, and let the practise wash away my worries, even if only temporarily.

After a couple of poses, I get into a plank. My arms and upper body start shaking after five minutes, and only then does my mind open and the screams begin once more. The cries for help. The helpless looks on their faces.

I bite my lip to contain my frustration, to just hold on a little longer.

Then all of a sudden, that prickling feeling of being watched slowly crawls up my neck to my head until it rests there, making me stiffen. It's hot, it's terrifying, and it makes me want to curl up in a small corner of my room with my knees up to my chest and shut my eyes tightly.

He's here.

He's here again, and just like clockwork, he has arrived at the exact moment my body breaks.

Like he knows this is my most vulnerable time, the only time when I let my demons take over, just so I can remind myself of the pain I caused others and how I deserve the same.

Nothing I do will fix it.

Instantly, I drop my knees forward and sit up.

With my hands shaking, I look away from the black mat in front of me and turn to glance outside my curved balcony. My curtains flap harder against the wind. Droplets of rain splatter on the marble floor of the balcony, a light warning of an incoming storm. And just like that, the calm night turns into one filled with terrors and fears. One that hides the worst of the monsters that lurk in the shadows, ready to take the souls of those who don't deserve to live.

Sometimes I wonder if I might be one of those few who will meet their fate like this.

My heart pounds inside of me.

For more than a month, I have caught glimpses of him.

Each night, without fail.

Slowly getting up on weak and shaky legs, I hold my breath as I step forward, pausing just at the threshold of the safety barrier of my house. With bare feet and nothing on my face to protect me from the dangers of the outside, no clothes that make me feel confident enough to fight back, I peek out.

And, as if muscle memory kicks in, my eyes move to that one spot on the right at the back garden. In the bushes, leaning against a tree, I see him.

And the skip in my heartbeat almost makes me stumble back a step.

Every day I see him standing there, and fear and curiosity have filled me in a way that I don't understand. I am terrified of the man who leans against the tree every night in my garden. His hood covers the top part of his face, leaving his lips visible as he smokes. The puff he releases makes me want to run far, far away.

The first time I saw the figure, I instantly called security. They searched the perimeter of the property, but they found no one, and I didn't see him again that night.

He was there the next day. And the next day. And the next day. I kept shouting at my security for being so damn useless that they weren't able to catch a man who was right there every night. I changed the security team and updated the security cameras, but I was never able to catch him. I thought I was going crazy and it could be my karma.

"He was right here. How could you not see him?"

"I'm sorry, miss, but there is nothing setting off the alarm system."

"You are working with him, aren't you?"

Now I am alone in a mansion that is bigger than any normal house should be, with only a few maids and my security detail to accompany me. I've never felt lonelier than I have these past two months.

It could be life playing its own twisted game and wanting me to suffer the way I made others suffer. Maybe it thought that me trying to fight my own demons every night wasn't enough and I needed to suffer greater fear.

So I learned to deal with it. To let the fear take over me as I watch his sinister smile take over his lips under the hood.

The sight grabs at my heartstring and pulls until I feel a painful ache.

My stalker has been here every night like a reminder that I will never escape the wrong I've done.

I hold still, leaning back slightly to avoid catching his attention any further, not moving a single bone or muscle in my body as I keep my eyes on him. He just stands there, his head dropped back against the tree. His sharp jaw comes into view, along with the grin that has me gasping for air.

I can't look at him.

I can't bear to see him.

Glancing behind me, I turn, then hesitantly close the doors to my balcony and shut the curtains, breathless and heaving.

And when sleep overtakes me, it's filled with nightmares,

which are getting worse. When I wake up, I go through the routine of showering and getting ready with nothing on my mind, and yet as soon as I grab the deep green heels that I wanted to contrast with my black suit with a mesh top, the image of a certain man with the same coloured eyes comes into my mind.

My grip tightens on the strap of the heels. Should I wear them or not?

Fuck him, and fuck his stupid smirk.

I will wear what I want.

So I do. Then I stride out of my house, climb into my Audi, and drive to the building that was supposed to be mine but is now in the hands of someone I am starting to despise. Actually, not starting to, because what I currently feel for Helia Nashwood is nothing but hate.

I hate him with all my might.

For taking my company.

For leaving me with nothing and now forcing me to accept whatever conditions he may set for working under him. Certainly, I can try to convince my younger sister to talk to her husband about this. Remo Cainn and Helia were both in the picture, so there is some link between them. I just need to know exactly what to do to get back what is mine.

For now, I have to accept a small defeat. But small losses are nothing but a stepping stone for the final battle.

I stride towards his office. When no one in the building stops me, I know he is expecting me. This twisted monster was expecting me, and that only makes me firmer in my decision. I feel everyone's eyes on me, curious but hesitant.

I look back at them all, sliding my gaze across each curious face.

"Is there a TV show going on? Get back to work." My tone is bitter, and it works to get them to look away. They scramble to grab papers, drop their eyes to the screen, and cough even. All six of them on this floor.

I knock twice on the door in front of me.

Upon hearing the 'come in', I turn the handle, take a deep breath, and steel my spine, ready to face him again, ready to lose my breath while I suffocate in his presence.

"Came back so soon?" He lifts his gaze from the papers in front of him, and I just want to hit him across the face for having that smile on his face. It's not one of sincerity but of mocking, one to tell me he knows I'm playing right into his hands.

I stand there.

Unmoving. Waiting. Contemplating.

I need to do this. For me. To survive.

Gritting my teeth and holding in my fight, I open my mouth to accept a small defeat. Just a small one.

"I accept." My voice turns hard.

Helia's dark eyebrows fly up. "That easily?"

I don't reply, nor do I move when I see a flash of amusement go across his face.

This fucker finds this funny.

"That doesn't mean I don't hate you or despise the fact that you snatched my company right out of my hand." A glare is set on my face, and I hope he sees the burning hate I have for him.

"And you want what? A job? How does a clerical position sound? Receptionist?"

My blood boils inside of me at his suggestion.

I have never worked a job at reception. The idea of having to keep a smile on my face to greet people who will test my patience every single day as I sit through hours of it sounds like torture.

"No. I have conditions of my own."

Helia drops his pen and leans back. The suit jacket he discarded hangs on the back of his chair, and his sleeves are rolled up to his elbows, revealing the thick tendons in his forearms and hinting at the muscles beneath the cotton fabric of his shirt. He rests his elbows on the table in front of him, sitting like he owns the place.

And he kind of fucking does.

Like a damn cheat.

"You think you are in a place to be negotiating?"

The grip on my bag tightens.

"Go ahead. I would like to hear it, nonetheless." He motions with a hand as if he is doing me a favour.

"I will keep my previous post and—"

"Not possible."

"—my responsibilities will remain the same."

"Also not possible."

"I will stay out of your way and you will stay out of mine—"

"That's also kind of not—"

"Would you let me finish?!"

Helia's eyes narrow, then he stands up and rounds the table. He stalks forward and stops right in front of me.

His hand darts out, then his fierce, brutal grip on my chin jerks my face up. I sneer at him, and his glare is just as dirty and disgusted. A shiver skitters through me at his harshness. I desperately want to sling my bag across his face, but the moment my eyes drop to his lips, my mind takes a different route altogether.

"Me letting you walk into this building is already a stretch. If I didn't need you, you wouldn't be standing in front of me speaking like this. Drop the attitude before I take care of it myself, and I assure you, Ms Torre, you will not like the reality of your tears staining your cheeks as you beg at my feet."

My eyes widen at his very clear threat and the truth behind those words. My eyes flit between his emerald eyes, catching on the dark shadow that falls over his face due to his jet-black hair.

"You will be my secretary, starting right fucking now. You will do as asked, like a good girl, and you will do so with no complaints. I may be a little laid back, but I promise you, the minute you decide to disobey me, the minute you decide to cross a line with me, I will destroy you." He lets go of my chin with a harsh jerk, making me stumble back a step.

I am breathing heavily, hands fisted around my bag while

I try to regulate my breathing.

He has been stomping all over me again and again ever since we met.

"If you need me, then this mouth and attitude will remain. Deal with it, *sir*, because I don't drop to my knees for any man, let alone you."

With those parting words, I head out, slamming the door behind me.

He's so frustrating.

I hate him so much I want to wrap my hands around his throat, choke the life out of him, and watch his soul leave his green eyes.

My eyes catch the vacant spot right opposite his office, the small room that was for my father's secretary. It's empty.

He knew.

He knew, and he wanted me to come back to him and beg like a fucking dog. To fall for his commands like a 'good girl', as he put it.

I will show him exactly who he is declaring war with.

3

HELIA

I know Ambrose inside and out, but there are gaps in my knowledge.

Toying with her last week was fun. I knew she would come back, full of fire and determination and ready to conquer me. And now she's come back to me, just a week later, confirming that I have her cornered.

She cannot under any circumstance regain her position in Glamorous. I forced her father to hand it over to me so I can hide my cash. Allowing her to work in the finance department would be asking for my own death sentence. Knowing her nature, her fierceness, and her desire to take back this company, she will do anything to bring me down; so I can't give her any freedom or wiggle room.

As Remo asked of me, I will keep Ambrose close. Hiring her as my secretary should do the trick.

Only, her attitude and the way she bites back just as hard

makes me want to bend her to my will.

I thought I was an easy-going guy, relaxed, calm, and a level-headed man in public, but something about Ambrose brings out a side of me that no one should ever see.

I want to conquer her. I want to break her to the point of no return, and I want to dim that fire in her. No one has presented me with a challenge like this before. I prefer my solitude, and I like my own company. Yet ever since I have been watching her, hidden in the shadows, I have been fascinated with the person she is at home and wondering exactly why she is so different from what she shows the world.

I'm only in London for two years, and I want to spend my time here well. Luckily for me, I've found myself a very interesting little obsession. One with such a strong fight in her that even if I grip her by the throat, she won't stop kicking, trying to get away from me.

Dinner with Aurora, Remo, and his sister, Venezia, this evening is especially fun. The hostile energy oozing off Remo can be felt for miles, but I smile through it. It's amusing to watch him be so protective of Aurora while she recovers from the aftermath of what happened to them both.

It surprised me that Aurora, for the second time, has wanted me here and extended the invitation to dinner. She should hate me for jeopardising her marriage with Remo, but she is grateful that I saved her. Regardless, I will take what I can get because not much has been given to me. I've always had to take what I wanted.

"How is your new role in Glamorous, Helia?" Aurora

asks, her soft voice overlapping Remo and Venezia's conversation.

I nod, glancing at my plate of lamb chops. Aurora made them, along with Caesar salad and a small side dish of garlic bread, which I discovered is a favourite of Venezia's. There is the option of parmesan pasta, too, but everyone is diving into the lamb chops more than anything.

"Good." A smirk travels across my face at the tasks I have thought up for Ambrose.

This morning, she was cooped up in her office. I could hear her grumbling whenever I stepped out of my office. She threw me a glare every time she saw me, but I gave her enough useless tasks to keep her busy and away from me as I try to form a new finance team with select hand-chosen people. I need people who are trustworthy.

"I know that look. Who are you thinking of torturing now?" Aurora raises a brow.

"Me? You got the wrong person, lady."

She narrows her eyes, and I let a little truth spill. I can't help it when I'm subjected to her intense gaze.

"Just a new hire at the company. She fights me too much, but her work is good. So I'm thinking of giving her some harder tasks."

Aurora looks at me a second longer before nodding. There is uncertainty in her eyes, but I don't care what she thinks about what I do.

"You kept her?" Remo asks, his dark eyes levelling on me.

His expression is bland, and he looks almost bored, but I know he has been listening the whole time. Remo Cainn is the epicentre of the elite circle in London. He is the owner of Vino Corporation, with its franchise of Giorgio Vino. The global wine company, founded by his grandfather, manufactures its wine in Italy and transports it across the globe. Many of its subsidiaries are tech companies reaching as far as Asia where its manufacturing plants are based, but he is also the supplier of glass wine bottles to his competitors, so he is able to stay ahead and keep a tight hold on them.

The power this man sitting in front of me holds is partly due to aid from me, but the reach and influence he has within the corporate world is insane. No other person has power even close to him. He has been able to hide his very dirty work while living in the heart of London because of me, a small shadow to be wielded as a ruthless weapon when necessary.

I helped Remo with his sister, Venezia, and in return, he owed me a favour. I cashed in that favour last year when I realised that my offshore account had been tracked down by US and UK intelligence and I needed a good-sized company to hide it.

"Hm… She was working until two weeks ago. I fired her because I don't need her looking into the finances. She came back, so I took pity and gave her another position." I shrug and look right into Remo's eyes. He won't find anything in mine, not with my years of practise of hiding my emotions.

Growing up on the streets makes you tough, and it helps you learn from your mistakes. Forces you to hide what you feel and makes you grow a spine of steel, so no one takes you lightly.

Remo nods once before his eyes slide to Aurora. She sits next to him, talking to Venezia, who sits next to me.

"Aurora, you have to bake me those croissants again. My stash is gone," I say.

"And why would she do that? That's for special people only. A.k.a. not you."

I turn towards Venezia. She shrugs like she is the oh-so-special person she is talking about.

"And you are? I didn't see you here when she was baking me all this." I raise my brows.

Venezia scrunches her nose at me.

"Sure am. I don't see you asking her politely. Fun fact, I am her favourite." She sticks out her tongue.

I snatch the cupcake—the last one—from her hand and shove it in my mouth in one go.

"Hey! Helia! That was my last cupcake!" Venezia shouts.

Aurora laughs. "You guys need to calm down."

Venezia whines about it like a damn child while I try to swallow the cupcake.

"Tastes like ass to me." I wink at Aurora, who bites her lip to stop herself from laughing again.

"I promise you didn't miss anything," I assure Venezia.

If I were to truly upset her or Aurora, Remo, who is glaring at me, would quite literally throw me out of the house, then send me a bill for the food.

"Mind yourself, Helia. Insulting my wife's cooking is not the way to keep getting invited here." His voice is low, a clear threat.

I raise my hands in surrender, finally swallowing the last bit of cupcake. It was actually quite delicious. A lemon sponge cake with vanilla frosting.

A faint ringing of the doorbell has us all pausing, and shortly, Isabella, Remo and Aurora's maid, walks into the dining area, her hands clasped softly in front of her. She's a sixty-year-old lady with a soft demeanour and a smile for everyone, except me. That woman hates me for no apparent reason, and I love to poke her. She's fun to mess with.

"Miss Ambrose Torre is here."

My eyebrows perk up while Remo's eyes narrow.

I give him a grin, getting up. "You guys continue. I'll see what she wants."

Aurora looks down at her plate, her mood instantly dropping, and Remo is quick to rub her back, murmuring something to her.

"Thanks, Isabella." I wink at her on my way out.

She grumbles, shakes her head, and walks away.

Seems my little fighter is here for a battle I wasn't invited to.

I step through the front door, softly shut it behind me, and cross my arms, leaning against the door frame, then watch her turn around. For some reason, that small action happens slowly, as if that moment was given to me to just…

take her in.

The long straight blond hair. The suit that moulds to her curves. My eyes drop to her shoes. They are a colour I didn't think she would ever wear. I've noticed her love for this colour, given the many little pieces she often wears. It makes me rage like never before when I spot her in it. My mind barely holding on at the sight of it on her. How could Ambrose, out of all the colours on this fucking earth, desire this colour?

Emerald.

A deep cool green colour associated with nature and freshness, a colour to balance everything. To see a woman like Ambrose wear it… It makes me want to rip off whatever article of clothing she has on with this colour. She shouldn't be wearing my favourite colour on her body.

I may be a little fascinated with her, but I know her history. Her background and the long list of sins she has committed are nearly not enough to influence my opinion of her.

She's quite foolish to be stepping a foot in this house.

We all make mistakes, and we all are forced to act upon wrong decisions when circumstances force us to, but Ambrose was anything but forced.

Everything was done by her own judgement, and with the power of her father, she was able to hide the fact that she ruined so many lives of people around her just because they made a small mistake.

I hate that I know this about her because it means that I care when I feel nothing but loathing towards her.

As soon as she turns around and those deep champagne eyes find me, rage fills them. Her hold on her bag tightens, as it always does when she tries to control her anger.

Her plump lips part. "Why are *you* here?" The distaste in her voice heats my own hatred.

I let an easy smile stretch across my face.

"I was invited for dinner. The question is, what are *you* doing here, Ambrose?"

Her name fills my mouth and softly glides off my tongue. It shouldn't.

It should feel like I just ate a cactus that is scratching at my throat with its spikes, but it doesn't. It's like my voice takes on a completely different tone when I say her name. It's heavy, deep, demanding attention.

Her nostrils flare, and her eyes narrow.

"Dinner? You? Here, of all places?" She scoffs.

She crosses her arms and shifts her weight to one leg while crossing them. Her straight blond hair sways behind her. I can't help but notice that the sharpness of her features enhances her fox-like appearance. Her eyes don't stray from my face. I keep expecting her to look away the minute her gaze falls on my scar, to not be able to handle the intense colour of my eyes.

My eyes trail from her white-painted toes up her long legs wrapped in black tights up to her very sheer top where her breasts are being held captive with a black bra held up by thin straps. A tease. Her body is a fucking tease. The moment my gaze falls back on her piercing eyes, I can't help the mental image of her stripping for me.

The desire in me doesn't dim the hate or disgust I feel toward her, but it's there, and it cannot be ignored.

"Were you possibly here to negotiate terms to outsmart me?" I take a step closer to her.

She doesn't move a single muscle in her body. Instead, she remains hyper-focused on me.

"No. But even if I were, that is none of your business." She huffs, turning her head away from me as if I am a measly little intern working under her. Like I am not even worth her goddamn precious time.

"Sure is when you are my employee and coming here to guilt trip your sister into getting you the company back."

She swallows, the pale skin on her neck glistening under the warm yellow porch light.

I take another step closer to her.

Her lips tighten, and her shoulders tense.

The smirk on my face widens.

"Don't assume things, Mr Nashwood." She sharply turns her head, and her hair almost slaps me across the face. Her face is mere inches from mine. Her dark peony perfume surrounds me, and I briefly wonder if she will bleed as dark as her personality.

Will she bleed a deep maroon? Or will she bleed bright red? The throbbing on the side of her smooth neck is such a tease.

When I look up at her eyes, I know she noticed my glance at her lips. Her hitched breath proves it.

What is shocking is that there is no tremble in her body. She looks rock solid. A stone wall that withstands even the most ferocious disasters, maybe even chipping but never breaking.

"Never said it was an assumption. If you think talking to Aurora or Remo will help you, then you'd better think again. It will be of no help. It's better if you walk away right now and save yourself the embarrassment."

Her lips tighten at my words, then she strides forward, shoving my shoulder.

Grabbing her hand, I twist it behind her back. She gasps.

She shuffles, twists, then groans, trying to escape my hold. I keep her in place, her cold skin making me hiss softly. How much icier can she get?

This is the first time I've touched her, and it feels fucking electric. My skin burns with the need to let her go. I shouldn't be touching filth like her.

"Stop it," I grit out.

She thrashes harder in my hold.

This minx.

"Let me fucking go! How dare you touch me like this?" She digs her sharp nails into my wrist.

I have to hold in a groan. Warmth spreads across my wrist, and alarm bells ring in my mind. She has made me bleed.

"Stop thrashing in my hold, or—"

"Or what?" She turns her head towards me, heaving. "Or fucking what? What will you do? You already took everything! So I would like to see you try to do something else to me!"

My heart rate spikes. She isn't afraid of me, and it makes me want to push her, to go to extreme lengths to make it happen.

She keeps fighting, and I hate it.

I whip her around and pin to the wall right under the porch lamp. My hand around her neck is tight enough to warn but not enough to cut off her oxygen. My hand flexes on her slim, translucent neck, my eyes on the throbbing vein on the side.

"God, you make me want to snuff this fire out of you. I want to see these eyes empty of life."

Her eyes widen at my words, then hateful fire flares in them, turning them into something different.

That fiery anger blazes to life, as if I just poured oil in it. A bright, dangerous wildfire that is out of control, heading straight towards me.

Her hands snap free and fly up, she scratches my hands again.

"I fucking hate you!" Her voice is hoarse, her eyes burning with defiance

"Feeling is mutual." I grind my teeth, tightening my hand just to see her eyes flare.

Her chest falls and rises like she is expecting more.

"A little more pressure and I can end your life right here and be free of your trouble."

I release my grip, and her knees collapse. She whimpers

and slumps against the wall. Her hands are clasped around her neck, and she gasps, taking in as much oxygen as she can.

"What is going on here?" a voice interrupts.

Ambrose blinks and steps out of my hold.

I clear my throat, my eyes trailing after her every movement as she turns to Aurora.

What would have happened if Aurora didn't come out?

Would I have done exactly as I said?

A little more pressure, one more second of seeing that fight in her, and what would I have done?

I can't exactly kill her because there is a stupid thing called friendship—more like me valuing my life—if I don't want Remo coming after me for killing his wife's sister.

"Aurora…" Ambrose says.

She tries to explain the situation to Aurora, who already knows. Aurora's eyes are wary as Ambrose tries to convince her, and I watch. The whole time.

I watch her try as Aurora stands there, indifferent, knowing her older sister has come to beg for something when she doesn't even know the hell Aurora has just come back from.

Ambrose doesn't bother to ask her how Aurora is even doing.

"Please, Aurora." Ambrose's voice drops to a whisper as she reaches for Aurora's hand.

Aurora steps back. She looks at me, her soft eyes flickering between me and her older sister.

"Let her keep the job, Helia. Whichever one, so she can

provide for herself, but don't ask me for anything more. And, Ambrose?"

The blond head looks up, her eyes vacant of any emotions now compared to how fiery she was with me.

"Never come back here again." Aurora nods at me to go inside the house, and I do, but not before I look over my shoulder one last time to see Ambrose's frozen figure as Aurora slams the door in her face.

All of this is a taste of karma for the way she treated her sister.

I know your dirty secret, Ambrose.

And it will ruin you.

4

AMBROSE

Every single day for the next week, Aurora's words echo in my head.

Never come back here again.

Didn't my mother say the same thing to her when she came to console us after Dad died, while I stood there watching? Didn't I stay there, unmoving, not even letting her talk to us?

Now the situation has flipped, and I am the one who is being thrown out. Left helpless…

What I would give to turn back time. But it's not possible. It's the one thing humanity cannot manipulate. I need to keep moving forward.

Aurora is a better person than me, to even listen to what I had to say, to let me be assured that I would have a job and will not lose it.

I have been at the mercy of Helia for the past two weeks, ever since I started my new role.

He tried to kill me in warning that night. He had me pinned against the wall, squeezing my throat. My life flashed before my eyes in those seconds. I never hated anyone more than I did him at that moment.

Helia doesn't come out to taunt me, but the tasks he gives me are a joke. What he is doing is a slow torture that will drive me insane. I really want to scream, then slit his throat with a knife. He keeps giving me tasks that require me to deliver and retrieve files and things to and from each department. Lucky for me, the elevator has been out of order for days. So. Many. Stairs.

I have been sending physical files to the staff downstairs, collecting photocopies, delivering them to Helia, and bringing him black coffee with no sugar—just like his dead heart—at least three times a day. And that coffee... He can't just have it from the twenty-grand coffee machine in the office. No, it has to be from the coffee shop two roads away. A good twenty-minute walk for me.

I don't complain.

Not once.

But it's getting too much for someone who loves working with numbers. I know it's a matter of time before I explode. Sure, I organise his schedule and accept calls and emails, but that is where it stops.

It's like he just doesn't want me to be involved in anything to do with the actual company.

He doesn't look up at me when I go into his office to give him the items.

At least there is peace in that.

He seems busy, constantly calling in the new finance manager he hired.

Soon enough, it's time for the first shoot for Glamorous under new management, and I have been given the task to oversee this new volume.

I hold my iPad and my bag, ready to head out, when the door in front of me opens and out walks my tormentor.

Energy lights with electrifying sparks. My heart quivers at the sight of him, knowing what hides beneath those ruthless eyes of his. They are a fortune teller's globe; the moment you look inside them, the only future you will see is your death. Helia doesn't look like the forgiving type.

I don't even want to look him in the eyes, but I need to keep up my fight.

He wears another black suit and a dark green dress shirt. Helia towers over me despite my height. Ever since I met him, he has constantly been in my personal space. His lean yet muscular body makes me feel like a small woman, even though I am five foot nine.

I'm not sure how, but we ended up matching today.

My black skirt hugs my hips and the flowy top is a deep emerald colour, just like his. Even my black heels match the exact shade of his dress shoes.

For the first time in days, Helia glances up at me. His tousled jet-black hair covers the scar on his eye today. My eyes trace his smooth sharp jaw and the muscles highlighted under his suit. My stomach dips for some unfathomable reason.

"My favourite assistant."

I frown at him and his stupid grin. He keeps acting like he didn't threaten me, and it's making me want to claw at him, to ruin that grin that he is always sporting around others.

"I'm your only assistant," I grumble back. I shoot a quick glance over my shoulder in my office to see if I missed anything, then follow Helia towards the... broken elevator?

"It's broken. Are you stupid or..." I trail off when the doors do in fact open.

Helia strides in, and I am left frozen in my spot.

"No. The only stupid one is you. You keep running up and down the steps, not realising the sign is fake." He leans against the back of the elevator, dropping his head back, his eyes lazily on me.

The elevator... wasn't it broken?

And I have been going up and down hundreds of steps for two weeks?

Like a damn fool? In my own company?

"Hurry up, or I will leave you here."

I blink, then quickly get into the elevator.

"You did this on purpose, didn't you?" I say with a gasp, still unable to believe my own stupidity. And here I was, calling him stupid.

"Seems so to me."

My eyes catch his in the mirroring elevator doors, and he is still in the same position, but the way his hands are in his pocket and his laid-back posture feels familiar.

"You did this to make my life more difficult. As if those useless tasks weren't enough to make me go crazy, you did this, too? You're doing this to make me quit, aren't you?"

He raises his hand to his heart.

"What will you do if the answer is a yes?"

He keeps his eyes on me as he steps closer. My hands turn clammy, and my breathing stutters.

His hot breath fans my shoulder, the heat searing through my shirt, and my grasp on the iPad tightens. My nails on my other hand dig into my bag. My heartbeat drums in my ears at his close proximity, and nerves twist my stomach.

Will he choke me again and look at me in that same antagonising way?

"You can't ruin me, Ambrose." His tone is mocking.

My head snaps to face him, only to be met with the sight of lush lips that are too close for my comfort.

"Fuck you, Helia," I spit.

His eyes narrow.

"You're staring too much." Helia's voice wraps around me tightly like a hot blanket that leaves me sweating.

"Yeah, people tend to stare at strange things for prolonged periods of time." I roll my eyes, trying to keep my cool.

I promised myself I wouldn't snap. I step back, away from him, fixing a disgusted expression on my face so he knows I hate his close proximity.

"I am strange?" He chuckles, and, God, I tried, but my eyes still betray me and hook onto the wide stretch of his mouth, the faint smile line at the corner of his lips as he grins.

My stomach dips for a completely different reason. A reason too dangerous to contemplate.

"Yes. You are the literal definition of a strange, rude, arrogant, and unapologetic man," I snap, my eyes narrowing at the way his cheeks lift higher and higher into a smile at each word I use to describe him.

And I notice it. I notice the shift in his eyes, like a sunrise behind the mass of a forest.

We don't like each other.

End of story.

"And you have a disgusting personality and no respect for others. You are selfish and a spoiled little princess whose tower I will destroy."

My mouth drops open, but I bite back my reply, and my hands clench into fists at my side.

Grabbing the front of his shirt in a tight hold, I lean towards him.

I ignore the masculine musk that fills the air around me and focus on extinguishing that light in his eyes.

"I. Hate. You," I grit out.

Helia gets in my face too, crowding my vision.

He grabs my hand holding his shirt, tears it away, then twists it behind my back. Pain sears through my shoulder, and I bite my lip to hold in a cry.

"Same. Here." His eyes harden. He looks very much like he'd like to kill me. And I hope he sees the exact same emotion in my own eyes.

"I want to kill you and bury your body in a forest," I bite back.

Helia pulls me closer to him, my chest mashed against his, and the pain in my shoulder pinches me harder.

"Is that all you've got?" His words make me want to scream in his face.

I thrash in his hold, trying my best to escape, but I know I have no chance against this man. He really is all strong muscles, taunting smiles, and menacing looks.

"If you try hard enough, you might actually make it." He smiles, his pearly white teeth on display.

Why the fuck are his teeth so perfect?

Why the fuck am I even thinking about his teeth?

What is wrong with me?

"The moment you let me go, I will claw at your face, Helia," I threaten.

His eyebrows rise as if he is really interested in finding out if I'll follow through. This fucker.

He pushes me away. The moment my hands are free, I carefully place my iPad in my bag, place it on the floor, then launch myself at him.

I grab his neck, wrapping both my hands around it, my nails digging into his boiling hot skin. His back is pressed against the elevator, but he doesn't fight me. His cocky smile as he watches me threaten him makes me want to press harder.

I hate him so much.

His twisted personality, his sick smile, and this hot-and-cold attitude he has.

"Didn't know you had this kink."

A frown twists at my face.

"Harder," he moans with an amused smile.

"You prick!"

"What does that make you? A masochist?"

"What?" My mind swims in confusion.

What the actual fuck is wrong with this man?

I apply pressure on his neck, but it seems to make no difference to his face. I even feel a drop of blood fall on my hand where I've pierced his skin. Guilt hits me, and I instantly reel back. No. I wasn't supposed to hurt another person like this.

Shaking my head, I think of something else so the voices in my head don't haunt me.

I never said I was giving up because of some small guilt.

I'm searching every small corner of my house for any evidence that could lead me to build a case against him in hopes of winning the rights to my company back.

Helia will suffer. He will suffer a big loss and I will come out to be the winner. I will get the last laugh in the end.

"I hate you, Helia Nashwood. I'm glad you wear black all the time. When I do manage to kill you, I won't have so much cleaning to do or blood to hide."

He laughs, throwing his head back.

The next moment, Helia's own hand is around my neck. He walks me backward until my back hits the elevator doors.

My eyes widen.

We are about to reach the ground floor. The doors could open at any moment, and I could fall right in front of everyone. That is just asking for humiliation.

The elevator dings, and my heart races.

No.

"Not before I make you beg at my feet. There is no ending this before I am done with you, Miss Torre."

The doors slowly slide open against my back. My heart is in my throat. I grab for his shirt.

"No…" My voice trails off.

The doors fully open and so does Helia's hold on my neck.

A small push and I stagger back. My heels catch in between the doors, and I go falling back.

A scream climbs up my throat, and my eyes widen as I fall back.

My eyes shut, but a jolt snaps them open.

Helia's glaring eyes are above me, and he holds me just a couple of inches above the ground.

"For all that barking you did, you sure are a coward."

He pulls me up with so much force that I get thrown against the wall of the elevator, effectively saving me the embarrassment of falling. I hate that his throwing me around like a rag doll just proves he is much stronger than me.

I don't care that he is. I want my company back, and he has made my life a living hell ever since he stepped into my life.

With my thirty-eight per cent of shares compared to his fifty-two per cent, it's a lot less, but the remainder are sold publicly. I have more than enough money to file a lawsuit against him.

I just need enough evidence that I should be the CEO of Glamorous. Not just the CEO but the owner. After all, I am the rightful heir to this company.

5
AMBROSE

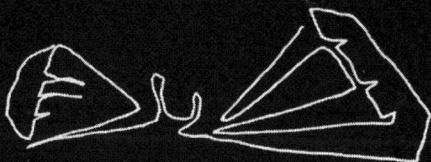

"I don't like this dress." Helia points at the pink dress Runa, one of the brunette models, is wearing.

The photographer, Arlo, sighs.

"How many more outfit changes do we need? I am a busy person, and you only have three more hours left with me," Arlo says.

Helia's eyes snap towards him with such cruel intensity, I don't know how Arlo isn't shaking.

The studio has a pink backdrop for the pictures, and there are five models lined up. The first two have already done their part, but Helia seems to be having a problem with Runa. She has already changed twice.

"I'm the one paying you, aren't I? Go change, Runa, and you—" He points at Arlo, who pushes his glasses up his nose. "If you want to keep your business going, I advise keeping your trap shut. If any of these pictures don't come out as I expect them to, I will drag you back here, be it midnight or during ungodly hours of the morning, and make you redo them."

Arlo swallows thickly.

"Understood?"

Arlo nods frantically, then waves a hand to his assistant, who walks Runa to the change room.

The models are too busy looking appreciatively at Helia to mind his behaviour or the way his voice drips with such authority and venom to suggest he might kill you if you made a mistake.

"Mr Nashwood?" Lilith, the second model, walks up to Helia, a soft smile on her face. She's a short model with olive skin and curly strawberry blond hair.

Helia looks up from his phone. His sleeves are rolled up to his elbows to reveal just a hint of his tattoos, and his shirt clings to his muscular chest. Each bump of his abs shows through the shirt, and the black slacks he wears emphasise his muscular thighs.

The minute his eyes fall on her, a small breath escapes from her lips. Her eyes widen a fraction as she moves closer to him.

"Do you want to have a quick coffee break with me while they get Runa ready?" She clasps her hands behind her, and she sways lightly, probably nervous, waiting for Helia's response.

He just keeps looking at her, unfazed and probably unaware she is nervous to ask him.

"Coffee?" he repeats, blinking.

She nods, keeping up her sweet smile.

Helia's lips twitch, and the minute they do, bitterness claws in my chest.

I push it down and glance down at my iPad, forcing my eyes to stay on the inspiration board I made, but a certain pull drives me to look up again, to find out if Helia has accepted or not.

They're on their way out, Lilith with a bounce in her step and Helia with a hand in his trouser pockets.

Helia glances over his shoulder. His eyes instantly find mine in the middle of the chaotic room, amongst the people, lights, and dresses being thrown around, and he winks at me. Then he turns around and disappears.

How dare he wink at me when Lilith clearly seems interested in him? Doesn't he have any respect for her?

Thirty minutes pass, and Runa returns wearing a short blue glittery dress. Helia and a smiling Lilith right behind him arrive shortly after. Runa spots them and walks over, her eyes on Helia, who is walking towards Arlo with an intense expression of concentration. For some weird reason, I find myself walking towards the water bottles placed behind the girls.

"How did it go?" Runa asks Lilith, a high pitch to her voice.

"I think it went well. He kind of just sat there and drank his coffee and looked at his cup the whole time. He seemed happy to be going, but he just stayed quiet while I was talking."

A stupid smirk makes its way onto my face, but I shut it down.

Exactly. Lilith should realise how fucked up Helia really is.

"Is that all?" Runa asks, her voice now a whisper.

"No. Towards the end, he finally looked at me and started talking about how good I was and how he thinks he could put a good word in for me to get more modelling jobs since I am so new to all this."

I glance over my shoulder at Lilith to see a faint blush on her cheeks.

No. Don't think that. Helia is manipulative.

Is he, though? Or does he just act like that with me?

His hate is so clear, so apparent, that I can't mistake it for anything else.

He despises me so much, loves to see me in trouble and struggling, and laughs when he sees me juggle problems, and yet, with Lilith, he seems so calm, so gentlemanly.

I turn from them and go to stand by Arlo, returning my focus to the task at hand and not on Helia's private affairs.

I shouldn't care what he does and doesn't do.

Throughout the shoot, I kept catching Lilith giving Helia longing glances. He keeps a soft smile on his face while she blushes profusely, and the makeup artists keep glancing at him from their corner of the room.

No one seems to care that he was being rude to Arlo. No one seems to notice his jaw ticking as if a timer is set for patience. And no one sees his fingers tapping on his crossed arms. He is running low on patience, trying to keep it together, but other than that, he looks so easy going.

So easily making himself out to be what everyone here wants him to be. A gentle, smiling charismatic boss.

What a manipulative fucker.

Near the end of the photoshoot when all models are together, a faint hot trail brushes my cheek, and I look up. Helia's intense eyes are on me. Something hot boils inside of me, probably my hatred for him. The sight of him makes me want to throttle him.

I lift a brow as if asking 'what?'

His eyes slide to Arlo, back to me, then down to my hand, which rests on Arlo's arm. His eyes harden, jaw locked while he keeps looking between me and Arlo. Maybe I am overstepping boundaries, but he didn't care when he went with Lilith, so me doing something simple shouldn't matter.

I shrug.

Helia narrows his eyes further. My body tenses.

I jut my chin towards all the models now together in front of the camera, silently asking him to pay attention.

His eyes dart to my hand once more.

I wink at him playfully. His nostrils flare, his body tense while he flexes his hand as if restraining himself from breaking something.

"Lilith, look towards me, love, at the camera," Arlo shouts.

Lilith blushes at being caught staring at, I can only assume, Helia. Her new little crush.

"Sorry," she mutters and looks towards the camera.

I hold in a small laugh, and it seems Helia catches me doing so. He strides over and shoulders his way between me and Arlo. His large body stands between us, his gardenia and dark musk scent looming around me like a caress.

"Get closer shots, Arlo. I don't want them all to look the same."

Arlo scrambles away at Helia's commanding tone.

To my surprise, Helia stays next to me.

His shoulder brushes against mine.

My breathing stutters.

I take a step to the left.

He casually takes one too.

I sigh, glaring at the side of his face. A soft smile is present on his face as he focuses on Lilith, who just keeps blushing.

"There is a thing called personal space," I grit out.

He glances down at me, smile frozen in place, but it isn't for me.

Two-faced fucker.

"Never heard of it."

I shove my shoulder against his. He bites his lip, holding in his laugh.

"Stop laughing. You keep flirting and not being professional. Maybe you should have left the company alone," I mutter, crossing my arms. "You weren't wanted here, anyway."

The humour drains from his eyes, and his jaw tightens and tics. His face darkens, and the easy-going smile on his face freezes in a way only I could notice.

My body runs cold, ice prickling under my skin like parasites.

Fuck.

"You seem to be very attentive for someone who isn't interested in my life. You want to see me fuck her? Is that what you want? A show? So that, what? You can label me as incapable of running the company?"

I choke on absolutely nothing. Helia takes a step closer to me and leans down to press his lips by my ear.

"Be careful how you speak to me, Ambrose. I won't hesitate to choke you on the very water you used as your disguise to listen in on the gossip."

My jaw drops open.

He strides away from me, his threat hanging like a dagger above my head.

I will never win against him if this keeps going. He has left me shocked and horrified after every single interaction. His parting words just now are an exact reflection of him.

Cruel. Disgusting. And a menace to society.

But watching him take control and be so commanding, it's twisting my opinion of this big bad guy who has stolen everything from me. I can see now that he's more than capable of keeping Glamorous afloat.

Doesn't mean I'll accept it.

Soon enough, we are all done, and I head home. I don't

tell Helia that I'm leaving. The workday is more than over. It's seven in the evening. I am tired.

Soaking in a beautiful hot bath is definitely what I need to soothe my muscles after being on my feet all day.

Tomorrow is Friday. Last day of the week.

As soon as I step foot inside my house, I catch movement in the corner of the hallway, and my mind instantly reels back to the mysterious hooded man. I take a deep breath, telling myself it's just security doing inside checks of the mansion.

My stalker doesn't just stand there watching my window anymore. He explores and wanders around the back garden as if he has no care in the world that my security guards, who patrol the property, will catch him. Every. Single. Night.

He is getting more confident.

I need to put a stop to this before it gets worse. Somehow.

I don't want to end up like my sister.

I don't want to be crazy and paranoid, obsessed that someone could easily end my life.

Helia would have no problem killing me if he truly had the chance, and I think he would do it.

His crude words flash through my mind. I can't believe he wanted me to watch him fuck Lilith like I am an exhibitionist who loves seeing that shit. Funnily enough, Helia seems the type to do exactly that. To get back at me. To make me angry. To piss me off, or to even just prove his point.

My eyes shut, and an image of his eyes on me as he kisses Lilith flickers through my mind. Disgusted with myself, this mental image makes me cringe. I won't give in. I could never see myself with someone like him. *Never* in my life.

My muscles finally relax under the hot water. The peace that consumes me is a rare reprieve. The water manages to release the tension from my body, and my shoulders drop, my body floating.

A loud thud comes from my bedroom. I flinch and snap my eyes open.

Water slouches around me, and I wrap my arms around my knees. The aroma of lavender is gone, and the cold air of the bathroom seeps into my bare skin, making goosebumps rise.

My heart beats erratically.

It's *him*.

It is definitely him.

I know it.

I knew he was growing far too confident.

With fear gripping my throat and my heart racing a hundred miles an hour in my chest, I snatch the towel off the hook and wrap it around me, rushing out of the bathroom and into my bedroom with bare feet and water dripping down my body. A piece of rolled paper wrapped in a green bow sits on top of my bed.

I shudder and gasp for air. My lungs squeeze as I struggle for oxygen, and my eyes water at the lack of it. I frantically look around. Am I alone? What made the thud?

I spot the open balcony window.

The curtains flare angrily, thrashing in the strong wind.

He was here.

He came through the window, and he left a fucking note.

I stand still, unable to move or do anything but watch the piece of paper like a hawk, willing it to disappear, to be a fragment of my imagination, but it's not.

A small cry climbs up my throat. My eyes sting, but I swallow the painful lump down.

With shaky fingers and weak legs, I stumble around, shutting the balcony doors before heading to my bed. With trembling fingers, I reach out and grab the paper, my eyes fixed on the balcony in case he comes back.

I tug on the ribbon and uncurl the paper.

Even the worst of sinners deserves to see a glimpse of heaven.

You've managed to bring hell on earth for everyone.

There is no signature, nor any indication of who this could be from, but I know. I just know it's from the man who has stood outside my balcony in my garden for the past few months.

The worst part is, I never imagined I'd be someone's object of obsession. I don't see myself ever stepping a foot into heaven after what I did.

He's right. I did that.

I did bring hell to everyone's life here.

That nineteen million won't be enough for me to survive on. It won't be enough to help the families of those I ruined in my desperate attempt to impress my father.

I destroyed people's lives. I ruined people's images and killed their self-esteem in fits of anger, jealousy, and boosts of ego.

A person like me doesn't deserve to be called an obsession.

It feels like this note is mocking me.

Maybe it is.

6

HELIA

"Ack."

My eyes snap to my black crow. He's flapping his wings as he flies around the living room. Glass windows take up three of the living room walls, facing a dense forest where the only thing you can see for miles is tall tree trunks. He's a common raven that I helped nurse back to health in Melbourne when I was visiting my client, a politician wanting votes for his campaign. I made it happen for that man. I also kept records of his secrets, knowing it would one day come in handy.

I kept Blaze with me when I couldn't let go, and he didn't mind travelling with me.

He is the only one I don't mind in my presence, nor do I mind him when I want to be alone. Somehow, he understands my need for silence. He always does.

Blaze comes back into the kitchen above me, circles the

kitchen island I am seated at two times, then alights on my shoulder. He tilts his head, bends down, and pokes me on the shoulder once.

"You want this too?" I point to the pathetic bowl of cereal I quickly made. I have to head out to meet with my personal accountant soon.

Picking some cereal out of the box, I hold it up to his beak. He nibbles it, then taps on my shoulder twice. I chuckle.

"Okay, now you want two? Little greedy shit. I already fed you." I give it to him nonetheless, and after being satisfied, he takes off, cawing loudly in the living room.

He only does this when he wants to get out. I can't take him anywhere; but now that I think about it… Would anyone say anything to me if I did? Remo granted me new-found power to help me live lavishly in London.

"Get ready, Blaze. We are going out."

I put away my dishes, then open the door and watch as Blaze swoops out. His caws are loud and cheerful. I laugh as I head to my black HR2 bike.

"Come on, on my shoulder!" I shout.

He flies up high, then dives, spinning in tight, graceful circles. He makes it seem like I never let him out when I do, every single day.

We reach my new accountant's office, and I am directed to the waiting room. My head drops back against the wall, and I pet Blaze, who perches on my shoulder as I wait. Blaze watches everyone go by in the office building. It's quite a popular place. I didn't think the accountant would be this busy, but Remo told me to consider him. Funnily enough, he readily accepted the money I presented to him to use Glamorous to launder my money. No one seems to care that I have a crow on my shoulder, but Blaze caws at the few who do, making them scramble away. I have to hold my laughter in.

As soon as the door in front of me opens, I rise to my feet and head to it, but the person walking out slams into me. Hard. Blaze screams, his wings flapping and brushing my ear.

"Watch where you're going! Are you blind?" The familiar sharp voice hits my ears, and when I look down at the woman picking up her file, an amused smile makes its way onto my face.

"So my little emerald is here," I drawl, my head tilting.

From the corner of my eye, I catch Blaze tilting his head, too, scrutinising Ambrose.

The nickname is a slip of my tongue.

She's in a white long-sleeved shirt with a cardigan and black leggings. I search for any emerald on her. And I find it in the earrings that wink at me the minute she tucks her hair behind her ear. A dip forms in my stomach.

Her eyes snap up, the brown in them bold and alluring.

"Why are you everywhere I go?" She frowns, her mouth twisting to the side.

"Here to launder money?" I ask, eyebrow quirked.

She scowls, and my loud laugh echoes down the hallway.

"You pay me perfectly fine. My presence here isn't your concern." Her shoulders slump as a sigh falls from her lips.

She rocks forward, and I swiftly step in front of her.

She huffs. "Really?"

I step closer, my eyes holding hers captive. Her gaze is sharp, like a fox ready to outsmart its prey and devour it.

"You are maddening. Do you know that?" Ambrose rushes out, throwing her hands up.

"Then does that make me your one and only special?"

"More like most hated."

"I beg to differ."

"Believe what you want. Now get out of my way."

I don't move.

"Helia."

My eyebrows rise at her using my name, though it shouldn't be a surprise. She loves pissing me off with her amusing empty threats.

"Don't look at me like that. We aren't in the office—"

"Doesn't mean you don't work for me,"

"And you should try giving people a thing called private space."

"I just can't seem to stay away from you."

Her eyes blaze at this comment. Not in a good way. She looks ready to murder me with her sharp claws. I can still feel the sting from the other day when she dug them into my neck. Another surprise.

"Would you stop interrupting me?" she snaps. Her jaw tics, and the vein on the side of her porcelain neck throbs angrily. She's a volcano about two seconds away from erupting.

"No," I grunt with a huff.

Her eyes move to Blaze, who sits silent and foreboding on my shoulder. The moment Ambrose notices him, her eyes widen. I'm not sure if it's in fear, astonishment, or just absolute confusion.

"Admit it. You're happy to see me." I smirk, knowing full well she hates the mere sight of me. She would rather make me choke on the papers in her hand, smash my head against the nearest wall, and watch with a sadistic smile than actually be happy in my presence.

And yet there is a magnetic force about her. How else would I explain this odd zap whenever we accidentally touch? With every passing moment, with every glance at her, there is this need, this desire, to feel her skin. Be it a mere touch to feel her cold skin burn against my warmth or to just have her in my sight.

I need her to always be in front of me.

"You are a piece of shit,"

I laugh harder.

Her eyes move to Blaze once more…

"Stealing animals doesn't seem like your type of hobby," Ambrose mutters, looking at Blaze every couple of seconds.

She scrunches her nose, but her eyes stay wide and soft.

Ambrose tentatively reaches out to pet Blaze, and I am frozen in place. I just stare. Like an idiot.

The world fades. Nothing is in focus anymore except

Ambrose.

Blaze caws in surprise, tilting his head at me, as if asking permission. Then he hops forward and settles on Ambrose's shoulder. She gasps, turning her head to look at him.

And I am still fucking frozen, as if I just witnessed something life altering.

"Why are you with this guy? I want to take you home with me and save you from him. He is really mean to me. Does he know you hide food from him? I know you do. I bet it's in a secret place."

I finally blink out of my frozen state.

Blaze caws like he understands what she just said.

"I wondered where the extra food went," I say.

Ambrose doesn't look my way or acknowledge me. And now I want her to. I want her to look at me like she looks at Blaze. I want to know what it feels like to be on the receiving end of it. And that thought is terrifying. I should be focusing on breaking this woman, not wanting her to look at me with wonder.

Ripping my eyes away from her, I step away and open the accountant's office door into her. She glares at me.

"Let's go, Blaze. If you'll excuse me, some of us have things to do." I walk inside without looking back, but I can very much feel her narrowed, angry eyes on the back of my head. Blaze caws faintly once more, then lands on my shoulder.

"You're not the only one who has shit to do, Helia. You—"

The door shuts behind me, and the man behind the desk rises from his chair.

His eyes go straight to my scar, and all the amusement drains from me.

He keeps staring, and I want to gouge his eyes out.

He clears his throat and nods at the seat before his desk. "Let's get started, Mr Nashwood. I have been given an idea of what you need from Mr Cainn. Could you tell me exactly how much money we are working with?"

I let my eyes go over the room before I roam around it, touching any place where there could be cameras or recording devices.

Once I am sure there is nothing of the sort, I take my seat in front of the older man.

"Seven hundred million British pounds." For now.

Once the two-hour meeting is over, I am ready to step out, but I pause.

"The woman who came in before me. What did she come to do?"

Mr Daveport looks up from his computer screen to fix his uncertain gaze on me. He hesitates, but I let an easy smile widen my lips. My head turns towards Blaze, who is looking at him, too.

"Don't worry. Your secret will stay safe with me. I'll transfer a good amount of money in exchange for this information."

He nods, and it irks me that it was that easy. Not a single fight in him or any hint of morals.

Maybe he isn't good enough to be doing my business. I need to keep an eye out for him.

"She came to take money out of her bank and transfer it to a shell account for safekeeping."

I frown. "Why?"

"Ms Ambrose has been saving money and setting it aside for over a year now. She mentioned she wants to give it to someone, but I am unaware of whom the intended recipient is. She did tell me that she doesn't want her name anywhere on the accounts because of her position. It wouldn't go well for her if this were ever to leak. Which I trust it won't." He gives me a pointed look.

I nod. I wouldn't tell a soul, but none of that answers my question.

I'll just ask her myself.

Tonight. I will be at her house tonight.

Just like every night.

I find that my thoughts around her take a completely different turn, but enough milling about.

The note I left her was supposed to be anything but sweet, and I know she isn't stupid to think it was. It was a way of saying she won't ever get to hear those words from anyone.

I will be there to destroy you tonight, Ambrose.

7

AMBROSE

"You will go to this dinner, and you will let Darci sweep you off your feet. It's the only way for us to get invited to the parties your father couldn't get into," my mother says.

I flinch.

She wasn't always like this. Once upon a time, she loved me and my sister and was an amazing mother. But living within the high walls of the oppressive Torre mansion has led to many depressive episodes. While I was working at the company with Dad, Aurora would come over and stay for a few days to help her through them, and when she slept, I would constantly check on Mum to make sure she was all right.

I monitored the food the staff prepared to ensure it was made to help her keep her strength. My efforts were silent. When Mum got better, Aurora never came back. She got out at the right time.

When Mum was well, it was my role to go to parties with her, ones she attended to escape the confinement of the mansion. I got used to it, but I was still a mere puppet for both of my parents.

Then Dad's death happened, and Mum's mental health took another hit. The minute she saw Aurora in the house, she dropped the blame on her and Remo.

I had seen Remo come out of the house the day of Father's death and had a feeling he had something to do with it, but there was no evidence, so I never pressed it. Remo wasn't the only dangerous man my dad had made deals with. Aurora left that day and never looked back. That was months ago. I used to see her regularly at family dinners, but now I don't.

There is silence in the house now.

Maddening silence that leaves me desperate for any kind of distraction.

"But why?"

Leysa, my mother, whose blond hair is just like mine, turns her sharp eyes to me. She wears a classic white dress paired with a sparkling diamond neck piece and matching heels.

"Why wouldn't you, Ambrose? You let Glamorous slip between your fingers, and now we need a different way to keep us afloat. You couldn't do it, and you've almost cost us everything in the two months I was gone, so now let me handle this." She walks past me and breezes through the front door of our house.

I follow, my glittering gold dress trailing behind me. It has long sleeves and dips low on my chest, showing a hint of cleavage. I've paired it with my diamond necklace and earrings, my white Louboutins, and a thin anklet.

"How are you finding this dinner?" Darci mutters in my ear, his cold breath fanning my neck.

I lean away and sip my water as I try to smile. God, I hate this.

"Why?" I drawl, looking at him.

He smiles.

It's a charming smile. He could be the epitome of class and money, with his million-pound watch, designer suit, and slicked hairstyle.

"If you weren't enjoying it, I'd have to try harder to keep you entertained, wouldn't I?"

I don't understand what he means until he drops his hand on my thigh under the table. I freeze.

My eyes sharpen in warning, and my grip on my glass tightens. I want to throw the drink in his face. I glance at Mum. She has noticed, but there is that look in her eyes that tells me to not fuck it up and just deal with it. Darci's parents in front of me are completely captivated by Mum's conversation.

I can't do this.

Why the fuck is he touching me like he has any right?

I wrap my fingers around his, then rip them off my thigh and throw his hand back to him. He raises his brows.

"You touch me like that again, Darci, and you won't have a chance at passing on your DNA."

For a second, I think he takes my threat seriously. Then he bursts out laughing.

"You are a fierce one."

Yet men like Darci cannot handle a fierce woman when she keeps that independence. They complain about not having a compliant partner and try to smother her spirit.

Something tickles along my spine, then travels up my neck. The heat and intensity of it makes me sit up straighter. The chatter around me fades into a murmur as I realise it's that same feeling I get when I am in my room near the balcony.

At night.

When my stalker is around.

He's *here*.

He's in this restaurant.

Awareness blossoms inside of me, and fear slithers around my heart in tight, painful bands. I press a hand to my chest and slowly turn around, scanning the restaurant. Nothing stands out.

Until my eyes fall on the figure sitting leaned back, legs spread wide, and the long legs out in front of him in a booth at the far back corner of the dimly lit restaurant.

The hoodie, the outfit, and figure. All of it is the same.

His hood is covering his head and face, but I can tell his eyes are on me. Fear chokes me, clamping around my throat with its sharp claws. He looks like he wants to murder someone. The glare is apparent even if I can't see his facial features.

My phone pings, and my fear spikes.

With shaky fingers, I take my phone out of my bag and wake up the screen.

Unknown: He touches you again, and he will meet a cruel fate by my hands

A different kind of rush goes through my body. This is the first time my stalker has contacted me through text message. And it's to threaten a man who was disrespectfully touching me.

"Who is it?" Darci tries to peek at my phone, but I shut my phone. My heart races inside of me as I slowly turn to Darci again. Trying to imagine what my stalker will do to him.

Will he cut his hands off for touching me?

Will he slit his throat for daring to disrespect me?

Would anyone even want to keep my pride and dignity preserved at all?

I haven't done anything to deserve anyone's mercy or kindness, and that thought alone has everything around me dimming as I force myself through this dinner.

"Ambrose is such a lovely woman. I think she is perfect for my boy, Darci," Viviana says.

My mother lights up at the suggestion, but it makes me nauseous.

I don't want this.

The feeling gets so intense that I need to leave.

"Excuse me," I say politely and rise from the table.

I walk swiftly to the restrooms and barely keep myself from puking in the toilet. Darci's wandering hands make me feel so disgusted.

I lean against the wall in the ladies' restroom and close my eyes. I suck in long breaths and release them slowly until my heartbeat calms and my hands stop shaking. I quickly check my reflection in the mirror, then walk back out. Everyone is ready to go, thankfully. I grab my purse, my eyes flying back to where I saw my stalker in the back, but he isn't there anymore.

No one has ever seen him before, nor have we caught him with any of our security cameras. Could he be a mere fragment of my imagination?

Could he be someone my mind created, pushing me to go insane? To tip over the last edge of sanity I have left?

The ride to the exclusive launch party of the new partnership between Anta Group and Fallum Corporation thrown by Darci Anta's parents is just as suffocating. I keep my window open a fraction to let some cool air into the car. My mother's presence, the thought of being in another event, the sight of people in the room, and the need to keep up a fake smile is all so exhausting.

My heart tightens with unease.

I take a shuddering breath in and let it out quietly. My hands shake, along with my chin, at the thought of putting up with Darci for the rest of the night.

My window gets shut just as flashes go off outside.

I jump when I feel a pinch on my thigh and look over to see Mum's retreating hand and a firm expression on her face.

"Do not, under any circumstance, ruin this, Ambrose."

I swallow thickly.

My door opens, and the flashes blind me. A hand reaches out, and I take it numbly, swinging my legs out, then placing one foot in front of the other as I exit the vehicle. I fix an unaffected, regal smile on my face as I wave and nod at the paparazzi, walking on the white carpet towards the steps leading up to Marigold Avenue . It's an elegant venue, situated right on the famous Marigold Avenue, which houses only the most exclusive event structures. Invitations to events here are extended to politicians, mayors, influential Chief Executives, and even to the state secretary. Some even come from the royal bloodline.

The Anta family ranks just below the Cainn Group, with their influence and wealth exceeding everyone in this group. With their hand in technology, they are always in demand. Their share prices keep increasing, and that rapid growth is exactly what shareholders and investors look for. It's been a quick, yet crazy, rise to the top for them.

What will happen if I reject Darci's advances?

What will happen if I walk away and don't attempt to make conversation with Darci?

Will it be the same as when I was in school?

Will I have to sacrifice myself once more for my family?

I have given up so much of myself for parents who had never cared.

Glamorous was my only avenue for escape, but even that has been snatched away from me.

Fuck Helia and Remo.

My eyes burn, and I blink away any trace of emotion from my face. My genial mask is firmly back in place when security greets me and guides me towards the grand doors of the venue.

The strong rose scent of my mother reaches my senses before I see her standing next to me.

"Follow me," she whispers.

Her heels click on the white marble, and I demurely follow her, as I have been doing my whole life.

I remain by her side and dutifully greet each and every person she introduces me to, my mind numb, silent, and hazy as I see nothing and everything at once.

The shine, the flaunt of money, the people. It's all a blur.

"This is my daughter, Ambrose." She pushes me in front of them.

"Pleasure to meet you." I greet each of them with a smile, then ask them about their business, their family, their favourite hobby. I have a file on almost every person in this room.

My mother and my father didn't let me slack in this department.

The chatter is loud, and faint music flows through the room. I engage in all the pleasantries, aware that even if I wanted to, I wouldn't be able to ask any of them for help. If something didn't benefit them, they wouldn't look twice.

Diamonds twinkle around throats, in earlobes, and around wrists, and crisp suits and beautiful dresses adorn the guests. I slowly move my gaze across it all, pausing on a man who is talking to the mayor of London.

He's tall and has dark hair and sharp features. A calm expression rests on his face as he sips his champagne.

Remo Cainn.

I quickly look around him. Is Aurora here too? She's never liked events like this. She wouldn't be here, and I can't see her.

Remo looks up, and I get caught looking. I tip my head before turning back to Talia Lonan, the daughter of one of the deputy mayors of London, Hayes Lonan.

"These events give me a serious headache sometimes. Do you feel that too?" she mutters, rubbing her forehead with well-manicured fingers and flashing the gold on her wrist. She's dressed in an impeccable, fitted silver dress with a V-neck and thick straps.

She's ten years younger than me, at twenty years old, but her beauty and elegance are unmatched. I like her. She's always at every event I am invited to, but she is also a confident woman who I sometimes fear is too bold and daring for this society.

To be in this circle, one must hold a certain power within London. To be here is to be among the most elite. The most powerful families and political figures mingle, hide their fucked-up actions, and call it a day, knowing their col-leagues will cover and vouch for them. Being a powerful and influential businessman or woman does not require a good heart. It usually involves the spilling of blood and a black heart.

It's no surprise that Remo's here, nor that we are invit-ed to these parties now that Mum has made acquaintances with the Anta family. Even if it came at the cost of tying me to Darci. While Remo is here, we haven't always been in-volved, which is exactly what Dad died trying to do. Funny how Mum is the one who got us here.

"It is. I don't know how these parties are always this long." I take another sip of my water, trying to keep my mind cool.

"Come with me. There is a small door leading out to the back. We can get some air before coming back in here."

Linking my arm with hers, she drags me with her, weav-ing through the crowd, turning men's heads everywhere she goes. Their gazes then take me in, too.

I can feel their hungry eyes, even if I don't turn my head.

I think Talia is the only person here whom I can toler-ate. She is quite fearless. She doesn't throw jabs at me, doesn't talk about anything other than light gossip, which just makes her easy to be around.

And I allow myself to breathe with her.

She pushes the fire exit door open, and we walk out. I let out a big breath, taking in the cold air. Light droplets of rain fall on us, and a soft gust of wind blows our hair.

"Thank God. I was about to die of suffocation in there."

Talia playfully slaps my arm, chuckling. "Don't be dramatic like that. I thought you would be used to this. You've been doing this for longer than I have."

I shake my head at her words. She couldn't be more wrong.

"So… I know I don't usually gossip, but I heard a little something." She turns her head towards me, leaning against the cool wall of the venue.

My gaze is on the starry night above me, watching the slow movement of the clouds making their way to cover the glow of the crescent moon.

"You and Darci…" She trails off.

I huff out a laugh. "I will do everything in my power to get that slimy shit away from me. You think I'll tie myself to a playboy like him who has probably fucked half of London? No way."

Talia laughs out loud, then quickly covers her mouth with her hand. Her wide eyes make me smile.

"Stop trying to act like a lady when you snort when you laugh." I poke her.

She frowns at me, crossing her arms. "And you, miss, are acting like you will find a gentleman with this little attitude you always have. Have you ever been nice to anyone?"

Helia's image flashes in my mind.

"Oh my God! What was that look?"

I blink, confused.

Her brown curls bounce as she shuffles over to me. "That

look! Ambrose, did someone just come to your mind? Who is he? Do I know him? Is he inside? Who is it? Tell me," she pleads, her big brown eyes wide.

"Stop. There is no one. And for your information, the last time my father decided to marry me off, the man requested Aurora instead of me at the last minute. You know I am the last person who wants to get married; not with what I am, the way I am."

Talia bites her lips, tucking a loose strand of hair behind her ear.

She turns and looks up at the sky. After a few quiet moments, she says, "You know, sometimes I wish—no, I dream—of marrying someone, anyone, who isn't a part of this whole… this… society, part of the elite. I can't imagine myself marrying someone who is so greedy, so addicted to money. I just… He would never put me first, you know?"

I nod and move my gaze to the bushes in front of me. Something moves in the corner of my eye, and I turn to look to my right. Someone smoking against the wall farther down the building. The flame of a lighter flares to life, and my heart explodes in a pounding frenzy.

That… that stance.

It cannot be.

That note was just for the sake of it. Right?

"I think you, on the other hand, you may have a little bit of a hard time, but you'll find yourself falling for someone who can easily handle your little mood swings; someone who sees you, who sees the struggles you hide, even from me."

Memories of Helia countering my arguments come to mind. Then the image of the hooded figure takes centre stage.

"I know everyone in the building behind us, but no one in there will work for what we want, what we need, we might have to fight against the strongest forces in London to get what we want," Talia comments with a sigh.

"Your sister married Mr Cainn, but I saw her, saw the newspapers and articles… She looks so happy, looking up at her husband with such love, such affection, and his eyes that are always on her." She sighs dreamily, but my attention is still stuck on the smoking figure.

My throat tightens, my mouth opening and closing, unsure if I should tell Talia.

"I guess she lucked out to be tied to such a powerful man who has proven me a little wrong. The picture of him on his knees for her that leaked? I never thought love like that existed. Deep, beautiful love…"

He blows a puff out, drops the cigarette onto the ground, then looks up, as if aware that I'm watching him.

"Ambrose? Are you listening?"

He shakes his head once, then turns around and disappears around the far corner. Only then do I finally let myself breathe. The way he walks with such ease makes my stomach twist. His height and broad shoulders make my heart drum loudly.

"Ambrose?" Talia shakes my shoulder.

"Huh?" I blink and focus on her.

She looks behind me. "What is it? Did you see someone?"

I shake my head. "I thought I saw someone, but it's nothing. Let's head back inside before my mom realises that I'm missing."

She nods but looks behind me once more before we head back inside.

Darci somehow finds his way to me, and Talia cannot hide her smile, aware of how much I hate this.

"Did I tell you how beautiful you look tonight?"

I smile, flashing my teeth, and shrug.

He leans in, his lips brushing my ear, and whispers, "You look hot, Ambrose. I wish I could take you out of here, right now, and see how you taste."

I shiver and hope he doesn't notice. "Not happening. There is nothing on this finger." I raise my left hand and wiggle my ring finger.

He laughs, shaking his head. "It will by adorned with the biggest diamond that will blind everyone in the room, and then I will get what I have been promised."

I catch Talia making gagging notions behind him, and I have to hold in a smile.

This stupid girl.

"I haven't promised anything," I counter.

The event continues, and it stretches long into the night. The speeches happen, and the crowd slowly starts to disperse after dinner, despite us already having eaten. And when I finally, finally, get to step out of the venue into the cold night, rain is splattering the pavement.

"I would love to see you again, Ambrose," Darci whispers in my ear, then places a kiss on my cheek and heads out. He looks back at me over his shoulder, a wink thrown my way before he gets in the car with his parents.

The cameras catch this. They catch every moment, and I know my face will be plastered all over the tabloids tomorrow morning.

"Good luck with the press coverage tomorrow." With an amused smile, Talia also walks away with an elegant wave.

"Good job. I think I can now sleep peacefully tonight knowing a wedding is on the horizon," Mum states when we are home.

She walks to her room, and I go to mine, my mind numb. The blank walls of our house seem so much taller today. Darker and haunting.

Locking my bedroom door behind me, I step out of my heels and make my way towards my bed.

My bag drops out of my hand.

I clamp my hands over my mouth to stop a scream from escaping past my lips.

Standing in all his dark glory is my stalker. He's tall, definitely over six-foot. His hood is down, and the angry curtains thrash behind him with the wind and harsh rain from the open doors of the balcony.

The drops falling into my room make me sigh; it will be a pain cleaning it.

The wind pulls at his untamed hair, and a trail of smoke surrounds him, the burning butt of the cigarette a glow in the dark. A cold sweat breaks out on my back, and my hands tremble. There is this unhinged atmosphere to him that makes him look absolutely terrifying. I fear if he were to reach out and demand to rip out my blackened heart, he could easily reach inside my chest and tear it out.

And no one would be able to stop him.

He looks like a reaper coming to collect my soul before its time.

8
AMBROSE

I feel sick.

My lower lip trembles while I keep my eyes from moving all over the place.

I lose my thoughts.

My fight-or-flight response leaves me frozen in place instead.

My voice doesn't come out when I try to speak.

He turns and looks ready to walk out, but at the very last minute, he turns his head, letting me have a glimpse of his sharp jaw. And then he is gone.

The fluidity at which he moves, the soundless steps despite his large figure as he rushes off, leaves me breathless.

As soon as I see him jump, I run towards the balcony, shutting the doors and locking them. I slide down the doors to the floor, then pull my knees up to my chest.

He left.

Thank God he left.

I wouldn't have been able to escape him if he stayed.

My head drops on my knees. Everything is spiralling out of my control.

I am tired of being who I am.

How much do I have to bear while being a puppet to my fear?

To my mother?

To what everyone expects of me?

I wish I could dig into my chest and rip out my heart and let myself be free of this slow, painful demise.

I rise to my feet and walk to the bathroom on unsteady legs, shedding all my clothes on the way. In the shower, I rub at my skin as if the steaming hot water can erase me. I rub, rub, and rub until my skin is red and raw, the scars burning and burning, but I don't feel satisfied.

A lone tear slides down my cheek, and I wipe it away.

A monster like me shouldn't hope for good things. I don't deserve it when people have suffered because of me.

9

AMBROSE

"He was what?" My voice carries pure shock.

Mom's expression is one of disappointment rather than pity or even sadness.

She just told me she got news that Darci's best friend has died.

Like… he is dead. Not alive anymore.

Darci has been put under lockdown, and the Antas have called off the engagement. The only heir to the Anta Group won't be put in danger. He was with him that night, according to Mum, and he could easily have been murdered in his place.

Investigations will now begin.

Could it have been… my stalker?

Did he do it in warning to Darci? Am I being delusional to think he did it because Darci touched me wrong?

Mum doesn't like this. She's missed her chance to marry me off to secure her position in society. Isn't that what Dad did with Aurora? Am I going to be met with a similar fate?

"Mum, aren't you tired of trying to be somewhere we don't belong? Look at Aurora. She—"

"Don't speak her name in this house!" she shrieks.

Red eyes glare at me, stopping me mid-bite. I swallow the avocado toast the cook prepared for us. Toast, fresh jam, green smoothies, pancakes, and so much more food that will be wasted sits on the table. Ever since Mum came back, she has kept up the expenses as if Dad is alive and bringing in money to keep up with them.

I've never visited his grave. His funeral was an event for people to play inspector, guessing why and how he died. Mum hid in the four walls of her bedroom for the first couple of days after it, then fled to Glasgow.

"What do you mean? Why can't I?"

"Grow up a little, would you? Do you not know that her husband is the one who killed your father? He was here that day!" She slams her hand on the table, but I don't feel frightened at all. Rather, I am angry. Furious, even.

"I think it's time you realise how fucking neglected you made Aurora feel; she was here every single day when you were having your depressive episodes. She was here when you needed her, but you discarded her the minute she wasn't useful anymore. What kind of mother are you?" I am heaving by the end of my short speech.

I am so tired of Mum tarnishing her name when she isn't

here. So tired of her casting her in such a bad light when she merely wanted love from her parents.

A lot like myself.

Mum chuckles, and it's taunting and intimidating.

Her eyes sharpen on me, and my blood chills. Ice pricks at my fingertips. Distaste leaks from her eyes, pooling around her.

"What about you, Ambrose? You are giving me a lecture on how I treated Aurora; have you forgotten the monster you are for doing what you did to her? For almost getting her killed? Do you not think your own actions have consequences? Did you forget about the scar she has on the back of her ear? It is there because you didn't stop your father. Did you forget her gasping for air when your father was threatening her? Did you forget that you were also closed off from her? Did you forget...."

As she replays each of my mistakes, one after the other, I feel myself shrink in my chair.

I know I shouldn't have behaved the way I did. I am thirty years old, not a fucking child, but how do I defend myself against this?

I can't.

So I blink the burn away. I grind my teeth, and my hands tighten into fists in my lap as my head hangs in shame. Mum shouts profanities, her anger hot and boiling. Every single word from her mouth is like lava searing through my skin.

The room spins, and Mum's face blurs. I reach up and massage my temple to keep the headache away until I faintly hear her walk away. I heave myself out of my chair and head to the office, shaking my head and ridding myself of the dizziness.

Swallowing, I enter my office in the Glamorous building, dropping my bag and taking a deep breath.

It hurts to even take a breath. It hurts to live. It hurts to want to be loved. It hurts. It hurts.

I did this. I did this. God, I did this to myself.

I need to search Helia's office today for documents of any kind to support my claim, but my mind feels foggy, and it just fucking hurts.

Taking my iPad in hand, I knock on Helia's door, then walk inside, only to stop short at the sight in front of me.

My whole body freezes, and I feel my whole world screech to a stop.

It's the woman whose life I also destroyed. One I was supposed to protect with all my might but didn't.

There sits my younger sister, Aurora Cainn, with my nemesis.

They both glance at me.

One in shock and one in annoyance.

"Did I tell you to come in?" Helia snaps, but my eyes are stuck on Aurora, who looks away from me.

"I... didn't know. I'll leave." I turn around, shutting Helia's door behind me, and rush back to my office.

I shove my hands under my thighs to stop them from shaking.

When they don't stop, I get up and walk on shaky legs

downstairs to the second floor to the small cafe. As soon as I am seated with a cup of coffee in front of me, I finally take my first deep breath.

It feels too much.

My body is still shaking, as if I'm afraid of everything around me.

I am not like this.

This is not me.

The tension in my shoulders and the shaking intensifies as I try to focus on my breathing. I concentrate on the feeling of sitting on my yoga mat as raindrops fall outside on my balcony. The cool air wrapping around me. The curtains softly flapping against the doors. The faint hum of wind flowing through the leaves outside.

My breathing finally slows, and my heart calms.

"I thank God every day that I have a secure job. Some people's arrogance gets the better of them, and when they are forced to their knees, it's a satisfying thing to see."

My eyes snap open and find the marketing intern, Naya Fash. She started working here just a year ago. I remember I rejected her designs. They were ugly, and I didn't sugarcoat my words.

She's talking to another intern, Selena Mell. A perfect match to her. They are both the same. Wouldn't be a surprise if they turned out to be sisters.

"Right? Everyone should stay humble. Ego can be bad for you, especially when your downfall follows right after," she says tartly, looking at me from the corner of her eye.

I don't respond. My head is swimming with thoughts about Aurora, but they don't let my mind stay quiet.

"I hope you are safe from the torments of people in this company. You can talk to me any time." Selena places a hand on Naya's shoulder.

Naya smiles. "Of course. It's quite hard, but I am glad that the management has changed, or I would have looked for a new job."

"Would have done us all a favour," I mutter, rolling my eyes.

Naya's black hair flicks over her shoulder as she turns to me, and Selena, whose red hair is up in a ponytail, also narrows her eyes at me as if I am the one talking shit about them.

"Excuse me?" Naya turns to me.

"You heard what I said. The changes in management don't mean that I have no power. I am still the second highest shareholder in the company.?"

Naya's face burns, the red hue spreading over her face and chest.

"But it doesn't mean you get to threaten to fire me," she spits back.

I chuckle at her words, and that makes them both straighten. I never intended to bully anyone anymore, and I won't, but they need to know to not overstep their boundaries.

"Sure, you can believe that if you like. It's not like I don't know every single employee in here and every single dirty thing they've done," I say, my eyebrow raised.

Selena opens her mouth. My attention snaps to her, and she shuts it under my harsh gaze.

"Let's go. There is no point in arguing with such entitled people." Selena all but drags Naya away.

I head back upstairs soon after, not wanting another encounter like this. It's part of the reason I rarely even leave my floor. I can feel the eyes of the managers on this floor follow me, a soft continuous murmur between them.

"She's beautiful and really kind. I wish she'd taken over Glamorous."

That one whisper sticks to me as I knock on Helia's door.

Dread settles deep in my stomach.

"Come in."

I do, only to find Helia on his way out. Aurora is still there, sitting on the chair in front of his desk.

His emerald eyes capture my own hostage as he leans down, his breath fanning my ear, burning it from the heat as he hoarsely whispers, "Take care of my guest, will you?"

A faint whisper of a touch lights the side of my neck on fire when he leaves, and a hot shiver runs up my spine as if he dragged his finger down my throat, but it was so faint I could have imagined it.

The door clicks shut, and silence takes over.

I can hear myself breathing as Aurora looks outside towards the gloomy London skyline.

Twisting pain hits me when I realise she is purposely not looking at me. She doesn't want to see my face.

And I deserve it, don't I?

When have I ever given her any reason to come back to me? To seek me out? To trust me?

My blood pumps hard against my eardrums. The silence is deafening. My lips dry as I open and close my mouth, trying to start a conversation or to just apologise.

Will she even forgive me?

She won't.

She doesn't have a reason to.

Tears pool in my eyes, but I blink them away quickly.

It's okay.

At least she is happy.

Your older sister will stop looking after you now.

Remo will protect you. He will keep you safe. I know it.

Don't worry, little sister. Don't worry anymore. And don't fear.

I stand next to Aurora, detached, caught up in my head.

She slowly drags her attention to me. Her chocolate eyes are soft, a painfully beautiful combination. Her brown hair cascades down her back in soft waves, and she wears a cream dress with matching heels. She's always loved wearing them. Not to mention the designer bag, the watch, and the diamonds decorating her. All of that is new, they must be gifts from Remo. He spoils her, and I couldn't be happier.

"Aurora, how are you?" I bite my lip, keeping my tears at bay.

"Just fine," she says quietly.

Your voice is still just as soft, just as sweet.

Silence follows.

Your eyes still hold dreams, Aurora.

Aurora lets out an empty laugh.

"You aren't even going to apologise for anything? You're not going to say you feel bad for what you did and how you treated me?"

You don't know how much those thoughts haunt me every night.

I swallow as a minute passes. I walk around and sit on the chair in front of her.

"I—" A lump forms in my throat, choking my words. So I try again. "Would you believe me if I said yes?"

The indifferent look in her eyes confirms she won't.

"I didn't—" My voice gets stuck in my throat. "I've wronged you, Aurora." My voice cracks. "I did so many bad things to you, and I left you when you needed me. I left you standing, fighting alone, when you needed your big sister, all to one day get the approval, the love, of a man whom I called my father, and yet I lost everything in between."

Aurora's eyes water, the soft brown now a muddy colour, reflecting her broken heart.

"Twenty-nine years you have been by my side, twenty-nine years of me leaving you to fend for yourself. H-How do you think I will ever forgive myself?" Leaning forward, I drop my knees to the cold hard floor, grasping her hands in my own trembling ones.

"The bullying in school when people liked you more than me, taunting you for doing what you loved, letting the abuse in our house happen to you instead of standing in front of you to protect you…" I shake my head, my chin quivering with the intense rush of emotions.

"Ambrose—"

"Let me speak, please. I hate myself for what I did to you, Aurora. To everyone. All when I lost myself. I should be ashamed. I am, and I'm trying to fix the damage I did. You are the biggest part of that. Your own sister is asking you for forgiveness, for tormenting you, for all the other things."

Tears gather in my eyes, blurring my vision. Aurora shakes her head, a lone tear falling down her face.

"You may not ever forgive me, but please know that I will do my best to help you, or I'll stay away from you if you want. I won't look in your direction, won't show up at your house, and won't ever stand in your way." I let her hands go, my eyes dropping to the ground. "Just know one thing. I hate myself for what I did, and I hope one day you'll find it in yourself to forgive me."

I blink up at the ceiling, willing the tears to go away, and then stand up.

"Ambrose, look at me." Aurora's shaky voice has me glancing down at her. "I can't look past your harshness, Ambrose."

I weakly smile, nodding.

She stands up too.

I will accept anything you give me.

"You ruined my self-confidence. You ruined the years

that were supposed to be most memorable to me. You ruined everything when all I had was a mere hope that my older sister would just… help me, guide me in life, but none of that happened." More tears fall from her eyes, and she looks to the side.

"I hate you for what you did to me," she says sharply, then turns her eyes to me. They brim with hate, but most of all, hurt. Deep, deep hurt. "I don't know how I can forgive you for it, but I know that it made me strong, almost immune to the hate and everything that comes with it from other people. But it hurts sometimes, you know?"

I sniffle, holding back my own pathetic tears.

"But I see you trying. I can see you fighting and holding on to a part of you that was once present before I joined your school. I see the Ambrose who loved bringing me snacks at midnight, the Ambrose who helped me bandage my knees when I fell, and the one who shared her dolls with me."

By the end of it, I have a hand in front of my mouth, holding in the sob. Aurora isn't ashamed to show her tears. They fall down her cheeks right in front of me.

"I hope you find a better purpose in life, Ambrose. Dad is gone, and Mum is slowly falling into his footsteps. I see it, and Remo tells me of her doings. Make your life better." She turns around and heads out, leaving me a mess.

My head drops, my hand covering my eyes as more tears fall and quiet sobs shake my body.

10
AMBROSE

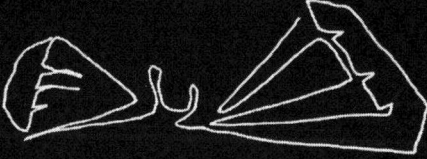

The talk with Aurora put me in a place that is pushing me to be a better person. She doesn't want me around her, and I understand. I will give her the space.

When I was watering my plants a few days ago, I felt the piercing gaze of my stalker, but the fear wasn't there anymore. If he comes to me again, I'm going to demand answers. I'm ready to take him on, because for how much longer will I suffer? The answer is, I won't anymore.

Why me?

For all these months, why me?

What is it about me that keeps him coming back, day after day?

What is his motivation?

So, when the heat crept from my back to my neck, I dropped everything and finally opened my bedside drawer and ripped open the rolled piece of paper he left a few nights ago.

Men who touch you will meet the same fate as Mr fucking Darci. This time, my bullet won't miss him by an inch. Be careful of who you allow to touch my obsession. It's not a pretty obsession. I will come to collect, to mark, and I will keep my promise of tasting my personal hell on earth.

It confirmed that the death of Darci's best friend wasn't simply an unfortunate car crash.

I worked up the courage to finally text my stalker.

Ambrose: You killed him?

The reply comes two minutes later.

Unknown: Yes.

I suck in a sharp breath at his unapologetic, one-word answer.

The headlines the next morning were all about the car crash. There were also pictures of Darci, his best friend, and me together at the event. I stayed in my office and went out the back entrance when I saw the rush of paparazzi in front of the office building.

My security footage is proof enough I was home, so they

let me go easily. Today, I am more determined than ever to search through Helia's office when he goes out for lunch. He asked me to book a reservation at a restaurant for two. He's meeting with Remo Cainn. He didn't invite me, and I didn't protest, too set on trying to find documents of any kind to support my reinstatement as CEO. Anything to help me get back my rightful company.

"I'm heading to lunch. Make sure you prepare for the board meeting tomorrow and email me all notes and what importance each board member has. I don't mean basic details; I mean, a good background check on them. And that new magazine volume being published for next month? I want further details and a final prototype before it's sent for mass printing. It's a spring edition, so make sure all the models we need are able to come. I want the location to be on a yacht on the Thames on a sunny day."

I note down everything Helia tells me on my iPad while he grabs his things.

As I look up, Helia walks past me. His shoulder brushes against mine, stealing my breath. I catch his glance at my lips, and the intensity in his eyes almost knocks me off my feet.

We still bicker, still disagree on many things. I used to manage most of Glamorous, so when he makes a decision I don't like, I voice my opinion. It often turns into a shouting match until I have to force myself to walk away and let him be.

Despite the tension between us, there are many instances where I believe Helia has touched my hand on purpose. Other times, he looks at me a second longer than necessary. Sometimes when I am writing something, I feel the tingles of awareness of his heavy looks.

Maybe it's just my imagination. But the racing beat of my heart, the shivers down my spine, the flutters in my stomach every time that brush of skin contact happens… How do I explain that?

The door shuts behind me.

The splatter of rain is soft against the floor to ceiling window to my left.

The only noise in the room is the soft ticking of the clock on the wall. I wait for five minutes at the least, making sure he doesn't come back, before I place my iPad on the table and rush to open the drawers.

There are files of the takeover, of the shares being handed to Helia. All these documents are public, so it's of no use to me. The second drawer holds copies of past magazine volumes. The third one is empty except for a small paperclip.

I search the left side of the table, but there is nothing in the drawers, leaving me frustrated. The shelf on the left wall displays every single volume Glamorous has ever published.

"Could there even be incriminating paperwork in here? He wouldn't leave it here, would he?" I run a hand through my hair, trying to work out where it could be. I can't go to his home, but maybe Remo has something.

I can't go to Remo's office to ask him.

Then I remember a hiding spot Dad had.

Peeking under the table, I find it. Pulling out a stack of papers, I quickly flick through it. It's a list of the finance team. Their names, addresses, previous jobs, and resumes. I peruse the five profiles. I could look them up, but why did Helia change the whole finance team?

Taking out my phone, I take pictures of each team member before placing the paperwork back the way it was under the table, then I head out.

Once seated at my own desk, I use my personal laptop and search for the names online. Each one comes up blank. I search again, adding the keyword *Glamorous*, and still nothing. There is nothing on them, not the job search websites, nor the search engines for jobs. For them to be in such a high position in Glamorous, they should have a professional profile, but they don't.

I let my head hang back against the chair, watching the light above me.

Is that how Helia works?

Just like the light flares out, covering every corner of the room, Helia might be doing the same. His touch and connections flaring out to cover every corner of what he owns. All this so he is aware of what is going on at all times.

I snap up, then search *Helia Nashwood*. I find pictures from the conference, and after some scrolling, I spot a picture of him walking behind Aurora a few months ago just outside her office building. She is frowning, looking down at the ground, while he walks behind her, looking around as if guarding her.

What kind of mystery are you, Helia?

Just the mere sight of his pictures has me squirming in my chair. Something a lot like discomfort mixed with irritation swims inside me. Why do his pictures make my heart race?

Scrolling up, I find a particular picture of him holding a mic and looking at the audience. There's a smirk on his face, and his eyes twinkle with wicked intention.

I can feel the power of his eyes, the hypnotic skill he has to capture everyone in the audience under his spell, keeping them hooked enough to get what he wants from them.

That vicious look in his serpent eyes is enough to make the audience squirm in fear, the sharpness of his facial structure setting him apart as a man with charisma and a good-looking face. Helia isn't the typical handsome man. He has this devious look to him that can only be described as Helia being a killer in a room full of sinners.

A grim reaper.

Every time I look at him, when my eyes connect with his, my skin tingles in awareness, telling me danger is close by. My instincts know that Helia is the epitome of a devil. And yet, my stomach doesn't hesitate to twist in his presence, to make me feel emotions that should absolutely never be felt for my nemesis.

I type *Remo Cainn* in the search bar, and pictures come up from his campaigns, the wine empire he has, and many are of his wedding with Aurora. I keep scrolling and scrolling, ready to give up until I find one of him standing outside my house.

Outside the Torre mansion with me in front of him.

I notice something in the corner of the picture. Right to the left of our house.

It's a hooded figure.

The same figure that reminds me of my stalker.

And my heart drops to my feet.

11
HELIA

With my hood up, I drop my burnt cigarette to the ground. My eyes do a slow sweep of the grounds. The guards never see me hidden in this place. Despite their schedules changing every night, it's easy to pick up on the pattern.

Easily rushing across the grass, I take hold of the pipe that leads up the side of the house and climb onto Ambrose's balcony. I am quick to drop to my feet onto the marble of the balcony. It's way too easy.

Many times, I've leaned against the railing of this very balcony and watched her sleep. I watched her thrash in her bed, small tears falling down her face as if she were reliving a nightmare.

My curiosity never dimmed.

It never strayed.

There has always been a why with her, and I am going

crazy with my unanswered questions.

Why the façade?

Why commit the sins when you couldn't bear the consequences?

Why be who you are when you know it would turn you ugly in the eyes of others?

One must repent in order to rebuild their life.

Ambrose didn't do that.

I step over the threshold and into her bedroom.

Her bed, with its plain white wooden bed frame, is pushed against the right wall. A rectangular mirror faces her bed, and there's an ensuite bathroom as soon as you enter her room on the left. A walk-in closet is in front of me, and there are a few tall plants here and there. The plants are the only hint of colour in her room.

The shower shuts off.

The minute the door creaks open and I hear the soft padding of feet, my eyes dart to it. I made sure to time the lights switching off at this very moment. They all go out except the ones visible to the guards, as to not raise suspicions.

The sight in front of me shatters my resolve. Her wet hair sticks to her body, and her black leggings and a tight shirt mould to her body. The sight of her top clinging to her breasts, her nipples peeking through the top makes me grind my teeth. Ambrose is wearing fucking plain leggings and a shirt that reveals nothing but everything at once. The view has my blood rushing south, and my hands ball at my side.

She looks up, brushes her hair with her fingers, and freezes when she spots me.

I should be advancing towards her to make her relive it all the torment she's inflicted upon others, but I am frozen too.

My eyes don't fix on a single thing. I take in all of her. Her blond wet hair trickling all around her face, the soft skin of her face, the paleness resembling an unreachable cloud. Her nails manicured and painted nude, her bare feet.

I hate her. But I also desire her. She just doesn't realise it yet.

"W-What…" Her voice is soft, and her lips part on a gasp. Her face is bare, as it always is when the earth is cloaked in darkness.

But today, for the first time, I have the privilege of looking at her closer, to see her face bare of any makeup at all. To discover the reddish hue to her cheeks and the paleness of her skin as if she were a doll. A weak, breakable doll that could shatter under the slightest pressure.

Ambrose with no makeup has me weak in my knees.

She looks… precious.

Delicate.

I would have never used these words to describe Ambrose, who is usually all harsh lines, scowls, and a bitter tongue.

I take a step forward, my combat boots thumping on the wooden flooring. She takes one back.

"Why are you here?" There is a tremor in her voice as

her eyes flick all around, possibly to find an escape, or maybe a weapon.

"I've caught you now, little sin." My voice is the same, and I fear she may know who I am, but when fear takes over people, they are usually unable to think rationally.

"What do you mean? Stop. Why are you walking towards me?" She takes one more step back and slams against her bedroom door, her hand frantically feeling around for the doorknob.

"The minute you exit through that door, I will catch you. What follows after that may not be as nice." I tilt my head, and a small frown turns her lips down.

"Tell me, little sin, have you ever thought of me?" The words slip out. My mind always takes a different turn when I'm around her.

"N-No. Did they send you? Why are you here?" She bites her lip, and her arms wrap around her chest as if she's trying to guard herself from me.

Is she expecting someone else? I haven't given her much to work with.

"Hm, how should I answer that question?"

I advance towards her, my footsteps like the tick of a clock. Her breaths come in short pants. Soon there is just one metre left between us.

She stands up straighter, jutting her chin out, and snaps, "I'm not scared of you, if that is your aim. For months, you've haunted me and my nightmares. How dare you just waltz in here as if it's your given right?"

I lift a brow at her standing up to me. Her strength is unmatched, and something a lot like pride blooms in my chest.

I close the distance between us and press her against the door, caging her in with my arms on either side of her face. I lean down, thankful for the balaclava that covers my face. I could wear contacts, but I don't really care if she finds out.

"Is that so?" I murmur, leaning my face forward.

The thrill of the unknown between us has me craving a taste of her. I want to press my lips to hers. To steal a kiss as a secret between us, but she won't know it's me.

So I restrain myself.

I let my eyes wander down her body, and my fingers skim up her thighs. She clamps them shut. I look at her. There is revulsion within those fierce eyes and yet something is brimming on the edge of it. Her eyes are drowning in fear mixed with ... something dirty.

"Yes. I know they sent you to make my life hell, but I'm already living with the consequences of my actions. If you have been watching me, surely you would know that." The honesty in her voice stops me.

Who are *they*? And why does she keep referring to them?

Is someone after her for what she has done?

I don't answer her question, wanting to see if she'll keep talking, but she doesn't utter anything else.

"I shouldn't be touching you like this, little sin. In fact, I should be staying outside, but I can't help but want to know if your daydreams ever have me touching you... like this..."

She frowns, but when she rubs her thighs together, and my interest spikes.

"No. Never. Get out. Right now, or I will shout for security."

Her threats don't scare me.

"Oh? But I told you to stay put. I don't want to resort to any harsher methods. I only want to touch you, to feel this porcelain skin that glows under the moonlight, to look at you from a step closer."

During the day, Ambrose would never let me. She would push me, hit me, and even bite to get away from my touch, but there is a vulnerability in her eyes right now. She thinks I was sent by someone.

That was long before this, and since I hired her, there is no need for me to be here anymore, yet here I am.

She takes a deep breath in, closing her eyes for a moment too long.

I take this time to watch her. To just look at her.

For one second.

Two seconds.

Three.

I keep looking at her, watching the way her slim nose twitches slightly when she breathes out. Her lower lip is just a fraction fuller than her top one. I see her dark lashes, the faint purple veins on her eyelids, the tinge of red to her cheeks from the shower, and the faint sparkle of water on her face.

Everything. I see everything.

And only then, just as I am about to count the droplets on her face, does she open her eyes.

Earthy brown, swirling with tinges of a softer honey colour.

They prove to be a lot softer, a lot warmer, than when she is biting at me.

My heart bounces inside me.

"What touch?" she whispers, her eyes wide and curious. "I-I will give you anything, but don't touch me."

When I raise my hand, she cringes back against the door, shutting her eyes tightly. I drop my hand.

"Why? Are you repulsed by me?" I tease.

"I hate my body. I hate to be touched. So please don't," she whispers.

My amusement flees.

12

AMBROSE

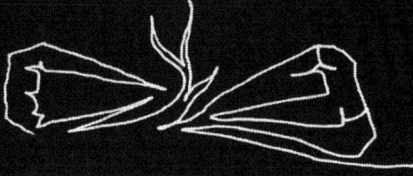

Age sixteen

"Make sure you don't talk to them, okay?"

Aurora nods, her lips pressed together as her determined eyes watch me.

How could I protect my sister from the horrors within the walls of this school?

Warning her would do her good. She will know what to expect, will know what to do, so she doesn't make the mistake I did.

Aurora smiles at me, then turns and walks away. It feels as if a piece of my heart has walked away with her.

It's my last year in secondary school, the last year before I can leave and never look back at this place. It may be a private school, and Dad has paid big amounts of money for us to study here, to get a good education, to live and learn amongst the elite. Yet the only thing I have learned to do is to hide my fear well.

My heart drums inside of me as I make my way towards my first class of the day, of a long final year, while my heart twists inside of me in terror.

One last year of fighting. One last year of surviving where no one sees my battles.

As soon as I enter the classroom, the lights dim and I realise no one is here. My breath catches in my throat, and panic sets in.

It's like I have been locked inside a small place with no way out, thrown into deep water with no oxygen tank as I struggle to breathe. Like something is wrapped around my neck, strangling the life out of me.

The door slams shut behind me. I flinch and spin around.

Three students.

Layla Madden. Gabriella Madden. Inara Madden.

Blond Layla, and brunette Gabriella and Inara.

"What happened, Ambrose?" Layla taunts, crossing her arms as she stalks towards me.

Every step, every echo of her shoe hitting the floor, chokes me a little more.

Every wicked grin, every dark twinkle in her eye, and every word coming out of her mouth has me wishing for death.

How could my father, who is spending each and every penny working his way up, barely paying our fees here to get us the best education in the whole United Kingdom amongst the elite, fight against the three daughters of the

pharmaceutical king of Britain? The internationally successful man who could crush our whole family like a mere
speck of dust in his way.

"Please let me go," I plead.

Layla tsks, shaking her head. "We just want to play like
friends do, and you, Ambrose…" She places a hand on my
shoulder, making my body jerk. Her hold turns rougher,
holding me in place as she walks around me. "You are our
dearest and most special friend. Friends help each other and
have fun, right?" She grabs both my shoulders and leans her
face next to mine from behind me.

Gabriella and Inara laugh and nod.

"Then, while we wait for the teacher, let's see you dance
for us." Layla pushes me farther into the classroom, her
words haunting me.

Last time, she made me take off my jacket, then made
me stand there as they threw balloons filled with paint, and
they laughed through it all. The bruises are still present on
my body. I hate them. They are a sign of my weakness.

I fought them in the first year, but how much can I fight
when I know one small squeak from me could ruin my
whole family?

"With no music?" Gabriella asks with a gasp before she
takes out her phone.

"Oh, put my favourite one on. She will look so good
dancing to this one." Inana hurries to her, and I just stand
there, shaking.

I go to shake my head, but the look in Layla's dark eyes

127

has me freezing in place.

"I heard your sister joined this school. Oh, how beautiful and innocent she is," she says.

My eyes widen, my lips parting. "No." I go to take a step forward, but Layla's grimace as she steps away from my touch stops me in place.

"Then get going. We put music on for you. Dance for us a little."

But they had something else in mind. They always did, and now, this time, to protect Aurora, I sit there as Gabriella and Inara hold my arms out and Layla uses small sharp razors to slice across my thighs. Blood spills from the wounds.

My screams reach high up to the heavens. They are ripped out of me with every swipe, every cackle and laugh they make. I bite my lip until it bleeds crimson. I shut my eyes, tears flowing out of me, but the thought of Aurora ever being in this position has me struggling. It has me sitting through it. I will never allow my sister to experience this.

"Look at her crying,"

"You had beautiful thighs. Just let us decorate them."

"Aw, cry a little harder, and I might stop."

And I bleed in the dark classroom to protect my family.

I bleed in the darkness while I lose my love for myself.

And I cry as my own happiness is ripped from me, my screams tearing up my insides.

***

"Ambrose?" Aurora's confused face is a blur, but I ignore her and walk away from her in the hallway.

The next day, the same thing happens, no matter if we come in the same car to school. Mum drops us off with a smile on her face, not realising what is hidden in the towering walls of this school.

"Ambrose, please listen to me!" I hear Aurora shout, but I run away from her as soon as my feet touch the ground.

And the next day.

And the next month.

I avoid her for the whole year until the very last month.

Feeling your own sister fade away as you dismiss her existence just for her protection has to be the worst feeling.

I tried protecting her from those who hurt me.

This party was supposed to be in honour of my school winning the football game. It was supposed to be the party I fought for myself. It was supposed to be the turning point in my life where it was only up from here. I was not expecting to come across part of my sister's pink dress peeking out from a small cupboard.

Bang.

Bang.

"Help me!"

I only just catch the muffled words through the heavy music, screams, and chatter of the crowd around the Madden estate. My heart drops. Anxiety twists my insides until all I feel is aching terror.

Time stops.

My blood freezes.

And right now, my personal hell on earth is right in front of my eyes.

My worst nightmare has come to life. Aurora is in there. Trapped. And the Madden sisters are laughing and recording as the doors of the cupboard shake with the force Aurora is using to try to open them.

Laughter. Laughter. Fucking laughter is all around.

Rushing forward and pushing people out of my way, I storm right up to them. Grabbing hold of Layla's phone, I smash it against the nearest wall. It explodes into pieces. I push Gabriella Madden into the pool behind her. Her eyes are wide, and she shrieks as she falls. Grabbing hold of Inara's hair, I push her to the floor. Her screams and clawing hands are nothing to me.

"How fucking dare you use your dirty hands on Aurora?" I scream in her face.

Her eyes snap open, and she sneers at me, wild and crazed.

A hand on my elbow pushes and tugs at my hand that is in Inara's hair, but I don't budge. Not a single muscle.

"Let her go, Ambrose, or this will not—"

I turn around and slap Layla in the face. Her head whips

to the side with the force.

"Shut the fuck up!" I snap.

Turning back to Inara, I pull her up and throw her in the pool.

Breathing heavily, I am barely able to keep my shaky hands from slipping off the knobs of the cupboard.

The doors slam open.

And there she is.

Aurora.

Shaking, shivering, with tears in her eyes.

"Ambrose," she chokes out, her words barely audible.

I tried protecting her. I took the brunt of everything to keep her from getting into trouble or ever having her body damaged. I let myself get ruined so she could stay pretty and happy.

So what in the world is she doing here?

"What are you doing here?" I shout. Guilt slams me when she flinches, but as soon as she steps out, she almost collapses on the floor.

"I-I just wanted to see—"

"See what? Did you not for one second think that just maybe I said no for your own good? Did you think I was joking? That this whole thing is the best thing ever and I am purposely keeping you from having fun?" My voice shakes and drops an octave, but I can't stop.

I was going to shut this whole thing down. I was going to end the bullying, so when I left it didn't follow her, and yet here she is, shoving her nose in business that isn't hers.

"No. I just didn't want to be left alone with Mum and Dad."

"I don't care! You should have asked me!" I scream.

A crowd starts to form around us, but I couldn't care less. She should have stayed at home. She shouldn't have come here.

"How could you be so fucking selfish that you decided to follow me? How could you think that you were going to have fun here when I want nothing to do with you? Ever! Get it through your thick head that you are not wanted."

Her mouth opens, her eyes water, and her hands shake.

"But—"

"But nothing. Never follow me and never, ever, get in my way ever again."

Grabbing her wrist, I drag her out, ignoring the eyes on me and the crowd that seems to want to swallow both me and Aurora.

I don't speak and let her hand go the second we are outside the front gates.

"Ambrose, I didn't mean it like that. You're my sister. I don't know why you were being so distant so suddenly," Aurora whispers from behind me.

"Don't. I don't want you near me. There is no bigger reason. It's the truth. Accept it now before it hurts you."

I am spun around suddenly to face a raging Aurora. The faint smell of rain hits my nose just as the dark clouds above us crack.

"How could you say that? I am your sister!" She shakes

me by my shoulders. "How could you push me away and act like I mean nothing to you? I have been with you my whole life. You protected and—"

"That's the thing, Aurora. I failed to protect you, clearly. Because you showed up. You let everyone know you are as big of a target as I am. So please, for your sake and mine, stay away from me. It's not going to be pretty."

I push off her hands, and the first couple of cold drops hit my skin, making me hiss.

"So that's it? There is nothing else?" Her hands ball at her sides, her pink dress crumbled and ruined.

I would have drawn hearts around all the bruises you may get. I would have got you transferred and still will do so. You didn't believe me when I said it's for your protection, Aurora.

"That's it."

Thunder booms and rain showers us. We both get drenched in no time. Hair sticks to our faces and emotions slowly dissolve as we both stand still, looking into each other's eyes as everything falls apart.

Piece by piece.

The dominoes fall.

And then she says the one word that will change our lives for the next decade.

"Fine."

13

AMBROSE

I installed cameras in my room and had a guard stationed right outside the door.

I can't have a repeat of two nights ago, no matter that I've seen him outside my window the past two days. My stalker is the first ever person I've admitted how much I hate my body. The reason I cover my legs, the reason I wear long sleeves, a jacket, or even black tights.

Going into work the following Monday, I knew I could just ignore everything and focus on my work, on my goal of getting my company back, and stupidly enough, I wanted to face Helia just so I could argue with him and let myself be free. To feel something other than my troubles that I always tuck away before walking outside of my home.

The mansion feels lonely and scary. It's an empty house that once housed monsters and has turned me into one. Mom has never felt the need to stay home often, I barely see her around.

I hate my father for making me who I am. For wanting me to do so well that I lost myself and destroyed so many lives.

I fired people, insulted them in front of everyone, and humiliated them far more than anyone can handle just to display the power I hold. I held the wrong, weaker people accountable just to show I could do it and manipulated everyone around me. That all resulted in resentment from others, including my sister. Now I didn't even know who I was anymore.

The day Dad died, it's like everything shut down and there was finally silence inside my head. It let me think about what I did and the day I made the biggest mistake of my life last year. Aurora's current state, trauma, and paranoia were heightened because of my mistake. I knew the road from then onwards was going to be rough, but it was one I needed to take.

I needed to make things right.

So I have been trying to locate the families, to ask and beg for forgiveness from them, getting on my knees, offering money in exchange for the losses they suffered. I am far from perfect. I still have a long list to go, but I have to start somewhere.

But still, even after trying to be better, Helia's words always keep reminding me of who I was. He brings out the past version of me that loved showing people I can do everything. I truly show what I feel for him clearly. I am truthful in what I say, but I know I can be a little harsh.

It's the way I am, after all.

"Ambrose, get these photocopied, and also, since it's almost lunch, can you get me a quick meal?"

I get up from my chair and head towards Helia, who is scrolling on his phone while holding a stack of papers. I grab them and wait for him to step aside since he is blocking the whole doorway.

Today, his white dress shirt is accompanied by green dice cufflinks that peak out. His sleeves are rolled to his elbows, showcasing the veins decorating his thick arms that hold enough strength and muscle to put many men to shame. His black slacks fit him perfectly and complement his jet-black hair. He looks every part the CEO today.

Something I realised over the past couple of weeks is that I notice Helia's arms a lot. Every. Single. Time. It's like some kind of stupid fetish that makes me want to run my hands along his arms, to feel every vein under my fingertips, to know if that buzzing around us would explode into flames or if he will wrap them around me, suffocating me.

His cologne wraps around me like a shadow. I know if I were any closer to him, it would be stronger, and I would be unable to stop myself from wanting to curl around him and placing my face in the crook of his neck to smell him.

He would take the chance to wrap me so tightly, surrounding my body until I am left gasping for air as he sucks the life out of me. His sharp eyes would watch me suffocate. Exactly as a deadly python would.

"Am I supposed to walk through you?" The sarcasm in my voice has him looking up, and I will never fail to feel my heart pound the minute those emerald eyes connect with mine.

They are so deep, swimming with such depth and darkness around the rims that it makes me want to take a picture or a video just so I could watch the colours blend so perfectly on repeat. The few locks of hair falling into his eyes accentuate the scar on his eye, but I rarely ever look at it. Not because it disgusts me but rather because it's not something that ever puts me off. It makes me curious as to how he got it more than anything.

"Funny," he muses with a deadpan look. He steps to the side and lets me walk through. Everyone has already gone for their lunch, so the floor is empty. I can feel his eyes on me, the intensity of them a slow torture my body recognises when he looks at me, even if I am not directly facing him.

"Did you run up the stairs today?" I hear him call out, humour in the words.

"Was your coffee to your liking today?" I counter, knowing I made it extra sweet when he prefers it plain with no added sugar. I get the photocopies and his lunch from the canteen, since he didn't specify where to get it from, and head back up.

I am about to knock on his door when I catch the faint sound of Helio's voice. I stop and press my ear against the door.

"The new finance team is ready and rolling. Two years

will pass easily for me and then I will be out of your hair, Remo. Don't worry."

There is a pause.

"She's working well. Tell Aurora not to worry. I didn't hurt her sister. I promised, didn't I?"

I bite my lip, heat expanding in my chest at hearing this.

Aurora asked him to be nice to me? He will leave after two years?

For the first time, happiness expands in my chest and there is a bounce in my step when I knock on the door and walk inside. He puts his phone away but keeps his eyes on me while I place the papers and his lunch on his desk.

"I need to eat, too, so I'll be heading out." I turn around, letting a smile stretch on my face once my back is to him and quickening my steps.

"Not so fast."

I halt right in front of the door.

Does he know I was eavesdropping?

He figured it out already?

Is there a camera stationed outside his office door?

Oh God.

What if he saw me snooping through his office that day?

"You missed one paper in this. You have one job and you cannot even do that properly."

I turn around and walk over, taking the paper from him.

"At least I am doing it better than anyone else would have done it," I mutter, shaking my head.

"Repeat that for me."

I glance over my shoulder. Helia is watching me with narrowed eyes.

"Did you not hear me the first time?"

His jaw tics.

"Here I was thinking you were being a good little obedient girl." He tilts his head.

I grit my teeth. "Girl," I drawl, turning around and facing him.

Don't say anything stupid, Ambrose. Don't do it.

"I'm a woman, and if I wasn't aware of your vulgar attitude, I would have thought you had hearing problems."

He lifts a brow at my comment, his hand fisting at his side on the table.

"Your insults don't faze me, Ambrose,"

"Sure, of course. With that personality, you probably got used to them." I don't realise what has come out of my mouth until I blink and see Helia right in front of me.

His hand snaps out and tightens around my throat, just like before.

So tight I can barely breathe.

I gasp for air in short pants, then I drop everything and claw at his hands, but he stands there unfazed, anger brimming in his eyes.

"I would love to fucking kill you right now," he grits out, his face so close to mine, his nose bumps against my own.

But I can't focus, my vision's blurring, and my ears are stuffed with cotton.

My chest heaves.

"You—"

He tsks, shaking his head, the hold tightening, and I fear if he clasped any harder, I would die right here, right this second, and Helia would feel no fucking remorse. I know it.

"Stay in your place, Ambrose. Remember who is in charge and who owns you right now."

I can only gasp. My words incoherent.

Tears gather in my eyes, and I blink them back quickly so I can still see him. It's all a blur. His dark green eyes are the only thing I can focus on.

"Fuck. You," I rasp out.

He throws me on the floor. I throw my hands out to stop the fall.

I heave and gasp, taking in oxygen after being starved of it for a few minutes, after being hung over my death bed like it was just another day. Helia dances with wrath at his fingertips, happy to destroy the world if something of his is taken from him.

My eyes slide to him, and he crouches in front of me, taking my jaw in his hands, holding me tight.

"I will say this one last time: fix that fucking attitude." His voice is laced with malice, hate, and rage all combined.

"You took everything from me and still expect me to bend to your will?" I don't know how I still have any fight left in me after he did all that to me.

He looms over me like an immortal monster, crowding my personal space as if it's his own and I don't deserve any. Everything around me darkens, and I can only see him.

"Yes. Yes, I fucking do. As long as I live."

He raises his hand, and I flinch, not shutting my eyes, instead locking them on his. When I feel his finger trace along my neck, I don't move a single muscle.

I won't show any weakness. Won't let him see that I'm scared of knowing he can end my life. Won't show him that just the sight of him evokes conflicting emotions, though wishing for his death steals the top spot.

He won't ever get anything from me.

His eyes, for some reason, show a glint of appreciation. For what? For me standing up for myself and not succumbing to his bullying? For trying to instil fear in me? For the marks he's left on my neck?

Why?

"Don't touch me with your disgusting hands." I slap his hand away before getting off the floor and walking away, slamming the door so loudly behind me that I spot someone at a desk jump at the sound.

How dare he?

How fucking dare he put hands on me after telling my sister he won't touch me?

That proves to me to never trust anything that comes out of Helia's mouth.

He's a monster.

The unapologetic villain in my story.

A fucking nightmare.

One I will not, under any circumstance, let win in my story.

14

AMBROSE

I stand before the house of one of the women I unfairly fired. I am shivering but ready to take her on. I know nothing will faze me, not after what Helia has done. She worked in Glamorous before I arrived, but the minute she messed up a small sum on the marketing budget report, I rained down on her in front of the whole staff and fired her on the spot.

She was supporting her small family of two children along with her husband, who had broken his leg and was unable to work. She was in a tight position.

I ring the bell, and when she opens her door, I am met with her widened eyes.

"Can I talk to you for a second, Savannah?"

Her lips part in shock, but she lets me inside.

"Are your children not home?"

"What is it you need, Ms Torre?" The cold tone she uses has me spinning around to find her arms crossed.

"I came to apologise."

She lifts a brow. "Do you need something?" she repeats stiffly.

"No, I don't need anything. I wanted to apologise for how I treated you. I am so sorry for the position I put you in years ago. You don't understand just how much... guilt I have been carrying around me, the weight on my shoulders is too heavy, and I cannot imagine what you went through after I fired you like that—"

"Are you done? Do you need a pat on the back?"

I shake my head. I knew not everyone would be accepting of my apology, and that's okay. As long as they know I am sincere and truly mean my apology.

"I came to give you money. I didn't realise you were struggling, and to be honest, I shouldn't have fired you at all. I am truly sorry, and I hope you accept my apology. Not because you feel bad for me or I am trying to guilt trip you, but because I know I did the wrong thing, and I am here to address that and make amends."

She looks at me for a second, and my heart quivers with uncertainty inside of me. She sighs and shakes her head.

"This is nearly not enough for what you made me go through. I had two kids to support. That job was providing for all four of us, and you took that away for such a small error. Rich kids like you will never understand the struggle to put food on your table, to be working while being under the pressure to provide everything for your family." Her words dowse me in ice water.

"You were rude, selfish, entitled, and the sickest person I had ever met. Your money now will not fix what you ruined years ago, Miss Torre. I suggest you leave before my kids get back from the park. I don't want to see you again. Please. Leave."

I open my mouth, but she looks away from me.

"I truly hope you find it in yourself to forgive me one day, Savannah," I whisper into the quietness of the house before walking out.

I left behind the cheque. Regardless of her reception of me, I don't want her to struggle.

The next two ex-employees did shout at me, but they also cried in my arms, making my own eyes tear up.

The old Ambrose never realised the severity of her actions.

God, I hate myself.

I'm fixing everything. I'm trying.

It doesn't matter that I can't fix myself.

"Come on, Ambrose, let loose a little." Talia says, then urges me to take a sip of the water she brought me, but being at this event while thinking about everything I have destroyed is hard.

I feel like I'm drowning in my own mistakes, in my own mind, and the water is so deep I can't seem to pull myself out of it.

"Is something wrong? Do you want to get out of here?"

I sigh into my drink, gazed fixed on the water, thinking if I were to jump off this yacht, if I were to let my body sink beneath the waves, would that bring me peace?

"I … I've made too many mistakes and wrong choices in my life. How can I stand here and enjoy this?" I look up from my glass.

Talia's head is tilted, her beautiful hair falling to the side, her bright eyes swimming with confusion.

"Don't we all? Don't we all wake up and have to decide to be better each day so we can correct that? Make up for it? Don't you think we all strive to better ourselves? So that we become a better person?"

Leaning against the railing, I watch the water, the ripples, as the yacht moves through it, pulling me in.

"Sometimes, the sins we commit are so big, so grand, that it could be deemed as unforgivable," I say quietly.

Talia stays quiet. Murmurs and laughter from inside the yacht trickle outside, the wind whips our hair in all directions. The music flowing out from the interior room feels like it's mocking me. It's so lively, so soft and warm, while I stand outside in the cold, letting the cool wind slash at my heart, taking it as a form of punishment.

"Do you want to know something?" Talia whispers.

I glance over at her. Her head is tilted back, her gaze fixed up at the cloudy sky. Her brows are pinched together, a small twist to her mouth.

"Remember when I told you months ago that I some-times wished I could do what I wanted? To not be born from money and do silly little things like sneak out to parties, to kiss a random boy recklessly, to go to a school where I could actually make friends because they genuinely like me?"

"I found that staying within the walls of my house is safer." She confesses.

I stand up, sharp pain twisting at my heart. Why does she sound so defeated?

"I fell in love once upon a time, Ambrose." Her words are just a whisper.

I suck in a sharp breath. I know exactly what is coming.

"He was my bodyguard, and I truly believed it would be something magical. I believed our differences didn't mat-ter." She sniffles, a sad smile pulling at her lips. "I made mistakes, too. I was ready to go against everyone and ev-erything for him, and I did. I went against my parents. I stood in front of them, and I have threatened them with such things that I truly hate myself for doing so. Only to find out my love came favourable to him. I was easy prey."

A lone tear slips down her cheek, and she turns to me, teary-eyed. "We all make mistakes. We all do things we re-gret. Mine may not be the same as yours, but each decision we make changes us, changes who we are."

"Take me, for example. I'm twenty years old, and I'm not the same person I was a year ago. I am still going through life, still getting used to things. You, though? You are old

146

enough to take the reins, to take action, and to forgive yourself before you try to amend things with other people."

"Is that… is that why you don't want anyone from the elite circle? So they don't judge you for what you did in the past?" She bites her lip, another tear rolling down her face, and a small pang hits me. She feels like Aurora to me, like a sister I should protect, and I can't help but reach across and wipe away the tear.

"Why are you giving me advice? Shouldn't I be the one doing that?"

She laughs and shakes her head, looping her arm through mine, and starts to walk towards the room of the event. "You need peace? You need to take your mind off things? Come with me."

I find myself on my back, my feet dipped into the water while I look up at the sky with Talia, pointing out the shapes of the clouds, trying to guess what they are.

"I think I see a crow there." I point to the cloud above us, the sound of the yacht engine a low hum under us.

A smile blooms on my face at the crow, remembering Blaze and the smart little crow he is. My thoughts drift to Helia instead, and I find myself thinking back to the bitter memory of him threatening my life again, in the office, with so many people right outside.

He had no remorse.

And neither did I.

I should have thought about what I was going to say before it came out of my mouth.

"Oh my God! I see it! The tail right there and the beak."

Should I apologise to Helia?

I'm trying to better myself, aren't I?

"Who is that over there? I haven't seen him, like, ever." Talia is hugging my arm, watching someone with narrowed eyes while we stand in the glass house of Aurora's fashion show of the winter collection.

Now that Dad is gone, I am the only one invited. My mother is not even aware of this event. She instead has gone to a dinner party with the ladies from her little friend group.

It's completely dark except for the green lights that are swiftly flashing all around. The show hasn't started, and everyone is mingling. The crowd is large, and I notice it is only people within the elite social circle.

Pride blooms in my heart for my little sister.

I feel happy to be invited here.

I'm wearing a baby blue, off-the-shoulder dress that falls to the floor, the fabric glittering each time the green lights flash over it. Talia is wearing a similar silver off shoulder dress.

"Who?" I ask.

"That guy. He's wearing a black suit and standing with Remo Cainn."

I follow her finger, and once I find Remo talking with

Hayes Lonan, Talia's dad, my eyes shift to the man next to him. My heart stops.

"No. No, no, no." I shake my head, my eyes widening. I blink to see if it really is him. "How can it be? How?"

"You know him? Who is it?"

"He—Talia, he is literally my tormentor. I fight with that man on a daily basis and hate his guts."

Talia looks back at Helia, who is laughing, the smile lines in the corner of his eyes and the extra line at his cheek making a show.

His black suit is tailored to his body, his muscles faintly visible under his suit. The crisp trousers, clean black dress shoes, and the double-breasted suit jacket he has on makes me falter in my insults. Women keep stealing glances at him. Of course they would. He's never shown up to these kinds of parties before. I see some women even blush, but he doesn't look away from the people in front of him. I blink once more, not knowing if I am just imagining him.

"What do you mean, tormentor? What kind of things have you been doing to be put in that position?" Talia bites her lip to stop from laughing.

"Shut up. This is not funny." I turn around quickly and glare at Talia.

"Do I sense a little romance blooming here?" She wiggles her eyebrows at me.

"No. Stop. This is serious, Talia. Believe me."

She doesn't know he quite literally cuts off my oxygen and threatens me to my face.

His emerald eyes turn so bleak, so black, that it scares me.

He looks like a monster.

"Why else would you describe another man in such great detail?"

I frown at her. I didn't even say anything.

"What…?"

"Ohh, *his suit is so black. His trousers hug his legs. Look at his watch, his eyes, his tousled, boyish hair.*" She flicks her hair, posing and shimmying her body to exaggerate each description.

My eyes widen and dart around us. A few people look over in confusion.

"Hahaha!" I force out, then reach out and grab her in a tight hug, stopping her.

But she is laughing. Loud. Her whole body shakes with mine while I try to keep her trapped in my arms.

"Stop this madness, or I swear I will announce that you are drunk and to stay clear of you. Let's see how fast that makes it to the tabloids," I growl.

Talia laughs harder against me. "I would like to see you try it at your own sister's event."

"Fuck." I sigh, knowing she's caught me in the lie. My lips pull up in a grudging smile as she continues to laugh.

She starts to sway as if we are dancing together, her arms going around me.

"So tell me more," she murmurs in my ear.

"There is nothing more. He is my boss, the temporary

CEO of Glamorous. That's it."

She hums. "And what is it that you hate about him?" She lets me go and leans back, brows raised, waiting.

"Of course you would want to know." I roll my eyes and turn to grab another drink, but she stops me.

"No, please, tell me. I can't live in suspense like this. Or else I will walk up to him and ask him myself. You know I will."

I watch her for a minute, and when I don't answer, she pulls from me and starts to walk away.

"Fuck, fine. You are really annoying. Do you know that?"

She shrugs, tapping her toe on the marble floor.

"He… He demands too many things from me. He has made me—the finance manager—his personal assistant. He plastered a fake Out-of-Order notice on the elevator to force me to go up and down the steps! He makes me buy him coffee from all the way down the road instead of the coffee shop or the machines in the building. His lunch, too. He finds every single miniscule mistake in my work.

"I hate him. God, I hate him so much. His eyes remind me of a snake that would literally suffocate you. His hair constantly falls into his eyes, and even that annoys me. Not to mention his disgusting smile, which he frequently throws my way." I let out a big sigh, closing my eyes before opening them again.

Talia is looking at me with her lips rolled in, a glint of amusement in her eyes.

"What?"

Her eyes flick over my shoulder, then back to me.

I freeze.

My whole body ignites as a trail of heat prickles across the back of my head.

"Is there anything else you hate about me, Emerald?" The deep, smooth gravel voice caresses my ears, and goosebumps erupt on my skin. I straighten my spine.

A ghost of a touch skims over my arm.

Something flicks my earring, and I snap my head to the side.

And there he stands.

Helia Nashwood.

A playful grin plays on his lips. His black hair is slicked to perfection, and his emerald eyes are hypnotic. Standing tall and proud, he towers over me, even in my heels. I watch as he slides his attention to Talia, whose gaze is darting back and forth between us.

"Helia Nashwood." He grabs her hand and places a kiss on it.

Her eyes widen at me, as if saying *He's a gentleman. After what you just said?*

I twist my mouth in a frown. *Yeah, he is a manipulator.*

"Talia Lanon," she replies.

"A beautiful name," he says smoothly.

Standing up straight, he looks over at me again. And somehow, my mind manages to admire the way he looks tonight. Dashing. Handsome.

"Do enlighten me. What else your friend here has been

saying about me?" he asks her, keeping his eyes on me the whole time.

I feel a weird twist in my stomach at his presence, at his close proximity. Especially when his hand keeps grazing mine every so often.

"Just describing my hate for you after what happened the last time we were in the office together," I grit out, my hands clenching into fists at my side.

"Last time? You should have been careful with what you said, Emerald." He shakes his head, and a lock of black hair falls into his eyes.

My hand twitches, and I fight the urge to tuck it back in his hair.

"What happened last time?" Talia so intelligently asks.

"Nothing."

"She tried to kiss me."

We both answer at the same time, and Talia bursts out laughing, placing a hand in front of her mouth.

I glare at Helia, who is smiling at me, his eyes wide. He looks just about ready to laugh out loud, too.

"Are you serious?!" I snap at him, then spin to glare at Talia. "And why are you laughing? It's not true!"

Helia wraps an arm around my shoulder, but I shove him off.

"But my beautiful emerald, you did try to kiss me when you were getting off the floor. You were…"

I walk away from the two very annoying people. Their laughter still faintly reaches me as I hurry to my seat.

"Stupid me. What was I thinking?" I slap myself on my forehead lightly, shaking my head.

"Ambrose."

I slow down and look up. Remo raises his glass to me with a nod, and I nod back.

Something must be up for Remo to acknowledge me.

Continuing on my quest to find my seat, I try to take deep breaths, knowing Remo just recognised me after so long at an event. Would it be wrong to ask him to help me get my position back? It won't be in my favour, though. I think Aurora may have told him about me. If she has, that would explain his cold shoulder to me and his lack of interest in me losing my company, while letting Helia be at the head of it.

I'm going to stay clear of him for now.

Several minutes later, Talia drops into her seat next to me.

I ignore her when she points out that Aurora arranged for chocolate-covered strawberries as one of the little snacks, and a small flicker of hope lights in my chest. I love chocolate-covered strawberries.

I quickly squash it down.

She probably didn't do it on purpose. She's probably forgotten that it's my favourite treat.

It's been so long since we have talked about what we liked or hated. We haven't spent time together in years.

"Are you ignoring me?"

I don't answer.

The lights dim, and everyone quietens down.

"Oh no." Talia stiffens, then rolls her lips together, humour dancing in her eyes.

When I follow her eyes, I find that Helia is seated directly in front of me.

Right. In. Front. Of. Me.

The lights focus on the start of the show.

Helia winks at me.

And my heart thunders inside of me, stealing my breath away.

Stupid heart indeed.

15

AMBROSE

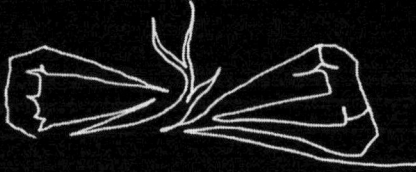

❝I am sick of your attitude!"

"And so am I. Do you see me making heart eyes at you?" I shout back at Helia, who is in my face.

This shouting match is all because I threw the documents on the table instead of placing them in his useless hand.

"I don't want your affection or your presence. Get out of my sight before I kill you," he grits out, taking a step closer to me. His strong gardenia scent irritates me more than anything.

I push his shoulder and grab the file off the table, then I grab his hand and slam the papers into it.

"There you fucking go. Happy?" I walk out, not waiting for his reply. I couldn't care less.

As soon as I sit down at my desk, an email pops up on my screen.

I scowl and click on it.

From: Helia Nashwood
To: Ambrose Torre

Knew you were submissive.

Love,
Helia

I want to strangle this man. He tests my patience every single day.

The little 'love' makes my hand twitch.

The day goes on without me shouting at him again. I silently hand him food at lunch. Then comes the meeting at the end of the day… Just one more hour and I will get to go home. In silence.

I sit next to him at the table, but he doesn't acknowledge me. He simply watches everyone present their reports. He doesn't speak, but everyone still tries to get a reaction or a smile out of him. Every time I look up, I find him looking at me.

Not a smile nor a smirk in place, just looking.

Something about it unsettles me, and I am not sure how to take it.

I raise a brow at him. *What?*

His lip quirks up at his side, and he shakes his head once.

Then I catch him again. This time, I mouth it. *What?*

But he just turns back to the projector in front of us.

The meeting ends, and everyone leaves. I drop my things off at my office, then turn around to head outside. Helia comes out of his office at the same time, and we quietly walk towards the elevator, then wait, watching the numbers on the display go up. It's working today.

"Do you know you chew your pen when you hate someone's idea?" Helia breaks the silence as we walk into the elevator.

"What?"

"Yeah, and you quite literally glare at the person when their idea is, in simple terms, trash."

I huff. "I think you need to get new interns."

"You don't like any of them?"

I turn to Helia. My heart rate skyrockets when I catch his relaxed posture against the elevator. His head is dropped back as he watches me with lazy eyes. He looks so relaxed and at ease, maybe a little sluggish like a drunk person would be, but he looks at me like there may be nothing more interesting than me. And that's a bit scary.

What would Helia be like drunk?

No. I don't want to know.

He would probably finish the job of killing me.

"No. Instead of doing something cliché and floral, like they suggested for the spring collection, we should do a shoot in a forest instead. Or dress the models in big poofy dresses against simple backgrounds. Then the focus will be on the dresses and what we are presenting rather than just a bunch of flowers, which is exactly what our competitors will be doing.

"Not only will the costs be lower, but we can invest in presenting bigger designers, hence remaining exclusive. Then the marketing budget can be used on better models." I lift my eyes from the grey wall of the elevator to find Helia watching me in silence.

I sigh.

"You don't like it, right? You wouldn't care anyway." Shaking my head, I turn around and head out into the parking garage the moment the doors slide open.

"It's good. Make a draft plan and send it to me."

I stop in my tracks and spin around to stare at his back as he climbs into his green Porsche.

"W-What…"

He drives away, and I am left, mouth gaping, in the middle of the silent parking lot.

He… agreed to my idea?

He didn't even argue about it.

16
HELIA

"You said the elevator was fixed and the poster was fake," Ambrose huffs out from next to me.

We are supposed to be on the fifth floor for a meeting with the board members in thirty minutes. And now we are stuck in this elevator, which has suddenly shut down.

How fucking great.

Just my luck to be stuck with her. Except the thought isn't as maddening as I thought it would be. Not after what I know now.

"Well done for being so smart and still using a broken elevator and making me use it too," she grumbles.

She's glaring at me as if it's my fault. I only purposely set that sign outside the elevator to make her job difficult and gave her the work to keep going up and down.

Except, now the broken elevator is actually broken, and I am stuck with her, of all people.

"Are you putting the blame on me?" I point to myself.

She crosses her arms, narrows her sharp eyes, and turns to face me.

"Yes. I am."

From here, I can clearly see the deep chestnut colour in her eyes that I never noticed before and a small mole right on top of her upper lip. Her eyes hold a familiar annoyance towards me.

It feels so familiar, so soothing, and yet chaotic.

We fit like this. Always arguing, always against each other, yet still have that feeling of familiarity.

And I hate to admit the fact that I truly look forward to having a moment alone with her.

"I could fire you for running your mouth with me like this."

She crooks a brow, as if daring me to. "Yeah? Go ahead, I would love to see you try." She looks so cocky right now, as if she knows I can't simply do that. And it's true, a small part of me doesn't want to let this little plaything go.

"I can send you a letter stating you are fired just like I did before. So don't test me, Ambrose."

She huffs, looking to the side before sliding those champagne-coloured eyes back to me.

"Right, and you think I won't fight back? Remember that I, too, am a board member."

I take a step closer to her, getting in her personal space, eyes narrowed. The urge to bend her over my knee to shut that sassy mouth of hers is pretty strong.

"Why didn't you just settle for that? Why make both of our lives difficult and be here?"

She clenches her hands into fists; a sign that she is very angry and trying to control it.

"Why would I when this company was supposed to be mine?" Her jaw tics, but her voice is firm and laced with loathing.

"And where is that written in your dear father's will?"

She blinks, and her eyes burn brighter than ever.

"You—" She jabs a finger into my chest, but I grab hold of it and pull her, making her smash against my chest.

"Let go!" She struggles, but she can't match my strength, and I smirk.

"Stop fighting, Emerald. Let the company go, and we can both live peacefully."

She rises to her tiptoes and narrows her eyes at me. She's five-foot-nine and doesn't come close to my six-foot-two, even with her heels.

"You will never win, Mr Nashwood."

I lean forward, dangerously close to her. Our lips hover right next to each other. Our breaths mingle. Her perfume dances with my cologne. And I catch her pulse throbbing on the side of her neck.

"Let… go," she whispers. Her eyes drop to my lips for a fraction.

"Never," I murmur, letting her feel the words against her lips.

Something electric stings my lips as they graze against

hers. My fingers twitch, wanting to touch her, to rake my hands through her hair, wishing those perfect lips were wet like the last time I'd seen them this close.

I lose against my fight and raise my finger to her lips, feathering my fingertip across them. Her mouth opens in a gasp. My heart explodes in a pounding clamour; I can feel each beat against my chest painfully.

"Ambrose, you—" My back meets the elevator walls.

Blinking, I realise she pushed me.

Her chest heaves as she mindlessly touches her lips.

"You…you touched me!" she stammers.

My ears are still drumming, so I shut my eyes and let my head fall back to rest against the elevator wall. I open my eyes after a second and watch her frown, biting her lip.

God, I should be the one doing that. I was close. So close.

"Stop biting that lip, Ambrose, or I will not stop this time."

Her eyes snap to mine but not in anger this time. In those champagne orbs, fire boils, drowning out the loathing and letting her desire for me show.

She instantly lets her lip go and crosses her arms.

"I would like to see you try. Don't touch me again."

I hold in my remark, hold in the words that could have us standing with hands around each other's throats. Spending a few moments alone with Ambrose is equivalent to summoning death and madness upon myself.

If she is fire, then I am the oil that feeds its flames.

If she is life, then I am the reaper.

All of that ends in death and destruction.

Never destined to be together.

Enemies.

We only are good against each other, ready to stake a claim and fight over anything we desire. And as in every war, there is only one winner, and I will be damned if it isn't me.

So, I stay quiet. Ten minutes pass. I can't forget she's stuck in here with me and certainly can't stop my eyes from going back to her every minute, regardless of the fact that I was ready to throttle her mere minutes ago.

And I manage to notice a few more things about her.

Like the white long-sleeved dress she is wearing. It reaches her calves and looks beautiful against her skin colour. The neck of the dress is high despite the heat that bathes London for the first time since I've been here. Her hair is tied up in a slicked-back ponytail with a side part, and the sharp eyeliner on her eyes and the emerald bracelet she has on almost make me smile.

There's my little finding of the day.

"Did you cut your hair, Emerald?" I reach for the shorter ponytail, but she steps back with a frown.

"Don't touch me."

I chuckle at her small huff.

A cute frown of disbelief paints her face.

"You did, didn't you?" I can tell she doesn't believe that I noticed, but I did.

"Cute." I wink at her with a grin, hoping to rile her up

more.

Her nostrils flare, and her lips purse, her jaw tightening.

"Don't call me cute. Do you hear me calling you—" Her mouth snaps closed.

"It's okay. You can say what is on your mind. I'll let it slide this once," I coo.

She takes a deep breath in, then lets it out slowly.

"No, sir. Nothing for me today here. Let's just wait in silence." She turns away from me and steps back against the elevator, her eyes fixed on the wall ahead.

She thinks calling me sir will remind me who she is to me, but that doesn't faze me. If anything, it makes me want to smile at her for trying her best.

I lean back against the back of the elevator too, crossing my feet at my ankles with my files on the floor. Every once in a while, I glance over at her, but she's never looking at me.

The third time my eyes stray back to her, her eyes are closed, and that's when I take my chance to take my fill.

The one question that has been running through my mind is why do I still stand outside her house every night when I see her every day at the office? Remo only asked me to monitor her so she was in my sight, but I hired her, so there is no need for me to follow her shopping, watch her do yoga at night, or find her social media accounts and stalk her online. I definitely shouldn't look at each smiling picture, each post about her shopping, each selfie with the mayor's daughter, and the many shots of her dressed in the most impeccable clothes that make her look like royalty and out of everyone's reach. The thirsty bastards in the comments didn't help to keep my annoyance in check.

There was also no need to know how much she loves eating different kinds of salads, watches reality TV a lot, loves thrillers, and loves the smell and sound of rain.

I love catching glimpses of her everyday routine. Sitting on the yoga mat every night and taking deep breaths. Watering the big plants in her room and petting them as if they are beloved pets. The bowls of fruit she brings upstairs with her sometimes while she reads magazines accompanied by a face mask.

My eyes trail from her nose down to her lips and the small mole I noticed on the other side of her face, but I stop at her lips. The bottom lip is slightly bigger than the top one painted a peachy brown.

It occurs to me that this is the first time there has ever been silence between us and we are both calm. I feel like I can hear every single beat of my heart, can feel every intake of my breath. It stutters the minute my eyes shamelessly trail down her body, taking in the way the dress hugs her gorgeous figure.

I find myself so captivated that I am leaning closer without intending to, to inhale the perfume she always wears. The fresh scent makes me close my eyes to commit it to my memory.

Until I feel the elevator jump and shake.

17

HELIA

I jab at the emergency button, but the speaker just buzz-es at me. Pulling my phone from my pocket, I realise there is no service available. I send a help signal through the software I created on my phone, but I know I will have to wait longer.

I sigh, letting my head drop back. We are both seated on the floor; though Ambrose is sitting on a handkerchief because she said, and I quote, 'my dress is too expensive to get dirty sitting on an elevator floor'. It had me rolling my eyes, but I didn't let my amusement show.

Ambrose is getting progressively more restless. She keeps looking through her documents, scrolling on her phone, and picking at her nails, but nothing keeps her oc-cupied for long. I tried to talk to her, but she gave me one-word answers, and now, even those are gone.

Her hands are shaking ever so slightly, but she crosses

her arms to hide them from me.

"I think it could be just one more hour now," I say.

A small part of me wants to ease her restlessness. Why do I want that to happen? I don't know. I should be happy she is feeling on edge; in fact, I should be encouraging it.

"Shaking because you can't handle being alone with me for too long?"

She looks at me, her eyes jittery as she manages to scoff. "As if. Not everything is about you."

"Really? Here I was thinking you are regretting stopping what could have happened—"

"Sure. Keep telling yourself that if it helps you sleep at night,"

A chuckle slips past my lips. "I'll be getting plenty of sleep tonight, and I'll enjoy it."

She doesn't look at me. Doesn't ask me why.

"Ask me why."

"Why?" She finally looks at me again after staring at the floor for too long. Those profound eyes that are usually bright and full of her passion for keeping her company, for standing up straight in front of a man like me, are dull. Seeing them flick around, in fear or even in wariness, leaves me confused.

"You will be in it."

She groans and covers her face. "Stop it." The trembling in her hands starts again.

Her whole body starts shaking, and worry takes over me.

"Ambrose?" I finally say.

She lowers her hands, and her eyes are wide as she looks at her hands. Her fingers still tremble, and the blue veins are prominent beneath her pale skin. The colour drains from her face, and her breathing turns into abnormal pattern of short pants.

The elevator shakes, and lights die, pitching us into complete darkness. Ambrose's panicked gasp is loud in the tomblike silence.

For the first time ever, I hear her whimper.

"No. I need the light. Please keep it on," she begs.

I fumble for my phone and tap the flashlight icon, then set it on the floor; but her shaking doesn't stop.

I slide over to her and grab her shaking hands.

She's ice cold.

Shaking.

Panicking.

The faint light from my phone reveals tears in her eyes and spilling down her cheeks.

"Ambrose," I say firmly. "Look at me."

"Tell them to open it. Please, please," she begs.

I freeze in shock.

Ambrose would never beg. Not like this.

My Ambrose is strong and a fighter.

My chest tightens in worry for her, my own thoughts not making sense as I watch her tremble in my hold. She looks so small, so fragile and frail, that I fear she may break apart like cracked glass in front of me.

And … the burning hate fades ever so slightly.

To justify what I am about to do, I tell myself that I can hate her and want her when we are out of here, but right now, I am worried and need to comfort her. She needs this.

She needs someone.

"Helia." Her whisper is quiet, so soft it feels like a caress on my cold skin. It wrenches at my heart, stripping away the hate I usually feel for her. I fear if she were to ask me anything in that tone, I would turn the world inside out to give it to her.

I would carve it out for her, and my ability to make that happen is so high it's dangerous to even think about it.

"Please, tell them to open it. Why did they lock us in here? Is it because of what I did?" Her voice shakes, and that's when I reach my limit.

I pull her close to me, sitting her on my lap. Her arms instantly go around my torso, her head burying into my chest.

"No," I whisper, but she shakes her head against me.

"No, no, no—" Ambrose pushes me away and starts to look around, her eyes not focusing on anything.

I need to stop her, to distract her.

I shouldn't do this.

I hate her.

Despise her.

She's made my life difficult.

But fuck it. Fuck my rules and fuck my hate.

Grabbing her chin, I kiss her.

She instantly grabs my wrists and freezes. I don't truly kiss her, just press my lips against hers. She slowly opens her mouth, and my mind shuts down. I go to pull back. I wasn't supposed to do this.

No.

Ambrose places a hand on my jaw and pulls me back, kissing me harder.

It's rushed, like she wants to use this lifeline to escape reality and she's running out of time. I follow her lead, kissing her back just as harshly, just as fast, just as desperately.

My skin burns with her touch, and explosions happen inside of me, fireworks that manage to wreck me. It's the dam finally breaking, rushing through us, wreaking destruction, and I know, beyond doubt, that this kiss will destroy us both, but I can't seem to care.

Her body relaxes, and she sighs into the kiss. She grabs hold of my hair, and her perfectly manicured nails dig into my scalp, making me quietly moan into her mouth.

Mistake. This is a mistake.

I almost killed her for insulting me.

But I want her to know that even with this kiss, I own her.

That's when the carnage takes over and the predator in me awakes.

I push my tongue into her mouth, swiping it against hers, and the instinct to pull her closer grows. I kiss her and kiss her until I feel her breathing slow. Her heart is pounding; I can feel it when my hand travels down her neck and back. I suck her tongue, slowly letting go, then dive back in.

Then I let her go, dropping my hands and pulling back.

Her eyes open.

Her lips glisten, and, fuck, if that sight isn't the most seductive sight ever…

"Ambrose, I—"

"Let's admit that it was a mistake. It's best for both of us. I freaked out, and you just did what you thought was best to distract me." Her words are exactly what I was going to say, but hearing her call it a mistake when the kiss felt so much deeper throws me off.

The want is still there.

To kiss her again.

But I nod and let it go.

Ambrose doesn't look at me when the elevator shakes.

The light comes back on, and the doors slide open.

And Ambrose still acts like nothing happened as we go into our meeting.

18

HELIA

❝She's lying."

Blaze caws, tilting his head on my shoulder. I'm walking through the forest right beside my house, the orange light seeping through the leaves lighting the way. The day is coming to an end soon.

"Why did she say that? She said it so fast, as if to keep me from saying anything else. She wanted to keep me away."

Blaze caws twice, as if to agree with me. Or to say *you are being stupid*.

"She could have been puzzled by me kissing her like that, but... how do I tell her that it was the first thought when she started freaking out because I can't stop thinking about kissing her? Constantly?"

Blaze takes flight, flying away as if he's had enough of me talking about her for the past twenty minutes.

I sigh, kicking a twig out of my way as I emerge from the

forest into a clearing.

I stand there, watching the sun fall from the sky, making the heavens bleed red. The mass of trees in front of me is silent, no sounds of cars or horns or people or anything.

Just Blaze's caws, birds chirping, and the faint sound of the ripples of water that flows just under the dip beneath my feet. A small waterfall.

And me.

Alone with my thoughts as I try to make sense of Ambrose's words.

"Blaze! Come back. I still need to—"

My phone rings.

As soon as I pick it up, I ask, "What does it mean when you kiss someone, and they immediately say it was a mistake?"

"Who even kissed you, Helia?" Aurora sounds baffled.

"That's not the point,"

Aurora hums. "It probably means they want you to ignore it. Maybe they don't want you to talk to them about it as they may feel guilty that they wanted it to turn into more. Or maybe they think it was done under wrong circumstances and—"

"Simple English, please," I mutter.

Aurora laughs. "Okay, I'm no expert, but I think it means they were flustered and didn't think their answer through, especially if they said it quickly after the kiss."

I hum in reply.

So, Ambrose said that because she wasn't thinking prop-

174

erly?

"How … has Ambrose been?"

I still, the sight in front of me disappearing for a second as the image of Ambrose and her bare face appears in front of me.

Wet hair, vulnerable, soft, fragile.

All these words I thought weren't made for her, but the episode in the elevator today has me a little conflicted.

"She's fine, the same firecracker she is. Always fighting tooth and nail against everything I throw her way."

Aurora chuckles. "She's always been like that, never one to lose. I'm glad. I hope she forgives herself one day."

"For what she did in her past? Highly unlikely," I comment.

Aurora is silent for a second. "You know?" Her voice is a soft whisper, as if she doesn't want anyone else to know. Remo knows, too, so she doesn't really need to hide it.

"Of course I know. Remo asked me to look after her when the news about the company hit the media in case she tried to make any false accusations or even build a case against us. I do research on my clients very well, Aurora."

There is another pause.

"Does she know that you know? That you are aware, and the dislike you have for her is because of it?"

"No."

Aurora sucks in a sharp breath, as if I admitted I killed someone, which isn't really far from the truth.

"Tell her. Please tell her."

I frown.

Aurora doesn't elaborate on the topic. "Do you have time to come over to the office? I have some new pieces. I'd like them to be featured in Glamorous if you like them."

That night, I watched Ambrose lay out a yoga mat and sit on it. She stretches, does stupid yoga poses, and then waters her plants in the same routine. And I keep watching, knowing she called our kiss a mistake and said to never let it happen again.

What will she say if she heard what I am thinking?

For the first time, I come early in the morning, too. I watch her pick out an outfit, but then she shakes her head and takes another one. She grabs one last one and then nods before going into her closet to change.

When I get home to change, I blindly pick the same colours. I don't want to match with her, no. I hate her too much for that.

I only pick it because I like green.

When she meets me in the hallway at the office, she looks at my deep green suit with the white dress shirt beneath, then glances down at her own green suit and white shirt and shakes her head. We turn and head to the scheduled meeting, and I can't help but steal glimpses at her. I catch other staff in the room noticing too.

She keeps glaring at them, and they look away, but it's obvious that they can't help their curiosity at the fact that we are matching.

I can't keep my smile in, so I let it slip free the minute I enter my office.

Running a hand down my face, I grin at the humour of the situation.

The day passes until lunch rolls around and I can't help myself.

"Ambrose?" I call her out, standing at the threshold of her office.

She looks up from her laptop, still in her office, regardless that it's lunchtime right now.

I am hit with a second of breathlessness when her eyes meet mine. She hasn't tried to avoid me today. In fact, she's acting like nothing happened. Fuck that.

I have proof that she didn't want to let go, and the tingling in my lips won't stop.

"Eat your lunch in my office. I need you to look over a few things."

I'm not doing this because she has looked lonely in her office the whole time she has been working for me. I am doing this to keep an eye out for her.

"Why?" She watches me, wary.

I shake my head and head to my office.

"Tell me why first. I'm not just going to sit in your office, wasting my time."

Minutes later, she is indeed sitting in my office, grumbling and giving me the stink eye. Clearly I won the argument there.

"Why do you always wear green?"

I run a hand along my jaw as I wait for her answer. She

doesn't reply. She just keeps looking at her screen.

"I'm talking to you." My voice is level, my eyes focused on her.

They aren't leaving her. I take in my fill of Ambrose as she swipes her hand through her hair to push it back off her shoulder.

She slowly tilts her head, and her eyes glide over to me.

The moment they connect with mine, the second I feel them look deep into my own, my heart dips into my stomach and this weird feeling inside of me expands. I shouldn't feel this way.

"Why? Am I not allowed to?" Her voice is crisp, feminine, clear, and full of the confidence she always has.

It makes me smile.

"I was wondering what makes you constantly wear green?"

It can't be because of my eyes. I watched her before we even met, and she wore this colour quite often.

Her eyes don't stray from mine as she answers.

"I just like it." She shrugs, no lie evident on her face.

"Right." I nod, forcing myself to look away before she notices that I am watching her.

But I physically can't look away from the goddess in front of me. Divine is the only word to describe her sharp beauty, her knowledge, her power, her confidence, her strong aura that pulls me to her.

My mind reels back once more to our kiss.

The next day, the moment I step into her office to ask

her to join me in my office for lunch, my eyes glide back to her lips.

"In my office for lunch, Ambrose."

She twists her mouth in disagreement, and I want to grab her chin and make her look at me, to see her fight and defy me so she can keep control of the situation.

Today, she's wearing a skirt paired with a top that has a straight neckline and wraps around her breasts and an over-sized blazer. My eyes are quick to try to find my emerald of the day, but I don't see it.

She walks past me with her laptop in hand, leaving a trail of her perfume. My eyes shut on their own, feeling her presence reach inside me, deep enough to evoke one emotion.

Want.

She sits on the sofa in front of me, but I can't find anything emerald today. Nothing.

Getting up, I grab the budget projections the accounting team has produced for the HR department and walk over to Ambrose.

I stand above her, and she looks up.

Her eyes capture me and send me into a daze.

Deep. Powerful.

What is going on with me?

"Do you think this is a good enough budget?" I hold out the papers.

Maybe she is wearing emerald earrings. I can't see her ears, as her hair is down.

She grabs the papers and studies them.

My hand reaches out. I don't think twice. I haven't been thinking at all since our elevator kiss.

All I see, hear, and even smell is Ambrose, and it's killing me slowly.

This obsession is growing bigger than it is supposed to.

Using my finger, I lift the curtain of blond hair, softly placing it behind her ear, revealing emerald stud earrings. They are surrounded by smaller diamonds. She has two more lobe piercings and one in her cartilage.

My eyes fall on Ambrose, who has frozen, her lips parted.

She's watching me.

Her eyes are soft. In wonder, almost.

But I can only focus on my finger gliding over the shell of her ear. My heart pounds. Each throb demands for me to capture her plump lips in a kiss.

Why does that thought make my heart race? More than being in a car chase. More than the rush of being in power, of holding something over someone and watching them wither in fear.

Why is this feeling so much stronger than anything I have experienced before?

"What are you doing?" Her voice is still strong, but I hear the faint quiver.

"Are you scared, Ambrose?"

She scoffs.

My hand trails down her neck until I let it drop. My gaze returns to her.

"And why would I be?" She crosses her arms, lifting her chin, but I see her eyes fighting to stay on mine. She holds my gaze for several moments before her gaze dips to my lips.

I grin.

"That's my girl," I murmur, my eyes drooping lazily, watching her.

She blinks, faltering for a second.

"You should be scared, a small fair warning." I wish my words were a lie.

I wish they were false, and that she didn't need to fear me. But as I walk away from her with my pulse thrumming in my eardrums, my body fights me. I know something is wrong.

Something that shouldn't be there.

Something very close to like.

For a woman I threatened to kill multiple times.

19
HELIA

"By changing the colour palette to a cooler tone, we can keep it timeless. The rebranding is necessary to keep Glamorous trending."

Who knew I would be so good at this job?

I've worked many jobs in the past, trying to keep myself occupied. So I'm not stupid. I wasn't blindly thrust into this role, and I won't run the company into the ground.

The board members nod around the table while I move onto my next topic.

Except, there is a certain distraction in front of me that my eyes can't help but travel to.

A certain blond woman whose presence has been taunting me ever since she started working for me. I was supposed to keep an eye on her, but every single day, my body reaches out to hers.

I feel myself drawn closer to her. I want to carve open

her head and demand the answers for my questions.

Why do you fucking do yoga at night?

Why water plants?

Why in the world do you like wearing emerald so much? That was supposed to be my favourite colour, not yours.

Why is she on my mind so much that I cannot fucking think when she is around? The minute she enters my office, my breathing stops and my eyes zone in on her. I notice every single thing about her, every part of her body and every change in her emotions.

I notice that she wears heels most days, bringing in a new bag every single day, as if she has an endless supply of them. She wears jewellery worth millions and is always dolled up, never to be seen without makeup. Except when she is at home, from what I have seen from outside her balcony.

That doesn't really provide much, since she is quite far from where I stand outside.

That night, that night when I was going to claim her, to give her more of me, as a stalker, I found a bastard trying to put his hands on her.

That was the end of it because all I saw was his dead body.

I fucked up his friend's car, driving him straight into his deathbed. God, I loved seeing his lifeless body lying limp, but unfortunately Darci didn't die. I don't care whose son he is, he needed a warning. All I know is that he touched Ambrose without consent, then kissed her on the damn cheek like she was his.

Like fuck she was.

Ambrose is mine.

Mine to obsess over.

That day, the small restraint on me snapped, and I lost it.

I sat at home, alone with my thoughts, and I realised that regardless of the hate I feel for her, I desire Ambrose sexually. I can't wait to see her bent over my knee as I treat her attitude.

"Moving on to the changes in the finance team. The new team is working hard to create a new budget specifically for the clothing pieces featured in the magazine volumes. From new couture pieces to bespoke designs by upcoming designers, we can be the face of featuring new work on fresh models. The new interns in the marketing team are bringing in fresh ideas..." I carry on, sharing my ideas and vision for this company, but my eyes keep straying to Ambrose sitting just to the right of me.

She nods, jotting down what other board members suggest, a faint frown between her brows when they speak about things she doesn't approve of. It makes me want to smile at how easily she can be read.

I often find her looking at me, a different glint in her eyes. Many times, I have caught her with her head tilted, as if she is trying to make sense of something.

After the meeting, we leave promptly. As I reach the threshold of my office, I glance over my shoulder to see Ambrose heading into her office, picking up a paper bag from the floor, and taking out her lunch.

I've noticed that she never eats in the cafeteria or even goes out to eat. She never talks to anyone in the company unless she's required to. She just stays in her office. All day.

Shaking my head, I walk inside my own office, but as the door shuts behind me, I can't move a single step farther into the office.

The place is just a temporary assignment for me.

My gaze drops to my shoes, the sleek black shoes that young Helia wouldn't be able to afford. I grin at the facade I currently wear. A fugitive trying to hide from the MI5 as a CEO.

They've been close to finding my accounts filled with money I make from providing personal information and background checks on people I see Remo interact with daily. They are people whose minds are sick and twisted and they want to ruin lives. I do blackmail work for people who want to ruin the weak, but I also serve them with a little bit of their own justice, a little taste of their own fucking poison if I know where and what may happen to the victim.

I let a little something leak, let a message pop up on someone's phone with information that could let them know that they shouldn't be going ahead with the deal. There is already so much bad in the world that I contribute even more to it.

I am unapologetic about it all.

I was raised on the streets, begging and crying for some-one to give me enough food to survive just another day, so how I get my money, how I live, is my personal choice, and everyone else can do what they want.

Not the woman outside, though.

After thirty-three years of living, I have finally found a skilled fighter in the same ring as me, someone who is putting up a great fight against me, keeping me entertained and curious about everything she does.

I have reign over her empire for two years before I leave with no destination in mind.

And I intend to crush but also conquer the woman who I snatched this fate from.

The next few days are me trying to put my changes in action, and I have been pulling many long nights trying to meet deadlines, sign paperwork, and get reports typed up. Ambrose has been working closely with me, sitting in front of me at my desk. Her sighs and huffs when she catches me looking at her leave me amused.

"Do you recognise who this is?" I point to the screen.

She rolls her eyes when she walks around to stand next to me.

Instantly her fresh and intoxicating scent has me closing my eyes to focus on it, to take in a deeper breath just so I can remember what she smells like.

"Who? Mr David?"

My eyes snap open, watching Ambrose click on the profile and lean closer. Her hip bumps into my shoulder, but I don't think she notices; she is too focused on reading the email.

I know who it is, but I want her close.

I want her here beside me.

Watching isn't enough for me anymore.

Twisting my chair, I let my finger graze the back of her thigh.

She freezes. "What are you doing?" There is a thickness in her voice, like she doesn't know whether to be angry or annoyed. Her eyes are on me, narrowed, but she stays in her position. Bent. Eyes bright, open, and curious.

What would she do if I were to break that barrier between us and bend her over? Would she fight me, crying and sobbing?

Or would she be submissive? Moaning and begging for more?

My hand abandons that place, and I let the tips of my fingers travel from her lower back down the curve of her ass and keep going down until I reach the back of her knee.

Emotion hits me in the chest when I realise she is letting me touch her. She threw off Darci's hand when he tried to touch her. And that same night, when I hid myself from her and wanted to touch her, she also fought back hard. But right now, her eyes are filled with blazing fire. She isn't moving, nor is she near tears.

There is something very clear in her eyes that makes me pause.

Trust.

"Seeing how you would feel bent in front of me." My voice is laced with lust.

"Stop it." She steps away, her eyes sharp.

"Would you like it if I touched you?" I lean forward, my eyes dropping to her lips.

"Very." She sarcastically remarks with a scoff.

"Sure you would,"

"I've seen you look at me, Ambrose,"

She turns to me, her eyes intent. "Like what?"

I lean closer, my lips brushing against hers as I whisper, "Like you want me to fuck you."

Her eyes widen. "I wouldn't even look twice in your direction, but you on the other hand…" Her eyes trail down, then she faintly brushes her hand against my crotch making me grit my teeth.

"Is this the game you are now playing, Emerald?" I smirk, grabbing her hand and palming myself using her hand.

Her mouth drops open, but she quickly recovers. She lifts a brow, amusement swimming in those dark chocolate irises.

"If we call getting each other hot and bothered a game, then sure."

I get up and lean even closer, letting the front of my body touch hers, letting my hard-on press against her stomach, so she feels it, so she knows no matter the hate, my desire for her is very prominent and there.

"Fuck yes,"

"Does this mean you are hot and bothered? Drenched at my words and touch?" I continue.

She scoffs under me, looking to the side, but gasps when I roll my hips into her.

Her eyes slide back to mine, this time burning with need.

"If I were to check right now, would you be wet, Emerald?"

She pushes at my shoulder, trying to walk away, but I grab hold of her and twist both her arms behind her back, pulling her against me, her front to my chest.

"Don't lie," I whisper, my lips ghosting over the shell of her ear.

She shudders against me.

Grabbing both her hands in one of mine, I use the other to draw small circles on her stomach. I feel it tighten under my hold.

"I hate you," she rasps out, her body pushing against me, leaning into me.

My hand travels higher until I am twirling her nipple through her dress. It pokes against the fabric.

"Still hate me?"

"Yes," she rushes out.

I laugh, my breath fanning her shoulder and neck.

"Your body says otherwise."

"I don't care. Desire and hate come from two different places," she says, bucking her hips against mine, making my hard-on way worse than it was.

I hum. One day, I will have her. I will get her.

She shakes out of my hold, and I let her. She walks out the door without even looking back, but I know she is seething, She wants me and hates herself for it.

"New pet, sir?"

I wink at the receptionist, making her laugh and shake her head at me.

My hands are in my trouser pockets as I walk into the elevator and watch it go up until I reach my floor.

"Your coffee, sir, and today's sche—" Ambrose stops short as she walks into my office. Her eyes instantly go to my shoulder.

"Blaze?" she whispers.

Blaze, the traitor, caws loudly and shoots off me. He circles her, making me see a sight that I felt starved for.

He sits on her shoulder, then pokes her with his beak.

She softly laughs, lips stretching into a wide smile.

And my heart stops.

My taunts pause, and I don't call Blaze back to me.

The laugh echoes around me, and my feelings reveal themselves. All these weeks of torture are coming to one conclusion. Like the calm ocean right before a storm is about to hit it, like the silence on a sunny morning. Peace that a person like me has never felt.

"Are you happy to see me? I'm happy to see you, too." Ambrose laughs as Blaze caws excitedly, flying around her once more before swooping all around the office. Ambrose's laugh trickles out again as he flies back to her.

And I know this is fucked.

My mind is fucked.

My heart is a traitor.

These feelings will break me. They'll ruin me.

I need Ambrose out of my system.

Thunder cracks the sky open.

Thousands of droplets decorate Helia's glass office walls, London a mere blur beyond. The wind howls outside; the sound weaves around my mind, bringing a sense of calmness over me.

I am sitting in the office, stuck on a deadline with Helia.

Another loud crack of thunder shakes the windows.

How will I get home?

Working with Helia for the past week has been torture. Not because of the tasks he gave me but because of the heightened tension between us. There are these almost-moments where I have to keep myself from touching him after that little breakdown I had in front of him.

I catch him looking at me in the elevator, and I have to look away. To avoid eye contact.

Now I am more aware of his presence and every single

small detail about him than ever.

But I don't hate what he has done. In fact, I am grateful he was able to stop me before I blurted out why I felt trapped in the elevator in the dark. So, in a way, I am grateful for the kiss.

I should have hated it, but I didn't.

The slow, seductive way he kissed me was breath-taking. My vulnerable state didn't allow me to think properly, and I pulled him closer to me. Instead of being ashamed, I was more aware of how he felt against my lips. More aware of how his big, strong hands that once wrapped around my neck to threaten me cupped my cheeks gently, so softly I felt myself turning into a puddle. I felt my emotions flare at his touch.

I couldn't believe it was the same man, and now, deep in my heart, an echo of a voice begs, demands, to kiss him again, and then I find myself watching his lips all over again.

How could I think about my nemesis like that?

After he helped me? The first to ever do so?

He makes sure to monitor my work and makes me sit in his office to do work with him, but he doesn't realise that lunches have started to feel less lonely for me. No matter if we bicker or argue or I am glaring and he is teasing me, they don't feel like the same empty lunches anymore.

In fact, I look forward to that part of my day when, instead of work, it's just me and him and our small arguments.

"Is rain that fascinating? I thought British people are used to it?" Helia's voice carries across the empty office as he walks in with two folders. His long legs carry him to stand right next to me in just a couple of steps.

'I thought British people are used to it'… Does that mean he isn't from the UK? Where is he from?

"I am. It's just really heavy, and it's getting late," I say, still worried about how I will get home.

Both of our phones ping at the same time. It's a warning about the thunderstorm that is approaching fast, recommending us to stay where we are for the next four hours.

"This—"

"A storm?" Helia interrupts.

"No, I need to be home."

I can't stay here. Mum will demand that I get home no matter the weather.

I stand up, ready to head out the door, but a firm grip on my shoulder stops me. I suck in a sharp breath and spin to face Helia. His emerald eyes look deep into my own, demanding me to stay in one place.

"You're not going anywhere, Emerald. Not in this weather." His voice is low, twisting my stomach.

"Are you worried about me, Mr Nashwood?" I tease, finding humour in the fact that he even said it.

He frowns, his brows dropping. "Of course I am. If I lose you, who will I torment? I am too lazy to hire someone else."

I step out of his hold. "Too bad. Get someone else to hire them for you, but I am leaving." Turning around, I open the door, only for it to be slammed shut with a hand.

"Helia, I need to go." I go to grab the handle, but he captures my hand in his. I bite my lip to stop my gasp.

His big hand consumes my own, its warmth wrapping me tightly. Goosebumps erupt all over my body at his touch. Those same veiny hands with those long fingers held my face, kissing me, and—

I shut my eyes, erasing the thought, and will my heart to calm down.

It was a mistake.

A mistake.

A mistake that can't happen again. And neither can that kiss.

I should want to kill him. He took my company. He tormented me. He hates me, and I hate him.

Then why? Why is my heart beating erratically inside of me?

Is it in fear of what he may do to me in his office?

Or… is it in anticipation of what other mistakes we might make?

"Let me go," I argue.

"First name basis with your boss? That is not professional at all," he murmurs in my ear, the velvety voice inciting an irregular heartbeat inside of me.

"What about you? Emerald, of all names? Very unique…" I can guess he uses it because I wear that colour often.

"It was my favourite colour, but then you stole it."

I turn around to face him. He narrows his eyes, but he looks at peace, relaxed. His breaths fall in soft puffs while his eyes watch me with heightened intensity.

"Stole it? Are you seriously arguing with me about a colour?"

He shrugs, leaning closer.

His cologne, that strong musk-and-gardenia scent, fills me to the brim. It's addictive. It's an unwelcome obsession.

"What if I said I want to argue about why you haven't been looking me in the eyes?"

If I didn't know him, I would have thought he cared for a second there, more than a boss would care about an employee.

I open my mouth, but there is no argument. I can't tell him it's because every time I look at him, the flashes of us kissing enter my mind, and I haven't been able to think straight.

Or the fact that even right now, with him so close to me, I can only focus on my pounding heart and the thudding in my ears.

Helia's eyes soften as if he found an answer in me. His body heat tempts me to curl into him to seek warmth, comfort, and safety.

With a mind of its own, my hand raises, my finger almost touching his lips, but when I realise what I am about to do, I go to drop it, but Helia takes hold of it.

A moment follows, his eyes captivating me.

Silence hangs between us, but it's like thousands of words are said.

We aren't meant to be, and we both know it.

If we took it even a step further, to just clench the thirst we feel, it would turn messy.

We are supposed to hate, kill, and defy each other, not try to find comfort, try to ignite a brighter fire between us.

Our breaths mingle, heavy, hot, and choking.

"Touch me," he rasps, his body slowly pressing into mine.

"Touch me the way you want to." He continues.

I feel my breath taken away the minute he allows me access.

"But I hate you." I weakly argue.

His eyes don't leave mine, not even for a mere second.

I am falling weak at the hands of the man who has written my demise. The sheer force and strength in his body would be out of this world, but right now, there is peacefulness around him that leaves me dazed.

It leaves me confused as to why I notice it, why I want those strong arms to wrap around me so he could be my armour while everyone tries to harm me for what I did.

What would Helia do if he knew about me?

He wouldn't be like this, would he?

He wouldn't show any mercy to me.

I'm trying to be better; so to think of him that way while not giving him the full truth… I can't do that. No more lies and deception on my part.

I can't keep another person in the dark. Can't let another person suffer at my hands.

Sucking in a sharp breath, I allow my fingers to ghost

over his lips, promising myself I'll tell him everything so he can go back to hating me and stop treating me like this. I can't see his eyes change while not knowing exactly who I was.

"You can hate me and want me, Emerald," he whispers, and the words cut deeper.

No. You will hate me more than you ever have.

I let my fingers graze his soft lips, my touch going up to his cheek, to his eye, then across his brows. He closes his eyes, soaking in my touch.

The tips of my fingers tingle, then light up with a spark.

He breathes in, and I breathe out.

"Open your eyes, Helia." My soft murmur opens what I believe is the portal to another world. The forest-green eyes that have trapped me with the poison they leak.

"I love the colour of your eyes."

At the mention of the colour of his eyes, they shine, like my words make him happy.

My finger hesitantly drags over his other eye, the one with the scar, but he doesn't move or flinch when I trace over it. The bumpy skin and the scar tissue seem from a knife wound. I would know from the many on my body.

I want to choke whoever did this to his face. Helia is handsome, and no matter if he had this scar or not, he's still attractive, but to think he suffered through intense pain makes me rage.

"Whoever did this to you, I hope they found their hell."

Something a lot like a proud smirk makes its way onto

Helia's face, but still, he doesn't utter a single word, allowing me to speak my thoughts in a daze.

My heart drops, and my hand follows.

My stomach twists and twists until I can't take it anymore. I feel sick.

"L-Let me go, Helia." I shake my head, but Helia leans closer to me.

"You should hate me. You shouldn't allow me to even touch you like this." I gasp when I feel his forehead drop on my shoulder.

The action is so small, but the pain inside of me twists so fucking hard that I choke.

It makes me want to cry out because I want this. I want him. But I don't deserve anything good.

"Ambrose—"

"Don't you get it, Helia? I have ruined lives. I deserve everything that has fallen upon me. I have bullied, humiliated, and broken people."

Helia's hand on my hip tightens, and I hear his breathing turn harsher.

"I have—"

"Stop." The force of his voice shuts me up.

Here it comes.

He lifts his head, his hands dropping from me, then he takes a step back, and the look in his eyes is gone. My hands clench tightly, my jaw ticking as I brace myself for his words.

"Get out."

Without hesitation, I leave.

There is no explanation needed.

None.

But I do leave behind a part of me that I don't think will ever come out as it did with Helia.

So then why, as I walk from my car to my house in the heavy rain, do I feel piercing pain inside my chest at the thought of Helia suddenly going back to the way he was?

So ruthless and unapologetic about everything?

Why does it hurt when it didn't before?

Was it because of the small moment when I almost felt as if someone could love me? That very small, miniscule hope?

21
HELIA

Age ten

Streets of London, people of London.

These places are supposed to hold people of high class. Of power. Admiration.

And by far, I have only seen the cruelty, the sheer hatred they have for people who have no money in their pocket.

Living by stealing the few scraps of food left behind has taught me that even the highest of royalty will sneer at one lower than them. Even ones you love, ones who smile in the spotlight and say they are helping those in need, when in fact, they are disgusted by the sight of homeless people.

With a ten-pound note in my hand, crumbled but still brand new, the smile on my face is wide. Nala will be so happy to see that someone gave me so much.

There is a bounce in my step.

Maybe she won't spend on the white powder she gets

and will get us food.

Maybe I should get food myself?

But what if she gets angry that I didn't share?

I shake my head and continue towards the small room we have. An abandoned building sits tall and cold, a window broken where it faces a small alleyway. We've made it our small home.

I can see my own breath, shivering despite my clothes. December is always the coldest month in London every year. The frilly scarf around my neck and the thin dirty sweater I have on don't help with the freezing temperatures.

As soon as I crawl through the window and jump into the room, I spot Nala pacing. Nala is my older sister, at seventeen years old. Some could say she is a little rude, but I know it's our situation that made her like that. One day, we were living in a warm house with Mum; the next, we were getting evicted. Mum didn't pay for the rent that month and was nowhere to be found.

That was three years ago.

Three years of being close to homeless until Nala started bringing in a few items worth keeping. Like a new sweater. Leftover food from her friend. New shoes, which she gave me.

But that scares me.

Mom used to do that and then she left all at once.

She used to tell us about her friend who gave her everything and how nice he was. He had money, and one day she'd take us with her to a good house. She promised, and she still left us.

We were both so confused and yet we waited for her for a year until Nala told me that she's gone. I didn't want to believe it, but it was true, wasn't it? She wasn't coming back.

She left us for a better life with that friend.

She left her kids behind and chased a life of luxury on her own.

And now I'm scared Nala may do the same.

Her head snaps up as soon as my shoes hit the ground.

"Helia, did you get any money?" Her eyes keep looking around, as if scared, but I know she isn't.

She gets like that when she takes that white powder.

My hand tightens around the crumbled note. It could be for food today, even tomorrow, and maybe some left for the day after.

If I gave it to Nala, she will take it for herself, and I will have to go to sleep hungry.

She will promise to bring food from her friend and then she won't.

My stomach twists, the lie on the tip of my tongue, but my sister needs it. She will stop being like this once I give her.

She's my only family.

Mum left, I never met my dad, and now I only have her.

So I swallow.

Squashing the need for food and wanting to help my sister, I slowly open my hand, revealing the ten-pound note.

Her eyes widen.

"Did you hide this from me?" she grits out.

I flinch. "No, I was going to give it to you for food and—"

"You hid it from me because I get to eat and you don't?"

How could she think that?

I shake my head, but her eyes look crazy.

"You did, didn't you? You think I can eat and dress well and you can't, so you hide money from me to keep it for yourself? You think I'm doing drugs and it is ruining your life, right?" She shakes me once more, her nails digging into my shoulder, and I hiss.

The wind picks up, wrapping around me, and my teeth start clattering.

"No, it hurts, Nala." I cry out when I feel her nails dig deeper, the pain searing through my skin, deep into my flesh.

"You hate me, is that right?" she shouts in my face, and for a second, I don't recognise her.

She shoves me away, grabs the money, and jumps out of the window. I am left in silence. For the next three days, I stay there, hungry, cold, and waiting for Nala. She never comes.

Just as the winter is freezing over London, it also slowly starts to freeze my heart.

A thud awakens me. I get up, blinking, only to see Nala. I smile, jumping up.

"Nala! I—"

She brought a friend with her.

A guy.

Now that I notice, she is dressed very nicely. She looks clean, showered, and her cheeks are a little red. Is she still cold?

"Helia, meet my boyfriend, Kaden."

I have a bad feeling.

Why did she bring him here when we have nothing to offer? In our hiding place?

And then I watch them take more of that powder. They laugh, drink alcohol, and then their frenzied eyes turn towards me. Nala watches as Kaden reaches out to the small corner I am huddled in and touches my eyes.

"Oh, how beautiful your eyes are," he murmurs, his speech slurred, his eyes bright red. "You will grow to be pretty. Pretty eyes, pretty hair, pretty face."

Something twists in my stomach, and I try to move away from his touch, but he slaps me, keeping me in place.

My cheek burns.

"You stay still, boy, or I might just carve these eyes out, so no one touches or wants you."

I frantically look for Nala, but she's lying motionless on the cold floor.

"I gave your sister a home. The least she can do is let me keep you."

I try to fight him off, but he keeps wanting to look at my eyes. He is a good-looking man. He shouldn't think like this.

"My dad told me no one would want me because I wasn't pretty. But I think everyone will want you. Let me test my theory out once I try to give you a gift."

I scream when he pulls out a knife and slowly starts to cut down my eye.

"I want to keep this eye. I want it," he murmurs.

I breathe faster.

I need to leave.

I need to get out.

I can feel the dripping of my blood.

Fear cuts at my throat.

No.

I kick Kaden in the stomach. He falls back with a thump. He is drunk, so he is slow to get up. I run towards the window, only to be pulled back by my hair.

"You need me. You need to stay with me. I own you both!" he shouts, trying to go for my eye again, but I kick his arm. The knife drops out of his hand. I grab an empty glass bottle and smash it on his head.

The pieces fall all over the floor, and I run towards the window.

I can't come back.

I will have to leave Nala behind and never look back.

My heart hurts. My eye hurts.

It's so cold.

I jump through the opening, hearing the pounding steps behind me. Then I run and run and run until my legs give out. I let my body sag against the back of a building.

And when I look up, snowflakes fall on my face. The cold barely touches my burning eye.

I can't sit around.

I can't wait for people to think they own me for giving me something. Every. Single. Time.

To have power over me just because they gave me one small piece of themselves.

As I bleed on the empty street in London, I know I am leaving my childhood behind, one that was ripped from me, one that was trampled upon, and one that took away my kindness for people.

22
HELIA

A mbrose is right.

    She did ruin lives.

Then why the fuck did I follow her in my car, in a thunderstorm, to see her walk through the front doors of her house?

Why in the world did I stand under that same tree in the rain, waiting for her to switch her bedroom light on?

I'm going crazy, and she is the sole cause of it.

She thinks I don't know anything about her. Aurora told me to tell her, but I didn't.

Whatever is going inside her head, I need to know.

I was falling weak because of her. I saw her look outside at the rain, fascination with a glimmer of worry on her face, and I felt myself give in.

She built up a wall in front of her the minute she saw me step over a line in the office.

Why would she want anything to do with me when I am her nightmare in person? When I am her tormentor? When she is everything I hate in a person?

These past few weeks, I was falling soft at the hands of Ambrose.

Not anymore.

The scar she touched? I'd been cut open by the hand of a person like her.

I'm glad she pushed me. I was losing sight of everything.

I hope you are ready, Ambrose.

I sit in the car, the rain still as heavy as ever, driving through the streets of London; the wet pavements and the rush of cars and red buses are a blur in my vision. My hands tighten around the wheel, my mind a mess. Driving to my house will take time. I've been driving for forty minutes already, and now the rain has lightened up.

I storm through my house, rushing past the living room and the staircase on my right and take a left through the glass doors to where my pool is. The glass walls surrounding it showcase the darkness that surrounds the house, the expanse of trees a frightening sight for a normal human being. Humans fear the unknown, but for a man like me, who is the unknown, one who rules it and lives in it, it's like coming home.

I rip off my shirt and my trousers, leaving my boxers. I faintly hear Blaze caw before I dive into the cold water.

The sound of water splashing quietens the loud thoughts in my head.

Hate her.

I should hate her.

I do hate.

I don't like her.

Not her soft blond hair that she recently cut.

Not the emerald parts of her.

Not the fierce look in her eyes.

Not her body.

Not her mind.

Nothing.

I hate her.

I fucking hate her so much it's an obsession.

I hate her so much that it's blurring the line between kill and lust.

I gasp, my head rising from the water before I dive back in, feeling my lungs burn as I swim laps in the water.

I go on and on for a good hour before I finally feel my lungs start to scream for me to stop. I am no swimmer, more of a runner, but this frustration with her lasts a good hour before I finally give in.

When I stand under the shower, my hands on the tiles in front of me, my head bowed and hair falling into my eyes, I shut my eyes.

No.

I don't want to admit it, but what good will it do?

Ambrose.

You've bewitched me.

You've ruined me.

You've made me mad for you. You've caught the eye of a killer, a hacker, and a man whom you may never have.

I don't stay in one place. I need to be untraceable. If I were to settle in London, in such a populated city, it would mean being alert at all times.

Why am I considering settling in such a dangerous city for a woman I'm supposed to hate?

I'm addicted to her small gasps of shock, her looks of puzzlement, her laugh.

My head falls back as my hand travels down until I grip my aching cock.

How would she look, wet hair, legs wrapped around my hips, her breasts bouncing as I pounded into her, her soft moans echoing in my ears?

My hand pumps harder as I imagine her grabbing my face and kissing me, hard, then soft, teasing me and bringing me to the edge as I fuck her into believing it is only me for her.

Her only saviour. Her only tormentor. Her only darkness.

And Ambrose?

She would be my emerald.

Mine.

I gasp when my stomach tightens, my muscles flexing, pulling me to reality. I slam my eyes open with a revelation just as my teeth grit and I release.

I know she is my doom.

She is my destruction.

She is my darkest desire. And once she realises who I

am, what I am, she will try to run, but I won't let her.

Serpents never let their prey go; they twist and tighten around them until they suffocate.

23

AMBROSE

It's May, mid spring. It's Aurora's birthday.

She got married last year, right after her birthday. It's been a year now.

I stand in front of Remo's house, gazing up at the mansion that puts the Torre mansion to shame. It doesn't feel cold, like my house. It doesn't look intimidating, like it might swallow you when you step inside.

It looks lively, warm, and inviting.

Peering past the gates, I can see cars lined up, and if I know my sister, I know she will have a birthday party at home with her friends.

My hands juggle the box I am holding, a small present for my sister, as longing wraps around my heart. I've bought her a present every year. Standing out here for the past thirty minutes is proof enough that I will not be giving this one to her either.

I'm proud of who she is now. Proud that she managed to come out the same person she always was.

Opening the passenger door of my car, I place the gift back inside and shut the door before looking back up at the mansion. The driveway leads up to the front door of the house, but it's caged with a gate and a buzzer next to it. Security lines the house's perimeter.

Of course, Remo has the best security around his home. He is the centre of the socialite circle. It's exactly why Dad wanted Aurora married to him.

He didn't want me married to Remo in case he didn't let me work after the marriage, and Dad needed me to help him with running Glamorous, and then that night, at the dinner when I was supposed to win him over, he requested to be tied to Aurora.

And what Remo wants, he gets. That man rules London with an iron fist and silent looks.

Dad granted him his wish, and I sagged in relief only to realise my younger sister would be at the mercy of the cold, ruthless man.

I tried to get her to work for Dad so I could look after her that way. I wanted her to know she had a safety net with me, but she was stubborn and wanted to do things her way. I let her be.

Whenever Dad visited her events, went to her office, I trailed behind to make sure he didn't do anything to her, played right into his act while keeping an eye out for Aurora.

I did so much for her, and I don't expect her to forgive me, but at least, she is happy.

"I miss you," I whisper into the night, watching the lights in the house, the cold night's wind ruffling my hair.

I tuck it behind my ear, my eyes dropping to my lap as I sit on the edge of the road. It's secluded, hidden from the cars driving down the road.

"I got you a beautiful pink diamond necklace. It has smaller diamonds surrounding it. It will look absolutely beautiful on you. It's your favourite colour too, pink," I whisper, trying to fill the void in my chest.

"You are turning thirty, and soon I will be thirty-one. How crazy has life been? It's moving so fast that your gifts are piling in my closet." A laugh slips out of me at a memory of us.

"Remember when you wanted to go out to this one fashion show because of how obsessed you were with them? I had to use Dad's name to get us both tickets. We kept running away from photographers in the show to avoid getting recognised, and we kept giggling about it." I shake my head, my lips pulling into a faint smile.

"I made almost all your wishes come true just to see you smile." My smile falls, and darkness seeps through me.

"And then a few years later, I lost it all the minute I pushed you away." I clear my throat, looking at my well-manicured nails, the nude colour clean and fresh.

"Are you talking to yourself?"

I jump up, a yelp leaving my lips. I look up and see someone walking towards me. They are smoking but drop the cigarette to the ground and step over the butt.

He takes one step closer, and my mouth drops open as I try to form an excuse as to why I am here.

Then I notice Blaze sitting on his shoulder, tilting his head, watching me.

"Would you look at that? Ambrose is now going crazy," Helia muses, slowly bending down and sitting next to me as if we are at some park and he wants to chat with an old pal.

I go to get up, my cheeks flushing with embarrassment, but Helia's hand stops me.

He is still looking forward, his eyes not moving away from Remo's house.

"Stay."

Something about it pulls at my heart. I feel it snatch my safety and yet... I don't want to leave.

So I stay.

A minute of silence passes between us. I feel Helia's hot, unwavering gaze on the side of my face, but I don't look at him, too busy trying to keep myself from giving him any ammunition against me.

He shouldn't want to be here with me.

He should hate me.

Hate me, Helia.

Hate me so I don't hope for anything.

You have to hate me.

"Why don't you give it to her?" His voice is soft, quiet.

I huff out a small laugh. "Okay. Sure. Great idea."

"So you prefer getting her a gift and then not giving it to her? What will you do with it, then?" he asks.

I'm silent, the gusts of wind ruffling my hair on the quiet street.

"I think I will send it to Santa. Make use of it, you know?"

The look I receive as an answer should be criminal. Helia looks annoyed by my pathetic attempt at a joke.

"Jokes don't work. Okay…" I whisper, turning my head back to save myself the embarrassment.

"Never try that again." He huffs.

Blaze turns to look at him, tilting his head before he looks at me.

"Why a crow?"

Helia's eyes narrow. I think I am giving him whiplash with the sudden changes in topic.

"Why not?" He shrugs, reaching up to run a finger down Blaze's back. Blaze nuzzles Helia with his head and gives a soft caw. My heart instantly melts.

"I would have never expected you to have a pet, never mind a crow."

Helia quietly chuckles, grasping my attention. I just can't seem to look away from him.

"Why aren't you there? With them?"

He looks down at the pavement under our feet, not moving or speaking for a couple of seconds. I almost give up waiting for an answer. He glances up at me, the wind stronger, ruffling his black hair into a mess.

His broad shoulders bump mine every once in a while. I wonder if he'd be able to lift me with one hand. That thought never crossed my mind until today.

"I stepped out for a smoke break, then I found a sad little fox outside." His answer prods at my heart, demanding answers that I will never be able to give.

His perspective of me, a sad girl sitting on the pavement with a gift in her hand, a solemn look on her face, creates an ache inside of me. I have never been perceived as a sad, lost girl.

I find myself giving in and whisper, "Sad?"

I'm not sad. I'm not weak.

They should be the least likely words used to describe me. The last time someone called me that, I lost so much of me that I still haven't recovered. Sometimes I feel like a broken glass vase that is still missing small, shattered pieces that will never be found.

I feel empty and forever will.

I will bear it and keep it tucked away. No one will witness this missing part of me.

"I didn't even know it was you until I recognised this long blond hair." He reaches out and gently tucks a loose stand of hair behind my ear, like he has done before. And like the previous few times, his eyes snap to my earrings, though I am not sure why.

Then his gaze drops to my wrist, to my fingers.

He slowly leans closer, his fingers brushing my hair off my shoulder, and when his eyes land on my emerald di-

amond necklace, they soften somehow. The look on Helia's face is similar to how Remo looks at Aurora, when his
shoulder drops a fraction and his hand instinctively reaches
out to her.

Looking into Helia's eyes feels like peeking into a world
that is bleak, dark, and powerful. It feels like stepping into
a silent place, where even one noise would awaken a beast
that hunts and kills to clench its thirst.

And yet, it also feels like there is a tree within that world
that provides warmth and comfort. Like that beast will sit
and watch you silently as you take your rest.

It feels comforting to be watched by a beast.

"Why do you hate me?" The questions falls out, and I
immediately want to slap myself. "Never mind. I'm just
going to walk into a ditch and drop dead," I mutter, turning
away from him.

His hand falls.

"I don't want the answer." Deep in my heart, I fear the
answer, and I fear what it may do to my heart.

Getting off the pavement, I walk away from him. There
is no need for goodbyes; we aren't close like that.

Then what was that moment in his office that rainy day?
What was that kiss you keep remembering?

Shaking my head at my own thoughts, I swallow, not
looking at the Cainn mansion in case any tears escape. If he
saw, Helia may destroy whatever is left of me.

"Ambrose." The thumping of shoes on the pavement and
the swift grip on my arm that turns me around has my stom-

ach dropping in fear.

I stand frozen. Helia takes a deep breath in before letting it out.

I wait.

The cold wind pierces my skin, and my hair flies out of my face, allowing more wind to freeze my face.

His green eyes focus on me with such intensity and emotion that my stomach churns. I finally manage to take in a few deep breaths, then we start to walk.

Pulling my jacket's zipper up, I dig my chin into its collar, seeking warmth.

He keeps looking at me like he is holding something in him and it's painful for him to speak about it.

His jaw tics as his hands clench into fists at his side.

His eyes look pained. He looks like he is trembling, his whole being fracturing.

"Helia—"

"Go home. Cry your tears in your bed."

I flinch.

Why did that hurt me?

Was I truly waiting for something kind from him?

Am I deluding myself again?

24

AMBROSE

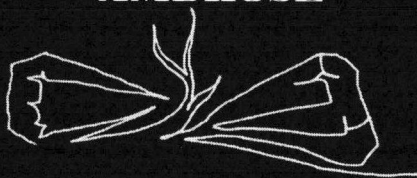

"Wake up, little sin."

My eyes fly open.

A hooded figure towers over me. The hood hangs low enough to cover his eyes, but I can see enough of his face to see his twisted smirk. His towering figure is dark and silently deadly.

I open my mouth to scream. Panic rises to the point where I can feel my heart thundering inside of my chest, but the cold hand on my mouth stops me. My muffled screams are quiet. Tears prick my eyes as I try to thrash in his hold, but I can't move. His thick thighs are on either side of my hips, pinning me in place. I'll probably be bruised tomorrow.

"Shh, wouldn't want to wake up your mummy and let her see you like this now."

That stops me. I know she would do exactly what Dad did to Aurora. She threw her out.

"Scared, are we? I thought you were strong," he taunts. His words reach inside my chest, wrapping my heart in shadows until not even a speck of light peeks out. Draining me of life. Draining me of peace and filling it with fear and terror.

I shake my head, my chest heaving. As if he knows what I am thinking, his head dips low, taking in the skimpy gown I wear, and my breasts, which are almost spilling out of it.

Cold metal hits my stomach, making me flinch and freeze.

My eyes widen, my breathing stopping at once.

"Want to say something?" He chuckles, knowing I can't speak. The laugh vibrates through my body.

I watch as he slowly draws small circles with the tip, climbing up my chest with the knife until he reaches my chin, forcing my head to tilt up. A pinch of pain sears through my jaw.

I stay still, careful not to move.

My breathing turns into quick, short pants.

"I won't hurt you," he murmurs, as if he isn't holding a knife to my damn throat.

Placing the knife on my bedside desk, he leans forward.

The next second, I feel his mouth near my ear.

My heart sprints louder than ever in my ear. The flicker of fright in me doesn't go anywhere, and with the knife close by, I know he can kill me if he wants to.

Who would even care if I was gone?

No one.

And the sad reality hits me hard.

Something hot and wet touches the side of my neck.

His body feels so familiar. He feels like Helia and my heart stutters.

His tongue draws a small circle on my neck, and my heart twists inside of me for a different reason. A shameful reason.

"You taste just as I imagined, little sin. Sinful, intoxicating, addictive." His deep voice is so strong, so masculine that it lights up a hot need in the pit of my stomach. My legs twist at his words.

Why do I feel turned on?

"I've wanted to hold you for so long." His tongue travels up my throat, then curls around the shell of my ear. "So, so long," he whispers, his hot breath fanning my ear. "And now you aren't fighting enough." His warm, wet tongue goes under my jaw until I feel him scrape his teeth, and that need starts throbbing in between my legs.

I shut my eyes.

Ashamed.

So fucking ashamed.

"Do you want this? Do you want me to take away this attitude you have?"

He lets go of my mouth, and just as I am about to scream profanities, he clamps down on my neck, making a gasp erupt from my lips.

I feel him smile against my neck.

His hand travels down all the way to my thighs, then he

raises the hem of my gown.

"No, please, stop."

He shakes his head, tilting it as if to say, *you really think I will stop?*

His cold hand against my warm skin sends tingling desire through me. Hot, disgusting, and perverted.

He's a killer, a stalker, for crying out loud.

What am I doing?

I shut my eyes, a troubled sigh leaving me.

"Helia, I—"

My stalker stops, and my eyes snap open.

Helia.

I said his fucking name.

His head snaps up, and I can feel anger rolling off him. I start to panic all over again.

His hand is at my throat, cutting off my oxygen.

"No, please—"

His other hand drops down to my hem, roughly pushing it up and finding me soaking wet despite the fear I have for my life. A deep chuckle escapes past his lips, the sound absolutely terrifying.

"Soaking like a fucking slut? You still want to be fucked, even if I could kill you within a second?"

I shake my head side to side, trying to twist out of his hold but failing to do so.

"No, let me go."

My eyes have adjusted to the dim light, and his face becomes clear to me. He looks like Helia; his smirk, his jaw, his rough hands that grab my thighs and push them apart.

He leans down, and even more wetness pools when I find his eyes peeking from beneath his hood. Green. Emerald green. He watches me dirty the sheets, twisting my legs, but his hold is like iron. Hot and strong. He exhales on my pussy, circling it with two thick fingers.

A whimper falls from my lips.

"Please." I try to push my hips up and away from him.

He thrusts two fingers right into me at once.

I choke, feeling full at the stretch. I have only been with one person in my life sexually, and it wasn't recently. His fingers thrust in and out of me ruthlessly. Then those thick, long fingers twist inside of me, and my toes curl at the painful pleasure.

"You seem to be loving this. What would happen if I just—"

"No!" I jerk up in bed.

My skimpy gown is stuck to me, and sweat covers my back. Cold shivers run through my body.

A dream.

I was having a dream where my stalker was Helia. I run a hand through my hair, my breathing quickening with every passing thought. Why him, of all people? Why would he star in my dream when I despise him?

Rushing to the shower, the faint glow of the sun rising makes me forget about going back to bed.

But how can I forget the moment my brain thought that Helia was my stalker? How could that be?

My burning body cools under the cold water, and when I am brushing my hair after getting ready, my eyes fall onto my bed. I gasp, then my mouth drops open at the wet spot. I was turned on from that; from the thought of Helia touching me. So much that my arousal had dripped down my thighs.

Then I saw the rolled up paper with a green ribbon around it beside my balcony door.

I run towards it and hastily unroll it.

Pleasure looks beautiful on your face.

My mouth drops open as my head snaps toward the balcony. It's daylight outside. He won't be here, and yet still my heart cracks with fear that he stood here.

He heard me.

He stayed.

And he watched me.

Needles prick my skin, a cold shiver running up my body. I tremble with such fear that my knees weaken. I take deep breaths in and out, calming myself before getting ready for the day, but not before rushing to get the sheets off the bed and into the laundry. I hurry around, not wanting to listen to my mother's morning lecture, and head out.

I am out of my mind.

Who could it be?

And why does my stalker show up day after day?

I think I've spent too long looking at Helia if I've started fantasising about him like that.

My fingers fidget with the watch on my wrist as I walk towards the elevator.

How could I?

I'm disgusted to even think about him like that. I was turned on by the thought of Helia taking me against my will. I need serious help.

The elevator dings open in front of me.

"Morning." The familiar smoky voice from over my shoulder has me straightening.

Helia walks inside, turning around to face me with a grin on his face. He motions to the space next to him, amusement flashing in his emerald eyes. Hesitantly, I step inside and stand next to him, my heart pounding like I've just run a marathon. My eyes keep finding him in the elevator doors, and I look away each time. I never do that.

Something is wrong with me today.

As the numbers slowly go up, I feel my body burning up, his presence loud yet calm. His strong musky cologne fills up my chest, expanding it in a way that I crave more.

He shifts, taking out his phone from his pocket, and I notice that too.

My breathing doesn't slow down at all.

He pockets his phone, his arm brushing against my own, and I have to stop myself from flinching.

Sweat breaks out on the back of my neck.

Just two more floors.

One more.

Ding.

Finally.

The door opens, and I let out the biggest breath, making Helia look at me sideways as he makes his way towards his office.

"In my office, Ambrose." His command is clear, but I know I will need to give him his schedule for the day.

Grabbing my things, I head into his office a few minutes later. He is on his phone when he notices me.

Walking around the table, my voice is shaky as I speak the first few sentences. My eyes fall on him rolling up his sleeves, and it makes me swallow thickly.

"Today you have a board meeting to update everyone on how everything is going within the company." As I detail his day, I feel him watching me from his position.

My eyes slide to his, and I catch him looking. Shamelessly. He doesn't look away, either.

His head is tilted. Just like the stalker in my dream.

God. I need this dream to vanish from my memories.

"Is there something you need to tell me, Ambrose?" There is something about the way he asks this sentence. It's as if he knows what I am thinking, but I shake my head.

"Why? Did I forget something?" I am never this civil with him.

Helia narrows his eyes and leans forward.

Then he stands up to his full, towering height. A creature of the night that feeds on the fear of people, smiling with bloody lips as he breaks you in two pieces for his own mad-dening thirst.

"No. But you keep looking at me like you are hiding something."

I scoff, moving away, only for him to grab my wrist and turn me around, smashing me against his chest.

"I don't like liars, Ambrose." His voice drops an octave.

I try to free my wrist, but he holds it tighter.

"Let go, Helia."

He brings his face closer to mine. "Not until you tell me what you are hiding."

"It's nothing,"

He lifts a brow, clearly not believing my lies. He turns me around until my front is against the table, then bends me forward with his hand clasped at the back of my neck until my cheek touches the table.

"W-What are you doing?" I stutter, like a child.

I need help. I need serious, serious help.

He steps into me, letting me feel every single thick inch of his warm body.

"I don't want lies, Ambrose. I won't stop until you tell me."

"How would you know? What if I was lying about not poisoning your coffee?"

He chuckles against my ear, his chin resting on my shoulder, the strong grip on my neck still not letting me look back at him.

"Oh, I know. The way you have been looking at me all

morning? That's not the look of a poisoner. It's the look of someone who is desperately begging for a fuck. Do you want me to fuck you, Ambrose?"

My breath catches in my throat, my body going still.

He presses harder against me, but I don't admit anything.

Was I that obvious?

Neither of us has admitted anything, despite what has happened between us in the past. In the office. The night of Aurora's birthday.

How could I ever hope for anything when Helia is not my final destination? How could we ever believe anything would come from hot, poisonous flames?

We'd only get burned in the end.

"Why would I want you to fuck me when I hate the very sight of you?"

His laugh is loud, booming in the office, and then I feel it. His cock straining in his trousers against my ass.

"Just like I want to fuck you every time I see you, and yet I still want to claw my hand into your chest to kill you for making me desire you, for being an inconvenience in my life." He rolls his hips into me, and my mouth falls open at the sheer length and girth of his cock.

If we were to ever fuck, I don't know how he would fit. He will have to force his way in, and I know for a fact that Helia isn't one to go slow.

"I will never make that mistake," I manage to say.

His hand tightens around my throat, and he thrusts against my ass.

Fuck.

"What—"

I feel his lips on my neck, robbing me of any coherent thoughts.

His kisses are light before he sucks sharply.

He keeps sucking, grazing his teeth across my skin, making my legs twist under me, desire pooling in between them.

"Helia," I whimper.

This isn't how it's supposed to go.

We aren't supposed to do this.

What am I doing standing here and feeling my body desire him?

"Admit it, or I will not let you go until I mark every inch of your milky skin," he says against my skin.

"No. We are in the office," I continue, but he growls, his teeth grabbing hold of my skin at the junction of my shoulder.

"Does it look like I give a fuck, Ambrose?"

No. No, he doesn't.

He nibbles on that part before he lets go and runs his hot, wet tongue over the bite as if to soothe it. I know I will be covered by many hickeys if I don't capitulate.

"If given the chance, I would fuck you here on the table so everyone outside knows that you belong to me." He mutters, his hand sprawled on my stomach, making me sigh in pleasure.

"Admit it, Ambrose."

His mouth latches onto the other side of my neck.

I can't have hickeys on display. My concealer can only hide so much. But he keeps going. He isn't stopping. His fingers on my stomach create small erotic circles that almost make me moan.

No. Stop.

If he doesn't stop, I might give in, and I don't want to lose this battle.

"Fine. Fuck," I snap.

He stops.

Waiting.

My harsh breaths echo in the office, the soft chatter from outside reminding me where we are. A laugh bounces around every once in a while, but there is only silence in Helia's office.

"I dreamt of you, in my bed, using... a knife to cut through..." I swallow. "Cut through my shirt."

His hands all fall from my body, and he steps back.

He's disgusted. He will fire me for admitting this. I know it.

Then a loud laugh booms through the office. I turn around and pin him with a glare.

"Oh, my little emerald likes knives," he murmurs before grabbing hold of the back of my neck and pressing a kiss to the corner of my lips.

"You—" He clamps a hand on my mouth, silencing my protests. "No fighting right now, baby. Not when you have given me this answer." A twisted smirk plays at his lips.

He's pleased.

A smile of a winner.

My heart dips.

What did I do?

I have a very bad feeling that if Helia ever held me like that again, he will get me to do anything he likes. If he smiles down at me like a man who has won everything, I will fall to my knees for him.

And that's fucking scary.

25

AMBROSE

I am mortified.

I cannot face Helia again, and the message I received yesterday gives me a good excuse to avoid him. Staying in my office all day doesn't really help with the embarrassment of what I said yesterday.

Forget trying to better myself, I am sitting here having told my boss I imagined him in my dreams in such a sick way that I don't know how he doesn't feel weirded out. But then again, a man like Helia wouldn't really feel like that now, would he?

He might even be having the time of his life with this information.

I breathe in and out, trying to regulate my heart, which wants to run out of my chest.

For the second time ever, I am standing in front of the Cainn mansion.

In front of the main door.

The jeans seem to be the wrong choice for today's breezy weather. I should have worn something else. At least the cream jumper is providing some kind of warmth.

If the door doesn't open within the next few minutes, I will run back to my car.

Cool wind ruffles my hair. It feels a lot colder now that I am out of my car, but even being here is making me feel a little sick.

What will I say?

I stretch my lips into a smile, but it hurts, so I drop it.

The flowers in my hand slip down to the ground, and I quickly pick them up, shaking them and getting rid of the dirt. Of course they had to fall now. The only day I wanted to gift them to someone.

The door opens in front of me, a warm soft glow of the lights filters out, and just as I lift my face to greet Aurora, the smile freezes on my face.

"Tell me why you are here every time I show up?" I speak through gritted teeth and the strained smile on my face.

Helia leans against the door, crossing his arms. His eyes follow a dark path down my body, making me clear my throat. I wait, but he doesn't do anything but observe me.

He just looks at me. His head resting on the side of the door, his eyes silent just like he is, and under his scrutiny I feel a little self-conscious. Not because I suddenly don't feel confident or he is making me wary but because those eyes of his. They feel like they are reaching deep inside me.

Seeking out something from me.

Like a lover's touch.

Tender. Soft. Patient.

"You look like…." he starts, his rumbling voice making my own heart tremble in need.

Why do I feel this way?

Where is the hate I always carry around with me?

"I don't want to hear it. Where is Aurora?" I look behind him to see her walking towards me, her chestnut hair bouncing.

"Move out of the way, Helia. I do not want any fights or arguments today" With a simple push from her, Helia turns and walks away but not before glancing over his shoulder at me.

His eyes are so deep and so achingly beautiful that it feels like they are physically calling out to me. I can feel his maddening eyes on me each time we are in a room together. I can see the antagonising way his eyes always do a slow sweep of my body.

"Ambrose," Aurora murmurs, a small soft smile on her face. "Welcome." She steps aside, and I finally take the first step inside her home, just like I am entering her heart.

Walking up to her, I hand her the pink roses. Her eyes fall upon them, and they light up. She looks up, and her lower lip trembles ever so slightly.

"Don't. Please don't cry," I whisper. I lift my hand to her cheek but stop mid-way.

I drop it, and her eyes mirror the pain in my heart. This is exactly what it feels like to rip out a piece of your heart and watch it sit still as a stone and lose life bit by bit.

"This way." She leads me through her home. A staircase to my right leads up to the second floor, and I spot blue accents all around the home as we pass a living room on my left. We pass another living room, but this one has a small little library on one of its walls.

At the end of the hallway, there is a wide door that opens to reveal a grand kitchen. Only the best of the best, the largest and most expensive things for Remo Cainn, after all.

He is the very epitome of the Elite. There is not a single powerful person that passes through London, that works in London, that Remo isn't aware of.

You cannot escape him. At all.

Despite there being a mayor, a head deputy mayor—Talia's father—Remo has his hands in everything. No wonder Dad wanted to get off his blacklist. To be blacklisted by Remo means to be removed from every connection, every tie, and everything you own.

"My friends are here. I promise they won't bother you. They are pretty easy-going."

I nod wordlessly as I follow her into the kitchen.

Navy-blue counter tops with white cupboards line the back and black stools surround the kitchen island. There is a dining table to the right of the wide kitchen, with sliding doors towards the back, covered by curtains.

I spot Remo amongst everyone. Standing tall with his

arms crossed, leaning against the counter on the far end of the kitchen. His eyes follow everyone around the counter with a small frown on his face. Aurora walks up to him, and instantly his expression melts and he gathers her in his arms. His tall figure almost engulfs her whole, his thick arms going around her small back.

She giggles, but that is drowned out by the sudden shouts of her friends.

Kamari is here and so is Ruel, as well as another brunette woman I haven't met yet. Helia is nowhere to be found despite walking this way.

But that doesn't mean I'm looking for him. No. I'm not.

"Everyone! Ambrose is here," Aurora shouts, and silence engulfs the room.

All eyes are on me, and I stand there. Unmoving.

"Don't be awkward, Ambrose. We will be making pizzas to eat while we watch a movie in the living room afterwards, though the vote is still out on what we will be watching." Aurora easily slides in to save me.

"Right. Do you need help?" I ask as I remove my scarf and go over to the dining table to put down my bag, scarf, and coat.

"Actually…" Kamari starts off, pushing Ruel out of her way and walking towards the middle of the kitchen and standing in front of me.

With long, luscious, curly hair, eyes hinting at the perfect honey colour, flared jeans that hug her hips, and a black jumper with the top few buttons popped open, Kamari looks like a dream.

Ruel looks like he belongs on the front of magazines, and I can't help but think that getting a famous football player on one of our covers would be a good idea. It could be an exclusive edition that we can sell, featuring the heart-throb football player of England that would have women screaming.

Black unruly hair and his athletic body give him a bad boy look. His playful flirty smile reminds me of Helia. He wears a navy-blue sweater that moulds to his muscles and blue washed jeans. His sleeves are rolled up to his elbows, revealing a sparkling watch and a glint of a chain around his neck.

"We will be in groups of two people. The teams are Aurora and Remo, Ruel and me, you and Helia, and Venezia…" She trails off as she looks over at the woman, who I assume is Remo's younger sister.

She has long, pin-straight brown hair, olive skin tone, matching Remo's, and similar dark eyes to him, too. She's quite slender and almost as tall as me, though I don't know her age. With an oversized white and brown striped jumper and black skinny jeans and white socks, she has young features, a soft touch to her cheeks, and a beautiful pearly white smile with a side parting in her hair.

She looks to be in her early twenties, possibly.

"I will be the judge, of course, and since I am left out, I'll pick the movie."

Protests start all around, and she shrugs with a victorious

smile, making my own heart fill with some sort of blasting light.

Everyone starts laughing and pointing to each other about their disgusting taste in movies. One suggests a Disney movie, while the other suggests a vampire series, and another votes for a dystopian series. It makes me swallow in longing.

The back of my head tickles, and the hair on the back of my neck rises in awareness.

And I know exactly who is here.

"You and I are together, Emerald," Helia's whisper in my ear makes my whole body stand up in attention.

He can breathe in a room and my eyes would find him.

How can I get rid of this? To stop this reaction I always get?

My mind, my traitorous body, and the way my soul wants to be pulled into his own, into the embrace of the one I am supposed to hate, is a complex puzzle in itself.

How am I going to keep up with this facade and keep denying my desire for Helia? And the small bundle of feelings that are being accompanied by this desire? I cannot look past it all and jump into this.

Our desires are out in the open. That much is clear.

Helia walks past me, his hand grazing from one end of my back to the other, leaving me breathless.

"We have a judge?" I say as I walk towards the counter and see three workstations. The kitchen island is so big, it could fit another two little stations for the pizza competition.

"Yes. Me. So try to impress me, Ambrose. Bribery works well." Venezia winks at me, making me laugh.

The suffocation that was wrapping around me disperses. We all gather around and stand in front of our stations. Kamari and Ruel are next to me, with Aurora and Remo next to Ruel. Helia walks around the counter and stands next to me.

Venezia is bouncing on her feet, a wide smile on her face as she points to the things on the counter.

"This was your idea, wasn't it?" I ask Venezia when she walks to me.

"Sure was. Though this man right here seems to hate the kitchen, so he voted against it. Thankfully, everyone in this was with me and not him." She narrows her eyes at Helia, who is leaning on the counter on his forearms.

He turns his head to me, and the minute his eyes catch mine, I hold my breath.

The intensity in his eyes makes me shift in place.

"Where has the little fox gone? Are you going to bite me for looking at you? For standing next to you?" he says quietly.

I huff at his words.

"Why? Seems like someone misses being insulted."

I look down at him and catch him biting his cheek with a smile.

"You came here. You could have taken care of this messy hair." I flick strands of his hair, his eyes shutting as I do.

241

"You guys can begin now!" Venezia shouts.

But I can't move my eyes away from him.

There is a pull between us that forces me to take a step closer to him. I want to reach out to him again, but how will I explain that?

Turning away, I clear my throat, grab the pizza dough, and start to roll it out.

"What will we be putting on the pizza?" Helia asks just as he grabs the tomato sauce.

Helia and I disagree on almost everything while making the godforsaken pizza. It left the others staring at us in shock. He didn't like what I did, and I couldn't let him win in any way at all.

"We don't need pepperoni." I push him away when he starts adding it.

"We might as well not put cheese on, and forget the tomato sauce too. I will just eat the base at this point," he counters with a glare.

I like my pizza with cheese only, and he likes it with lots of different toppings, but we are making one pizza.

"Remo, let me do it!" Aurora calls out, frustrated.

I glance over to see that he is telling her to let him do the work so she can relax, but she looks ready to kill him.

"That's not how you do it!" Kamari screams as she sees Ruel pick the pizza up, effectively making the sauce and the cheese almost fall off it. The pizza is not on the tray, just on the table counter.

I hide a smile. We aren't the only ones fighting and it's

kind of fun to argue over something so little.

"Say cheese, guys!"

We all look up at once. Venezia is holding up her phone, taking pictures of us with the flash on.

"Make me blind, why don't you?" Helia grumbles, shutting his eyes.

"Sure will." She walks over and takes close-up pictures of him with the flash on.

My hand flies to my mouth, holding in a laugh.

Helia leans over the counter to grab her phone, and she screams, running back to the living room.

"It's okay. A flash won't blind you," I mutter, admiring my plain cheese pizza, which is ready to be put into the oven.

Helia looks over at me. His eyes are a glittering colour today, sage green in contrast to his pitch-black hair. His sharp jaw and the tendons in his neck make my mouth water. I want to press my lips there, to feel his heartbeat.

I shut down that thought really fast.

The scar running down his eye really intrigues me. It makes him look devastatingly hot. Just looking at him makes my ears burn hot. It evokes turmoil within me, like molten lava is roiling in the pit of my stomach, and it burns hotter the longer he looks at me.

I am aware of his presence like never before.

Every time he passes me, every time he is in a room with me, my body buzzes with excitement.

It's not possible to ignore any of this.

"In the oven now," I mutter softly, grabbing the tray and placing the pizza in the oven behind us. Kamari follows soon after me, and so does Aurora.

We all are now piled into the living room, a movie ready to be turned on.

But a problem has arisen: the seating plan.

"Someone can sit on the sofa, if they don't mind." Aurora motions towards the sofa.

The living room is grand; there is no need to sit on the sofa. But everyone wants to sit close together. That means sitting in front of the four-seater sofa facing the TV mounted on the wall. There are pillows and blankets on the floor, and a blanket on the sofa with throw pillows all around.

"I will take the ground." Kamari places herself in front of the sofa on the ground, while Remo and Helia grab the coffee table and place it on the far end of the living room on the right.

I am sitting on the sofa, a little out of place as everyone takes their seats as if they already have done this multiple times. I haven't.

"Do you want me to sit next to you, Ambrose?"

I look up to see Aurora holding out a bowl of popcorn for me. My eyes fall to the empty space next to me and to the people on the floor. I don't want her to feel left out or to not sit with her friends just because of me.

"Sit with Remo or Kamari. It's okay, I'll have the whole sofa to myself." I lift my cheeks into a smile, hoping she believes it and agrees.

She opens her mouth to say something, her eyes narrowing, only to stop short a heavy arm falls on my shoulder.

"I'll keep her accompanied," the velvet voice drawls.

Aurora's eyes light up, and she nods. "Perfect. You don't mind Helia sitting with you, right? If he does anything, you tell me. I know exactly what kind of mischief he is always up to." She narrows her eyes at him with a pointed finger.

To see her care for me, trying to keep me company, helping me settle in, so I don't feel lonely or left out, warms my heart. I truly feel like she is getting closer to forgiving me. I hope she does. It's not easy to forgive someone who tormented you.

But I am grateful for it. I will take whatever crumbs she gives me.

A laugh vibrates in Helia's chest, raising goosebumps all over me.

"You have so little faith in me. I just want to keep Ambrose company. She doesn't talk to me in the office much. It will be great to get to know each other, right?"

I sigh, shaking my head.

"It's okay, Aurora. Go sit down. I will be fine." I hit Helia in the ribs with my elbow.

"Ow!"

Aurora narrows her eyes in warning once more, making me grin.

"Remo, reel in your misses. She's out for blood today."

Remo looks up from my right where he is seated in front of Helia, his build so big that his shoulders sit higher than the sofa. Aurora settles into his arms and looks so small.

Remo's one look, his jaw ticking just once, has Helia raising his hands.

He doesn't need to say anything for everyone in the room to tremble. Quite like Helia. They truly do suit each other. No wonder they are friends.

"You both are so alike yet so different," I murmur, watching the opening scene of the murder mystery Venezia chose.

Kamari is next to Aurora, then Ruel, then Venezia, who is sitting in the corner on the left, a whole blanket to herself. She's got an excited smile on her face as she watches with intrigue. It's her movie, after all.

"You guys are going to love it," she tells us.

"Sure, because we love watching murder and gore," Kamari grumbles, making Aurora laugh.

"I'll protect you, sweetheart." Ruel wraps an arm around her shoulder and pulls her to him.

"Get away from me." She scrunches her nose at him.

Ruel grins in return, as if he knows something she doesn't.

"I hope not. I wouldn't want to see Remo look at you the way I do," Helia answers quietly and softly in my ear.

I thought he hadn't heard me, but I catch him settle in next to me, his thigh pressed right to mine.

Touching.

His shoulder, too. His body is so close that I can smell his strong gardenia cologne. I can see the small tattoos that are creeping up his shirt collar, can feel the heat from his body seeping into mine.

My heart races at being so close to him in the dark, on the sofa, alone.

He could reach over, and his hand would be in my lap. He could rip the blanket off of me; he could kiss me and no one would notice.

He could—

I shut my eyes tightly.

What is going on with me today?

The movie starts, and everyone grows quiet. I don't reply nor look at Helia beside me.

I force myself to keep my eyes on the TV when he shifts.

I don't look at him when we reach forty minutes into the movie and a soft sigh falls from his lips. Lips I have kissed.

I don't let my curiosity win when I feel his hand graze mine under the blanket on my thigh. My legs are crossed, touching his big, strong thigh next to me.

My heart spikes when I feel a feathery touch on my neck. Thinking it's a trick of my mind, I don't look over.

My stomach dips when I feel it again, as if he's brushing a strand of my hair away from my neck.

The girl in the movie is running through the woods, a hooded figure running after her with a knife in hand, and the music in the background is getting louder and louder. The girls in the room grab their blankets and cover the lower half of their faces.

But I'm not scared. I am too aware of what Helia is doing.

"I'm bored," he whispers in my ear, his hot breath fanning my bare shoulder.

The girl in the movie trips.

The music grows louder, and my heart thunders.

"I've watched you all night long, Ambrose," he continues, his lips softly skimming over my shoulder, making me suck in a sharp breath.

"You make me lose my mind."

The killer reaches the girl with his knife, the music louder than ever.

"You make me a crazy, crazy man."

The killer lifts his knife and slams it down on the girl.

And Helia's lips kiss my throbbing pulse. I gasp along with others in the room, though not for the same reason.

Helia grazes my shoulder with his teeth, licking and nibbling at the skin there, and I don't do anything to stop him. My hands tightly fist the blanket on my lap, my eyes on everyone else while they watch the scene intently.

"Helia," I whisper, pushing at his chest softly.

A pulse throbs between my legs.

He lets go, his eyes hooded. The light from the TV illuminates his face, revealing lust, desire. His eyes hold mine, and I have a hard time looking away.

"We shouldn't be doing this," I murmur.

He drops his head back against the sofa, jaw tense, looking up at the ceiling while I watch him.

His arm rests behind me on the back of the sofa, and once I know he isn't going to do anything else, I turn back to the TV. The girl is sitting in her house shivering wet as rain splatters loudly outside.

Just as she goes upstairs, a loud bang sounds at the door. She screams, along with the girls in the room.

Helia's hand behind me grabs hold of the back of my neck and pulls me to him in a quick, bruising kiss.

He lets me go a moment later, and I am left breathless, not knowing what just happened.

"Helia." My fingers go to my tingling lips, my eyes wide.

The look on his face… He looks tortured, his brows furrowed, his lips pulled down as his eyes beg me to let him. Let him what?

What does he want?

Why the kisses?

Shouldn't he hate me?

"You—you…" I blink, turning back to the TV. "Don't do that again. I will walk away Helia,"

"Don't you want this, Ambrose?" he whispers hoarsely.

"Wrong place, wrong time to ask a stupid question like that." I jab him in the ribs, but he grabs my elbow and almost pulls me into his lap.

"Then tell me that you aren't dripping from the fear of getting caught, from just the thought of kissing me, of letting me touch you right there, right now. Tell me I'm lying," he whispers in my ear.

I stay silent.

He isn't lying.

"Fuck." He runs a hand through his hair, watching me,

but I don't look at him.

I have no answer. On more than one occasion, I have imagined him in such a dirty, disgusting way that I was ashamed to think of him like that.

To have him ask me about it?

For him to almost beg to touch me?

In my sister's home?

I don't know what to do, and my heart is too muddled for me to think properly.

There is still an hour left of the movie.

Everyone is engrossed in the movie, keeping them on edge. Though Remo seems to be bored more than anything.

And Helia's body right next to mine is making it hard to think.

My heart is still racing from what has happened.

Fuck. Fuck. Fuck.

I shouldn't want him. Shouldn't accept this invitation from him.

It's wrong.

So, so wrong to want my enemy like this. Whose hands held my throat, ready to kill me.

But my hand travels over to his lap, grabbing his large hand in mine, and I bring it over to my lap, to the hem of my jeans. I can't find it in me to stop myself at all.

When I glance over for a quick mere second, I catch Helia's eyes darken. They look seductive and crazy. He looks like he is ready to snap at any second.

"We shouldn't be doing this," I mutter once more, biting

my lip, my eyes shutting when I feel his fingers slide down my jeans, under my underwear, to my soaking pussy.

We are enemies.

On the opposite side of the battlefield.

But I want him.

26

AMBROSE

If you'd told me I would be in this position a couple of months ago, I would have laughed in your face. I would have cursed you out for daring to even imagine Helia's fingers inside of me while I sat in Aurora's home.

With my bottom lip trapped between my teeth and my breath falling in short pants, I can't do anything but focus on the pleasurable ride Helia is giving me.

With each ruthless pump, I can feel him branding me. Soft sighs fall on my shoulder from his lips.

Everyone is too engrossed in the movie that is gripping their throats to notice or even look back. Even if one of them knew what was going on, I wouldn't know, too blinded by pleasure.

My hand grips Helia's muscled arm. It's probably going to leave nail marks.

"Fuck. Seeing this look on your face makes me weak in

my knees, Ambrose," Helia grumbles.

He's fucking me so hard and fast that I am breathless, unable to intake even a simple breath.

"Give it to me, Ambrose."

I break apart, shutting my eyes tightly, and pressing my lips together. I collapse, heaving. His fingers slip from my body, leaving me feeling cold and empty. My whole being gravitates towards him.

"Helia." My head falls back against the sofa, my eyes shut.

I lost my battle.

I lost my control, my composure, and my hold on my tightly caged heart.

A finger softly traces my cheek, but I don't want to open my eyes and face reality. Of what I have done and exactly what this means.

I can't do this.

Getting up from the sofa, I walk out of the living room and into the bathroom next to the kitchen.

"Fuck, fuck, fuck!" I stare at myself in the mirror. My dirty brown eyes are wide in horror as my chest recovers from being deprived of oxygen.

"What have I done? What have I fucking done?" I shake my head, walking back and forth in the massive bathroom.

How will I walk out?

What will I do? How will I face him after this?

Punching the marble counter, I try to focus on the pain, on the searing prickles up my arm.

Shutting my eyes, I take a deep breath, shaking my arms and my head, erasing all thoughts.

I agreed to this. I accepted it. I wanted it.

I shouldn't be ashamed. I shouldn't be insecure about wanting something natural.

I am who I am.

I am firm in my decision. Whatever happens from here on out, I will just follow along. I will bend it to my will if it goes against my morals.

When I return to the living room, the movie is paused, and everyone is in the kitchen.

"Ambrose, your pizza is ready. It looks good." Venezia points to the tray with my pizza.

"Isabella, our maid, was kind enough to take them out or else they would have been burnt by now." Aurora laughs, shaking her head.

She hands one pizza cutter to Kamari and the other to Venezi,a who hands it to me when I get there. As soon as my eyes lift from the pizza cutter, they connect with Helia's dark ones.

He's standing there with a fucking smirk on his face.

My hand tightens around the cutter.

It's like a push and pull war.

He knows that I am at war with myself over what has happened. He knows it. His eyes drop to my red knuckles, then they rise to the crook of my neck, where he licked, where his soft lips were pressed, and then his jaw tics, though I can clearly see it isn't in anger.

Him leaning against the counter with his arms crossed, a dark smile playing at his lips while he watches me approach him, proves to me that he is enjoying this far more than me. When I reach him, his broad chest instantly covers me, guarding me from everyone else.

"How do you like the pizza?" he asks me casually.

I scowl at him, making him chuckle. It makes me freeze in place to soak it in. His genuine smile, his eyes a forest at sunset, his hair a starless night. Helia is a masterpiece.

"I mean, I didn't put any toppings on it for your boring self. Do you not see me sacrificing my dinner for you?" He flutters his lashes at me, making my lips twitch into a smile, but I shut it down quickly.

"Everyone likes cheese," I state like it's a fact, jutting my chin out.

We are both toying around the subject of what has happened, speaking with our eyes while something entirely different comes out of our mouths.

Helia raises a brow.

"Again, no fighting." Venezia comes in between us, pushing Helia and me away from each other.

"I love all kinds of pizza, but Aurora and Remo win." She points over to their pizza. It's round and has chicken and cheese for toppings.

I look at Kamari's. It looks very messy with almost everything on it: chicken, black olives, jalapeno, and all you can think of.

And mine... looks bland.

"Now grab your pizzas, and let's head back into the living room," Venezia shouts and skips to the living room.

We all pile in together, back into our positions. The lights dim, and my heart starts to race, though the pizza plate in between me and Helia is sort of a barrier.

And we still haven't talked about it.

About anything, and I don't know if we will.

We should just ignore it.

Just like we did with the kiss.

Like the office night.

Like everything else.

It should be erased from existence.

The rest of the night, Helia keeps throwing heated glances at me, though he isn't moving over to touch me. He's teasing me with soft strokes and long looks that make me feel like I will fall apart if he doesn't touch me again.

Having Helia's eyes on me the whole night, every time I was scared in the movie, a soft touch from Helia would calm me knowing he is here. Despite the harshness that surrounds him, despite the danger and the havoc, he quietens my mind like no other.

I shouldn't feel like this with him.

His eyes, they haunt me, warn me that he will kill me with his bare hands if he has to, and that doesn't even begin to cover the psychotic tendencies he has. Pleasing people, a gentleman to others, all while hiding a psychopath personality under it all.

Helia is the definition of chaos.

Of the deadliest serpent.

27

AMBROSE

I walk into the office, and I cannot hide the small smile on my face, knowing that Aurora isn't as angry nor as detached from me as before. I don't know if sending her a bouquet of flowers with a thank you note would suffice.

I should tell her that I am thankful she decided to take this step towards me.

So I do.

I buy a beautiful argyle pink diamond tennis bracelet with a rose bouquet and decide to drop it off myself rather than have someone else do so for me. Happy with my idea, I get started on the tasks for today.

My stomach dips every time someone opens a door. I keep thinking Helia will walk out, that he will look at me with dark, heated eyes and I will fall apart.

He will lean over to touch me, and I will lose all control. But that will never happen. Internally, I may be breaking and not knowing how to control my emotions, but on the outside, I am keeping my composure.

"Ambrose, my office. Now."

My head snaps up towards Helia's office. He is standing in the doorway of his office, his expression blank of any emotions.

Fear wraps around my throat.

What is it?

What have I done?

I try to remember if I let anything slip through, but I can't seem to think of anything.

Getting up, I take a deep breath, putting on a brave face, and walk right past him into his office.

I will stand my ground if anything happens.

I am Ambrose Torre.

And I do not back down from any challenge.

"Whatever stupid mistake you may have found—" I turn around and bump into Helia. He is standing right in front of me. Not a single inch of space between us.

I look up at him, filled with determination, ready to fight him, but I stagger at the softness in his eyes. His brows are pulled down, a crinkle in his eyes as passion swirls in those maddening eyes of his.

"Are you going to call this a mistake, too?"

My brows twist in a frown. "Call what a mistake?"

His hand snakes around my waist and pulls me to him. I push at his chest, but getting him to let me go is like trying to bend metal with my bare hands. It won't work.

So I give up, huffing, as I look back up at him.

"What happened last night, Ambrose?" His voice is hard, commanding.

He wants no lies.

But am I ready to accept that whatever happened last night was, in fact, something I truly wanted and not a mistake?

"Yes." I jut my chin out.

Helia's eyes drop. The black takes over the green in them, and he suddenly seems too tall, too muscular, too strong, and too large against me.

He feels threatening.

So why does my stomach drop in anticipation at seeing what he may demand in retribution of me denying it?

"You will deny something you begged for? You will deny something you wanted?" he grits out, his hold on my waist tightening. His other hand slowly climbs up my body, past my breasts until it reaches under my jaw.

"It didn't mean anything. A moment of weakness. We all have them." I try to shrug, but it's not possible with him holding me so tightly to him.

With each intake of breath, my nipples brush against his chest. I feel the zaps run through my veins, the pit of my stomach fluttering and my knees weakening at his possession.

"So your pussy didn't beg for my fingers? Your pussy didn't weep as soon as I pushed my fingers inside?"

I shake my head, then lean forward, brushing my lips

softly against his. "No," I whisper.

"On your knees."

I reel my head back from his demand. One I am supposed to comply with. "What?"

He dips his chin to the floor. "On your knees, Ambrose."

He must be joking.

"No. I never have and never will bow to a man. Find yourself another woman." I push at his chest, and he lets me go but instantly cages me against the edge of his desk, his arms on either side of me.

"You will get on your knees for me, right fucking now," he grits out.

"And I said no." I cross my arms and turn my face away from him. He grabs my chin between two fingers and wrenches me back towards him.

"On. Your. Knees." His eyes leave no room for argument.

He looks menacing. He looks crazy. Helia looks terrifying in this moment.

And I am shamelessly begging him in my mind to push me more.

His dominance is calling out to my dark pleasures.

"I will open this door, dip my hand in your trousers, knowing exactly how wet your pussy is, and watch you scream out my name in front of everyone on this floor." He leans closer, his lips brushing my ear.

"You know how fast gossip travels around this company, don't you? You know how many people in this building hate you. How about I humiliate you and add disdain to the general sentiment?"

My eyes burn. I clench my hands into fists but just the image he has painted in my hand of him fucking me with his fingers again, wrenching out orgasm after orgasm with the door open while my moans echo down the hallway has me panting for more.

Like the dirty woman I am, my desire leaks through my underwear.

"You want to play that game? I will not only win, I will destroy everything you stand for; so get on your knees, Ambrose."

It's hard, but as I narrow my eyes at him, I know I will do it.

Not because of his threat, but because of the disgusting anticipation bubbling in my chest.

"I see the look in your eyes. I see the want and need for me, so let me give it to you," he murmurs, rubbing his thumb over my chin, back and forth.

"You want me and it's killing you to admit it. Ambrose doesn't admit defeat in front of a man, does she?" He looks at me like he can read me, and maybe he can.

How could he recite everything, the war I am in with myself, and still want me?

To know how difficult I am and yet still love the fight?

"I hate you." I get down on one knee. "I despise you." The other knee hits the floor. "I want to fucking throttle you and kill you."

A dangerous gleam shines through Helia's eyes.

"But I want you to fuck me all the same," I admit. It's out in the open now.

He knows it.

I know it.

"That doesn't mean my feelings for you have changed." It's a lie.

They have changed. And I did not, under any circumstance, want them to change.

So I am avoiding them.

His hands go to his belt, and my lips fall open with a small inaudible gasp. The clinking of the buckle echoes around the office, and my hands turn clammy. The zipper goes down, and the flaps of his trousers open. My pussy clenches around nothing, wanting attention.

Fuck this.

How could I want someone I hate? Someone who is set on destroying my life?

"Be a good girl, Emerald, and I might give a little attention to that pretty pussy that is craving me." His voice drops to a soft tone, making my heart melt, but I shake my head internally.

How does he know that too now?

My eyes focus on the outline of his cock beneath his black boxers. It's thick and huge, pressed against the stretchy material.

"Take my cock out," he demands.

My hands fly up, perfectly manicured nails dragging along the waistband of his underwear, then I tug.

My mouth waters at the length and girth of his cock. As soon as it's completely out, it almost hits me in the face. I swallow, just imagining it ripping through me with Helia pounding above me, making me reach impossibly pleasurable heights.

It's not my first time seeing a cock, but I've never seen one this size. My chest constricts, excitement rushing through my veins as I lean forward, sticking my tongue out and licking the pre-cum leaking from it.

"Fuck, don't you dare tease me," Helia grumbles from above me.

So, I don't.

Leaning forward, with a hand on his thick muscular thigh and the other holding his cock at the base, I suck him into my mouth.

Helia's hand grabs at the desk behind me, his other one on the back of my head.

"You look so good on your knees for me," Helia grits out.

And he picks up his pace.

And fucks me. Fucks my mouth.

He keeps going, and desire starts to pool between my legs.

"You are doing so well," he grumbles.

A whine slips out of me, and I find myself aching to be touched, but that hum alone has Helia groaning above me.

When I look up, I see his head fallen back, his hair falling recklessly around his face, the tendons in his neck popping.

The sight of him in his black suit, stretched across his chest and broad shoulders, completely at my mercy as I suck him off, makes me want to pleasure him more.

I have this big manically psycho man, losing control at my hands.

And I fucking love it.

"Take me like I am yours. Take me just like that… Yes, hmm," he groans, his words ringing in my mind.

His chest heaves, and a moan slips from his mouth, making me smile.

"You're such a dirty girl. Ambrose," he grunts, then releases his load into my mouth, breathing heavily above me.

And I swallow.

Fuck if he doesn't taste good.

He lets go of the back of my head, and the sharp edge of the desk hits the back of my head. I realise he held me there the whole time to avoid me hitting my head. Something pinches in my chest at that thought.

"You look good, being ruined by me, being owned and marked by me." He rubs his thumb across my bottom lip, his eyes darkening when I lick that lip.

"And I still hate you." I narrow my eyes, making him laugh.

He presses his thumb softly onto my lip, and I open my mouth, taking it in and sucking it, rolling my eyes, knowing I have his full attention.

Just as I open my eyes, Helia pulls me up and places me on the edge of the desk.

He unbuttons my trousers, pulls them down with my underwear, and gets on his knees.

"Now let me reward my pretty fox." And he does.

I am in the office an hour later, coming down from the high, and still not recovering from what he has done to me. I don't let myself think too much of it. Not the soft touches I got every so often, not the long glances, not the low murmurs in my ears, and certainly not the fact that my own heart beat an extra beat for him.

He took it from me.

My submission.

And a truth that no man ever has before.

That I want him.

It doesn't matter that it's in the name of desire.

The next day, when I am in his office, he pulls me to his lap, making me sit and type up an email to the marketing team while he has his hand so deep between my legs that they shake with pleasure.

And every time I came into his office over the next couple of weeks, I found myself in some kind of position at his mercy, and yet I kept uttering the same words.

"I hate you." With his fingers inside of me.

"I despise you." When he kissed down my neck.

"I feel repulsed by you." While he was deep down in my throat.

And yet, the one thing we never did was kiss.

We never did it. It felt too intimate.

And a small question arose in my mind.

Was I just a means to an end for him?

To satisfy his need?

Is that why he didn't want to fuck me?

Does being secretive about our pleasures while hating each other, a reckless thing to do?

Especially for someone like me, whom no one has ever spoken softly to?

For someone who lost her virginity, then never went within arm's reach of another man again?

Helia may as well be my first. No man has touched me a second time. I never let them. My life never let me. My priorities were different.

Instead of drowning in alcohol or sex, I found myself constantly on the move to better Glamorous, to look over my shoulder in case someone was planning to overthrow me, to looking out for Aurora and making sure she was safe.

And I never realised that maybe I needed time for myself, too.

I lost too much of myself to the point where I don't know what I want except to have Glamorous under my control.

Now, as I stand beside Helia at Remo's new product launch event, I think about exactly what position I am in.

Vulnerable.

Then why does my heart refuse to push Helia away?

Why can't I deny him when he asks?

Where is my strength when his eyes look over at me and my heart skips a beat?

What is happening to me?

28

HELIA

I am more than ready to admit everything.

   More than ready to gather Ambrose into my arms to keep her there forever.

It doesn't matter that no one finds comfort in darkness; I know my emerald will.

I walk into the office and notice that Ambrose's desk is empty. A frown makes its way onto my face as I enter my office, only to stop short when I see her on her way out.

She looks at me, then her eyes dart away and she walks past me like nothing has ever happened between us. Her strong perfume was a reminder of last night. It's stronger at the junction of her neck, where I'd pressed my face, breathing her in, unable to entirely get my fill.

My hands twitch at my sides, wanting to grab her and place her on the desk in front of me.

The soft click of the door shutting fills the silence, and

my eyes find my coffee on the table next to a pile of folders. They should contain the pictures of models for the next volume. I will have to approve them for the marketing team.

We need to be there on set tomorrow.

Why does the silence in my office bother me right now?

The light outside on my left shifts my attention.

London's skyline is clear as the clouds make way for the sun, slowly swimming away while a beautiful day rises for the people of London.

And yet, something is wrong. Something doesn't feel right.

My shoes click on the floor as I walk over to grab the folder with the models, then I walk back out to find Ambrose sticking up papers on her board, a pencil in her mouth, frowning before changing the papers.

My eyes catch onto what she is doing, and I realise she is piecing together drafts of how she wants a specific spread to look like. I gave her this task because one thing I cannot ignore is how good Ambrose is at her work.

My heart stammers inside of me, yesterday flashing on repeat.

She's wearing a white flowy shirt, a matching flowy skirt that reaches her knees, black tights, and heels.

"Ambrose," I call out, holding the list of models in my hand.

She turns her head, flicking her hair off her shoulder, and in that one swift movement, the softness that wraps around her face almost has me stepping back.

"This list? I don't like it. Research some other models and get them for me." I throw the file on her table, then turn and stride back to my desk, feeling her eyes on me the whole way.

Two hours later, she knocks on my door and enters the office. My eyes instantly find hers once more. They are drawn to her like good is to bad.

"The new list. The marketing team approved it."

She places a file on my desk, her eyes careful, and that's when my eyes fall on her neck. The white silk scarf wrapped around her neck makes me smirk.

I open the file and see the models, but the thing is, I liked the first ones fine. I don't care who they are so long as they fit within the theme of the newest volume of the magazine.

"No."

Ambrose frowns. "Why? I think they are fine. They fit with the fitness theme of the month. They are influencers, and—"

"Didn't I say no? Do you know better or me?"

She clamps her mouth shut, her eyes narrowing. "Well, I am here to tell you that you are being unreasonable. Those are the best choices."

I lean back in my seat.

"Why are you looking at me like that? You know I'm right." Her frown deepens, and she crosses her arms.

I lift a brow, amused by her offended tone.

"I didn't say anything." I shrug, making her scoff.

Before she can say anything, someone walks into the of-

270

fice. Unannounced. Without knocking.

"Helia, here you are. I went to your house, and you weren't there. Remo said that—" Venezia stops short once she notices Ambrose standing there too.

Her long brown hair is braided, and she's wearing brown trousers with a fitted black long-sleeved shirt. Her chocolate eyes flicker between us. From Ambrose, who is ready to fight me, to me, sitting here, nonchalant.

"I'm sorry. I should have knocked. The receptionist let me in," Venezia says.

I frown. "I never approved you to come in whenever you like."

She shrugs, and I know Remo did it.

"Remo insisted on giving you these files and says to be prepared. He wouldn't email because he wanted it to be special." She shrugs again, as if really not knowing what she is here to give me.

She hands it over to Ambrose, then turns around and leaves.

"She didn't have an appointment, but I guess being Remo's sister has its perks," Ambrose mutters, looking down at the file.

She doesn't open it as I expect her to; instead, she hands it over to me and then turns to walk away.

"I didn't say you could leave."

She looks at me over her shoulder. "You didn't say I can't either." Then she leaves. The door shuts behind her, and I let out a small laugh.

I leave the file to one side and open the rest of the work I have piled up, looking through documents.

Someone walks in through the door, and I sigh, slamming my hand on the table.

"Who the fuck keeps letting everyone in?" I raise my head, then sigh even louder.

"Tell me why you keep showing up? Your sister and now you? Give me a break. If Aurora wants to invite me to another dinner, or if you want my help with getting a different therapist who will agree to your terms, then come another time."

Remo raises a brow, then sits down in front of me, his eyes slowly looking over the office. I changed nothing, knowing I will leave soon. London was never my home. I thought it never would be, but that thought is changing now.

"It's been more than a couple of months now."

I know what he is about to say next.

"I guess I need to deal with it this time, huh? Can't run away to Mexico, Spain, or even Tokyo?"

Remo doesn't look amused. His face relaxed, bored.

A man like him, a man with such power? No one can ever harm him.

Me? I'm the one living in the shadows; the one who does his dirty work.

Once caught, I won't be able to turn back.

"Did you read the papers I sent you?"

"No."

A moment of silence follows.

"You left many bodies behind, Helia."

The realisation makes its way into me, and my hold on the arm of the chair tightens, my knuckles turning white with the force.

The bodies of people who touched Ambrose wrong: in the past, in the few months I have known her, anyone her mother may have considered worthy to marry her to. I did so without thinking then, not realising something was about to overtake me. That was the effect Ambrose had on me.

A crushing, maddening effect.

"Were they all truly for her? I thought you hated her? What do you see in her? I don't even know…"

His words weave around my chest and slowly sink in. I let my head drop back, exhaling loudly.

"She is the one who allowed Aurora to get kidnapped. She is the one who allowed Aurora to almost get killed, bringing her to the point of suicide. If it weren't for sheer luck on her part, Aurora wouldn't be here." His voice hardens, his hate for Ambrose taking over. "Did you tell her you know? That you know everything because of a simple background check? The day Aurora told me, I was about to kill her. I would have if Aurora hadn't stopped me."

I suck in a breath through my teeth, clenching my jaw.

I should hate her. I should.

Why the fuck am I thinking about smashing in Remo's face for speaking about Ambrose like this?

"You've been watching her more than you needed to. You hired her, and I didn't say anything. You killed for her, and I still covered you. But now? You need to let her go. You need to—"

"No."

Remo slowly turns his head, looking right at me.

"Just because I warned Aurora about you doesn't mean you should do the same to me. Give it your best, Remo. I will not do what you just said." I get up and turn away from him, looking out at the city.

I know what he is doing.

He's striking back since he almost lost Aurora because of me.

How was I supposed to know that he was falling for her?

She seemed sweet to me, a small piece of the puzzle that fell in between our plans.

I warned her while I could, but Remo didn't like that at all.

I'll tell Ambrose tomorrow that I know of her past, but I'm not letting her go. If anything, I am holding on tighter, knowing something is brimming and Remo will not back down.

"You asked me if it's possible to leave dead bodies behind for someone. Do you remember my answer?" Remo asks.

My shoulders tighten.

I asked him that when I saw him kill for Aurora after a decade of staying clean.

"I said yes."

That's when it dawns on me why he is telling me this. He

274

wants me to acknowledge what I feel for Ambrose.

It cannot be what he feels for Aurora.

That's love.

What he has with Aurora is love.

What I have with Ambrose?

That's hate.

Right?

That's why I'm killing so many people for her... Right?

29
HELIA

Age twenty-one

Living within the walls of a library has taught me many things.

Knowledge cannot be taken away.

Knowledge will always remain the most powerful tool.

For the past eleven years, I have been hiding, sneaking into libraries, sitting and reading through everything, making use of a card I stole from a kid so I could use the computers. I mastered the artificial intelligence humankind has made.

I hacked into smaller places, seeing the kind of information not many others were able to gather. Then I stumbled upon Peccator, a search engine that allows me to find information on people. I can be anonymous and still get blackmail material.

And so I took advantage of it.

I blackmailed people, took their money, then expanded into gathering blackmail material for others.

I didn't care. No one cared about me. Not a single one.

Until I stumble upon the heir of the Vino Corporation.

Remo Cainn.

And then I decided I wanted his help, knowing a deep secret of his that was about to be revealed to him after 'someone'—me—decided to threaten to leak that the Cainns had another child, a daughter they didn't want.

Power hungry people do that.

I wait outside his fight, watching from the shadows as his assistant walks over to him and tells him. I watch him punch the wall, knowing he is about to hit rock bottom, and then I step in.

"All I ask is for you to support me while I destroy the very people who hid your sister. Your parents. I can get rid of them, or I can help you find your sister," I tell him.

He falters, his eyes turning towards me, trying to look at my face but unable to, due to the fact that it's nighttime and I have a hood over my face.

Remo will help me become more powerful, give me his resources while I find his sister for him. Remo Cainn, the soon-to-be CEO of Vino Cooperation and the famous wine company, Giorgio Vino, will help me stay anonymous and enjoy my life while he covers for me as I do for him.

I researched enough.

I know enough.

This step will force Remo to take over his grandfather's dying company and flip it around, since he needs the money and resources to find his sister, whom his parents very strategically hid from him and the world.

I know they've moved her again by now, but I will track her down.

"Take it as an offer from a new friend of yours. They are Mr and Mrs Cainn, so they will have more than enough resources to hide her very well, and I can be of help. All I ask for in return is one favour in the future when the time comes. How does that sound, Remo Cainn?"

I can tell he doesn't believe me by the way he narrows his eyes.

"And what do you possess that I can't buy with my money?" he asks, wary.

And then I show him, lowering my hood.

The bruises covering my face, the scar, the eyes that people scatter away from in fear.

"Skill. I understand computers. I understand the very language that can destroy humanity, a skill that is too good to be left on the streets like this. Artificial intelligence. Pro tip, it's good for when you need blackmail material. Just saying." I shrug.

I see the moment he decides. His eyes change.

The moment my life changes.

Remo and I build up our lives for the next decade.

Me gaining power and knowledge no one else has ever had over the elite, and Remo using it for his blackmail and finding his sister.

Both of us swore to achieve what we wanted from this partnership.

Remo wanted his sister back home, and me? I wanted freedom.

And I am granted my wish.

I only twist the fate of those in power, watching them clash together.

I keep my morals close to myself, to my heart, and don't let them go astray.

Never.

Never will I let someone take control over me again. Especially someone who finds it fun to bully those weaker than them.

30

AMBROSE

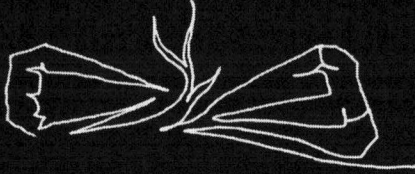

Unknown: ready for me?

I got that text an hour ago.

Right after I got the email from the hackers I hired. No matter my mixed feelings for Helia, I still want my company.

I can't let go of that part of me.

Ms Ambrose Torre,

Thank you for the drive. I will be working on it for the next week to retrieve the CCTV footage you have asked for from that specific date. It may take some time as it was very skilfully done and little to no mistakes are shown, but we are confident we will succeed.

I release a sigh of relief, sagging against my chair in my bedroom.

As soon as I saw my stalker in the corner of the picture taken on the day Dad died, I went home, retrieved the CCTV security footage and hard drive. As I went through it, I realised the stalker wasn't shown on any of it, and I knew someone had tampered with it. So I had tried to find a good enough hacker to recover the deleted footage.

I'm not sure what my next step will be, but since Dad was brutally killed, and the case has now gone cold, it's not that I am seeking justice for him but rather answers as to why I saw my stalker in that picture and exactly how long he has been meddling with the CCTV footage of my home.

Since Remo visited Helia in his office, there has been a change in him. He has been mostly at home instead of the office, but Remo's presence here has me on alert. That man is powerful, and even if Helia and he have the same power and authority, Remo feels more like the patient predator that pounces all at once, the one that seems to think carefully, who plans and sits and watches his chess pieces fall just as he forced them to. While Helia, he is one that does it all based on his own mood, reckless, dangerous, rogue, and quite literally unpredictable. Both are vicious in their own way, both commanding.

There is something striking, something alluring in Helia that keeps pulling my eyes back to him.

I hate to admit it, but Helia has been on my mind a lot

these past few months. Somewhere along the hateful looks and arguments, something is cripling inside of me.

And I fear this change.

I fear it could ruin me once my secret is out. I fear I'll be ruined and left with nothing, not even my company if Helia finds out my secret about Aurora, and because he wants me gone, he will use any means to get rid of me. Even if that secret is a wrongfully manipulated situation.

Helia is teasing me day after day, catching me off guard. The small confession from me that day about when I dreamt of him changed something within me. It snapped a small string of control, and now Helia looks at me like he knows everything about me.

Now that we have crossed a line, there is no going back.

There is absolutely no forgetting what we have done, what sin we keep committing.

Why am I risking it all? Why do I feel my heart pound inside of me when he is near me? Why do I want to hold on to a small hope that can only mean I want him when I cannot have him?

Then there is the problem with the stalker.

I don't know what to do.

Should I tell Helia? Could he get rid of him? Could he do it?

Something in me tells me he could. Maybe I should tell him. This small part of me trusts him, and even if that burning hate for him has diminished, the small ounce of trust he got from me is there. He didn't use what happened in the elevator that day against me, nor did he use how I pushed him away against me, either. He stayed the same. I need to tell him something about me.

Maybe... maybe he could look past it and we can both trust each other enough?

I'm so confused about how to go about this.

He won't think I am doing this to get back my company, will he?

What I feel for Helia is different from wanting my company back. I will do that myself, but what if... what if he thinks so? What if he rejects me because I was a ploy to him?

I fear it.

I need to be clear about myself if I ever want something from him.

I've never hoped for a partner, for love, affection, or anything.

Not until Helia has done such small things for me that really left me thinking for days. Giving me better tasks, making me eat lunch with him, looking at me like he actually wants and desires me.

And being there at Aurora's birthday party when I felt left out, watching the consequence of my actions break me apart. He was there, in silence, his presence a blanket of comfort.

Not long ago I found out that he sent an email to all the staff of Glamorous telling them to respect each other just the day after the interns were mouthing me off, and he *ex-*

cluded me from that email.

His threat was very obvious, hinting at the fact that he knows who did it and to whom.

I sat at my desk in silence for ten minutes when I found that out.

He includes me and asks me questions in board meetings and other smaller meetings, something Dad never did, so he didn't seem like he is asking for help, and he doesn't let anyone disrespect me as Dad did.

Dad forced me to deal with people ruthlessly while Helia's one look is enough.

My phone is in my hand, against my chest as I stare at his contact.

I should tell him. Get clear. And just hope.

Is it wrong for me to think that I don't see hate for me in his eyes anymore?

"Ambrose? We have guests downstairs!" Mom shouts.

I flinch, almost dropping my phone. I quickly rush out and head downstairs, dismissing texting Helia for later tonight, only to stop in my tracks as I spot my *friends*.

The friends I dropped.

Friends who ruined my skin, my body, and my life.

The Madden sisters.

Layla, Gabriella, and Inara Madden.

The daughters of the pharmaceutical giant who bullied me in school.

My hands tighten into fists, but I won't back down today.

Why are they here?

"What the fuck are you doing in my home?"

They look at each other, smiling.

Like they didn't just step into my own home. Like they didn't love bullying ones below them; like they weren't part of making me who I am today. Like they don't fucking care that I suffered so much because of them.

I will never be that weak Ambrose again.

Nor will I ever go back to the way Dad wanted to shape me.

"Oh, we missed you, Ambrose. Remember us? Layla, Gabriella, and Inara?" Layla raises her brows.

"I don't remember anyone in my life because of how insignificant they always are to me." I shrug, and their faces fall.

The Ambrose from before Dad's death is here. She's here to fight back.

"Don't be like that now. We came to go for a day out." Layla takes a step forward, but I raise a hand.

"Don't be rude to our guests, Ambrose."

My eyes sharpen on Mum, who stops in her tracks. "Stay out of this."

She frowns, a glare set on her face for talking like this to her. "Ambrose—"

"Mum. Leave," I force through my teeth.

She gives the women one last look before scoffing and leaving.

I turn back around towards Layla, who is standing there, arms crossed with a brow raised. Dressed impeccably, a gold watch, perfectly done hair and makeup, dresses screaming thousands of pounds, they are dripping in money thanks to their daddy.

"Get out. I have no time to entertain you, much less people who supposedly claim to know me. Why does security let in unwanted people?" I throw this remark while looking at them.

They all gasp, looking at each as if silently asking if they heard the same thing.

"You will regret disrespecting us, Ambrose."

I huff a laugh at Gabriella's offended tone. "Sure. There's the door." I point behind them, and they turn around and leave without another word.

I know they will strike back. They will do something. For now, I can't do anything.

Running back up the stairs, I shake their memories that are fresh in my mind. My throat is parched. I should get some water, but just as I go to shut the door, a hand with sharp nails clamps on my arm, stopping me.

A hiss falls from my lips while pain sears through my shirt, the nails digging into my skin.

My mother.

A sneer is on her face, and the hallway lights casting a yellow shadow on the side of her face.

She doesn't look like the mother I thought she was.

She looks different.

She looks manic, like a madwoman.

"How dare you turn away the Madden sisters? Do you

know what you have just done?" Her low voice and the sharp sting travelling up my arm make my eyes water.

"Yes." I grind my teeth.

She's choosing them over me.

"I have arranged a marriage. Between you and the son of the tech giant, Eric Kallias. You know they had some conversations with your father in the past of an alleged alliance, and I am here to secure it and make it true. You will give up your shares in Glamorous and allow us to invest in this marriage."

My whole world falls apart beneath my feet.

"And you will not, under any circumstance, ruin this for me. Understood?" She gets in my face, her voice raspy and empty.

Empty of emotions. Empty of her relationship to me as my mother. Empty. Empty. Empty.

Just like my father.

She is just like my father.

"Now go to your room because I don't want to see your face." She shoves me away from her, her nails scraping against my arm. Blood oozes from the deep scratch of her nails, and I lose my balance.

I see her back, walking away from me as my knee hits the floor, my head falling forward, hitting against the edge of a table, making white dots cover my vision.

I take in deep breaths, blinking away the dizziness, pain emanating from my head.

Placing my hand on my head, I look at it and see red.

Blood.

My breaths turn shallow, but I swallow thickly and get up, walking to my room with a dizzy vision.

As soon as the door shuts behind me, I drop to the floor. *Thud. Thud. Thud.*

My heartbeat is so loud, my head lolls to the side, my vision turning black in spaces. Something trickles down my head.

I drop my head back and blink up at the empty ceiling, tears streaming down my face.

I became them, didn't I? The Madden sisters made me just like them.

Why would anyone want me in their life when they know what I have done?

Getting off the floor, I swallow through the thick bundle of thorns stuck in my throat and walk tentatively towards the bathroom, feeling numb, empty, and tired.

Sighing, I remove my clothes, walk under the shower, turn the water on, and stand under the steaming hot water. Clouds form all around me, my vision blurring as the scalding hot water burns my skin.

Grabbing hold of the loofah, I put soap on it and scrub.

I scrub at the slash marks on my arms.

On my legs.

The cuts and burn marks on my stomach.

I scrub till I feel my skin burn.

I scrub harder until the skin turns from pale to red.

The hot water makes me hiss in pain as the blazing sensation sears through my whole body.

And I keep going.

Doesn't she have perfect porcelain skin?

How would it look decorated?

Scream louder. I love hearing the sounds of people screaming. It makes me giddy. Beg for my mercy.

No. No.

These gifts might stay with you for the rest of your life.

Your parents may see this and feel sad, or is your dad too power hungry to even know his daughter gets these marks because of how weak she is?

Please.

A sob climbs up my throat as tears coat my eyes, and my hand gets tired. The loofah drops from my grip.

Pressing a hand to my mouth, I drop to my knees, my eyes shutting, and the memories take over.

There is no reason to believe I deserve anything like love, hope, and a happy future. I became who I feared the most.

I am a monster.

I am ruthless.

I made the weak cry.

I am the worst of them all. I shouldn't have taken that step.

I am such a disappointment.

Sobs wreck my body, my walls crumbling as each brick falls to the floor into a broken mess, the world behind the wall witnessing my destruction. When will it be enough for me?

When will it stop?

I try to take deep breaths to calm myself, but it only gets worse, and I struggle to breathe under the hot water. The steam in the bathroom is so thick, I am barely able to see my arms, legs, or any part of myself.

Shutting off the water, I dry myself before walking out and changing into black leggings and a sports bra.

A moment of emptiness fills me as I stand in the middle of my room. Slowly bending down and crossing my legs under me right in front of my bed, I watch the window to my left, my open balcony doors, the curtains flaring softly against the glass doors.

The soft ruffle of the trees outside swoops into my room, weaving around and helping my mind to calm down. The faint crunch of leaves only means that guards are patrolling around the house.

Crossing my arms and placing them on my knees, I rest my head on my arms and just look out.

Silence envelopes me.

What would happen if I were to not exist?

Mother doesn't care.

Aurora wouldn't suffer because of me. She wouldn't face the bullying both by me and the Madden sisters.

I don't have actual friends to consider them to be worried about me.

Helia wouldn't.

I feel something wet trickle down my forehead, but I don't pay it mind.

"Little sin."

My head snaps up to the hooded figure standing on my balcony.

And my heart drops.

31

AMBROSE

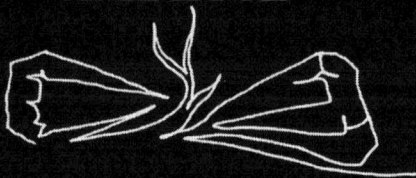

Why? Why me?

I feel exhausted from fighting.

My eyes fall to the wooden floor, moving away from my stalker.

Why couldn't I hope for something simple like love in my life?

Why couldn't anyone just… hold me?

And tell me that it will be fine and that they will keep me safe from the dangers of the world.

More and more tears drip out of my eyes, falling onto the floor. I hear the stalker take steps toward me.

Maybe this is it.

Maybe I should let him just kill me and accept death. Maybe the world is better without me.

No one would miss me. No one would want me here.

Nothing will change.

Helia's life would be better.

Mom will get my inherited money.

Aurora wouldn't look twice.

And everything will be fine. The same.

The steps get closer.

My hands tremble in my lap.

When I lift my head, he's right in front of me.

"Kill me," I whisper into the darkness of my room, hoping the monsters in it hear me and make my wish come true. "Just kill me, please. Rid me of this mess," I continue.

He falters. Instead of the usual smirk, there is a twisted expression on his face.

"Little sin." His nickname doesn't even compare to the one Helia gave me.

Is it wrong to wish he would miss me when I'm gone?

A laugh trickles out of me.

"My enemy, my tormentor, gave me a nickname, too. Emerald. He calls me emerald because I always wear a piece of that colour every day. It's also his favourite." I sniffle, lifting my eyes to his figure.

"I think... I wish he—" I swallow, my throat closing up on me, not allowing the words to come out of me.

He takes one last step into my space.

"Why are you here? Why are you always here in my most vulnerable moments? What is it you find fascinating?"

He tilts his head, similar to how Helia does.

"Why are you always here?!" I shout.

Without thinking, I go to grab his hood, but my hand meets air.

I blink.

He's gone.

It was… a hallucination. It wasn't real.

Why do I keep seeing Helia everywhere?

He keeps running through my mind. He keeps showing up, even in my dreams. In my nightmares.

He is in every aspect of my life.

In my fear, in my happiness, in my curiosity, and has even become a crucial part of my journey to become better.

He is even in my hope.

A hope for something.

I'm finding it with the wrong man. I know I am.

But I can't help but think that I should tell him. The truth about Aurora. About me.

Is it because I want my stupid feelings to be reciprocated?

Is it because I want to feel something before I destroy this too?

I stand in front of the house made of glass and black marble, peering up at the home that looks exactly like Helia.

I can't believe I am here.

Flat ceilings, panels of wooden frames, glass walls that are tinted, grey marble steps leading up to wide double main doors. A balcony sits on the second floor with a glass railing. A faint hint of a bedroom is visible from my position in the clearing in front of the house.

Forest surrounds the whole area perimeter, and the sun setting behind the home is painting a beautiful orange colour while Helia's house sits tall and dark.

His green Porsche is parked to the left, a black bike right next to it.

I didn't know he rode a bike too.

Taking careful steps towards the house, my feet softly thump on the marble stairs as I reach the front door.

I ring the bell beside the door with a pounding heart.

Why am I here?

Shaking my head to rid the unnecessary thoughts and questions, I wait patiently.

A lock softly clicks before the door opens.

And there stands Helia.

Black sweatpants ride low on his hips, and he wears an open sweatshirt with nothing under it. His tattoos are on display, and I instantly spot a small crow near his rib, a snake wrapped around an arrow just above his hip bone, and a small spider on the other side of his hip. My eyes trace his extremely sculpted body, every line and bump of his six-pack so clear that I would be able to count them blindly if I were to put my hand on his stomach.

The V-line of his hip leads down into his sweatpants, his jet-black hair falling into his darkened forest eyes.

"Ambrose?" He lifts a brow, stepping aside and letting me walk into his home.

I open my mouth to answer, to give him an explanation, anything. But nothing comes out.

My throat closes, and I am once again reminded of my past and exactly why I am here.

I turn around, my fingers unclenching, my body slowly relaxing when I look into his eyes.

"I had… nowhere… I didn't know what—where to go," I whisper, feeling absolutely helpless.

If I think about it, I truly had no one.

What the fuck am I even doing here in my enemy's home where he could easily kill me?

Helia tilts his hand, taking a step closer to me, and another, then another until he is right in front of me.

Strengthening my resolve, I wait.

Is he going to kick me out?

Keep me?

What will he do?

"You had nowhere to go?" he says carefully, observing me.

I nod.

"So you came here?"

I nod once more.

Helia doesn't say anything more. His eyes move to my forehead, to my black zipped-up hoodie with black leggings. I didn't bother changing. Everything is still covered. Every single scar burns in reminder, but I stand still in front of him.

Helia raises a hand, reaching for the side of my face, and a breath leaves me just as his hand makes skin contact. The warmth from his hand feels soft. It feels like patience and home.

Of calm waters.

Of a final destination.

His hand moves under my jaw, tilting my head softly side to side as if inspecting me before he drags his fingers softly to my forehead, pushing away strands of blond hair. The softness in his touch makes my heart burst. He has never touched me this tenderly, never with the intention of just looking at me, of feeling me.

And it feels out of place, and yet, it feels right.

My eyes shut on their own record when Helia takes a step closer, his body almost caging me in with how tall and broad his chest is. His touch travels from my forehead down to my cheek once more, going over my eyebrows, my nose, my lips, and my chin.

I release a shuddering breath.

"Helia." The soft whisper falls from my lips. I open my eyes.

And the look in his eyes, the concentration mixed with rage and worry. It's different.

Grabbing his wrist, I pull his hand away from my face and take a step back.

"You shouldn't be touching me like this." I look away from his eyes, too ashamed to admit why.

It makes me hope. And hope isn't good for me. It's wrong.

"You should hate me, kick me out of your house, so I can get rid of this misunderstanding."

There is only silence on his end, forcing me to slide my eyes back to him. His hands are clenched at his side as he heaves, his nostrils flaring. The emerald in his eyes is engulfed by black while his hair sits messily on his head.

Right now, with his hoodie open and his black sweatpants, he looks every bit of the monstrous serpent I think of him to be. He looks ready to kill, and I am ready to take on whatever he will throw at me.

My vulnerability today has made me delusional.

"Misunderstanding?" Helia grits out harshly.

I wordlessly nod.

Narrowing his eyes, he takes a step, then another until he is right in front of me. His hands grasp my forearms, then Helia gets in my face.

"A fucking misunderstanding? You are telling me that every time you looked at me, it wasn't to seek me out but because I *misunderstood* and you were just glaring at me in hate? You are telling me that every time you touched me, it was out of obligation and not because you craved my touch?" He heaves. "Your words, your secret smiles, your care for me, and your heart are nothing but a lie?"

A frown twists on my face at his words.

Why would he notice any of it when he merely hates me?

"Were we not fooling around? Was this not just a game for you?"

Helia's hold on my arms tightens. "A game?" His words rumble in his chest. "It's a game to you?" he shouts, letting go of me. "I would very much like to kill you right now for uttering those words. Have you ever seen me take an interest in a woman like this? Do you think I merely wanted to use you? For what? Your company? Did you think all this time… everything I did was for… personal gain?"

I can hear my own heart drumming inside of me, the painful thud against my chest making me swallow in pain.

Helia's words cut deep because it's not true. I thought each time he touched was because he liked to, each time he looked my way, he wanted to find his emerald of the day, each and every single time he smiled at me, it was because I entered the room and his eyes found me.

I had been delusional. I had denied it.

And now I'm denying it in front of Helia.

"Tell me!" he screams in my face. "Tell me that it's true. Tell me that your disgusting mind got to you." He keeps shouting, running a frustrated hand through his hair.

"Did my touch ever feel like hate?" he mutters, his eyes blazing.

No. It never did, but I never dared to hope.

"Tell me, dammit!"

"No!" I roar back.

I slam a hand on his chest, frustration and anger getting to me.

"How dare you make me hope?" I shove at his shoulder.

His wide eyes are stuck on me.

"How dare you make me believe your touch was for anything but my company!" I push at his shoulder again, and he lets me. "How fucking dare you make me want you?

How dare you bring me to my knees, to make me beg for you, to make me crave you like crazy, to the point where I can't think." My hands grasp at my hair, my throat scratchy. "How dare you make me want a forever with you when I was told to never believe in one!" My voice turns hoarse as I push a finger at his hard chest. "Did you do this on purpose? Make me fall for you so I come bearing my weaknesses to you, allowing you to take advantage of it?" My voice grows loud once more.

Helia grabs my fingers and pushes it away from him, getting in my face. "I fucking hate how much I want you!"

"Same here!" I shout.

Our eyes connect as we both breathe heavily, our chests rising and falling from the exposed secrets.

"I hate how crazy you made me, and how I cannot think when I'm around you," Helia continues, and I feel my eyes tear up.

He won't keep me.

"I hate it all, and yet I kept you standing. I kept coming back to you again and again." His voice lowers. "I hate that I am willing to risk my life to stay here with you, Emerald."

A tear rolls down my cheek, and my lip trembles.

Helia's eyes follow the tear's trail before they slam back to my eyes.

And then his lips crash against mine.

I'm frozen for a split second, then I kiss him back. I grab his shoulders in a tight hold, and my stomach clenches. Desire, pain, and overwhelming emotions grasp at me like never before.

Kissing him deeper, I feel his tongue slip into my mouth as his arm wraps around my waist. His fingers grip my jaw, and he tilts my head up. I kiss him and kiss him, feeling more tears roll down my face.

I will never have him.

I will never be able to have him if I want my company.

I can't have both.

He's the only one who has ever made me feel so special. He's the only one who has made me feel like I could conquer the world, and he would be there to push me further.

His care, his sharp eyes, his strong hold, his heart that cares so deeply yet so quietly, it makes me weep.

I wish...

I wish for you to fall in love with me as madly as I am in love with you.

Helia dips, his lips softly pulling at my upper lip, then diving back in for another kiss. And I am grasping at his hair, his shoulders, everything he can give me.

When we pull apart, we are both gasping, but all I can think about is just how we will go back to how we were, at each other's throat.

But for now, I want to stay right here. In his arms.

"Helia." My voice is a soft, pained whisper as I look at him through my lashes.

He shakes his head, keeping his arm around my waist.

"No. Don't say anything. I don't want to hear it." His eyes drop to the floor for a second before he looks back up at me.

He stills for a moment, watching me, his body warmth seeping beneath my freezing skin. His gaze travels from my eyes to my forehead. Lifting a hand, he runs his fingertips over the cut there, though the pain from there doesn't compare to what my heart feels.

The upcoming betrayal, knowing I will be filing a lawsuit against him while wanting him, while being here in his arms, it breaks me.

My world is about to collapse, and I can do nothing about it.

"Why are you here, Ambrose?"

My heart sinks.

"I came to tell you the truth."

32
AMBROSE

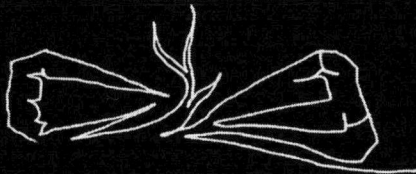

"What truth?" Helia asks.

I step away from his embrace. I can't confess my secret, knowing I will feel his body pulling from mine after this.

I would rather do it myself to save the hurt.

My eyes fall on the open-plan kitchen to my right with a counter in front of it.

I can't look at him while I say this.

"You need to know something about me, Helia."

I swallow, the words crumpling like a piece of paper inside of me.

"Aurora had a stalker, and it was going on for three years until four months before her wedding, she was kidnapped. She…" I blink at the ceiling, trying not to remember or think of the images in my mind.

"Everyone, including her, thought it was me who gave

her location to the stalker because Dad so strategically told her that I was the one who dropped her location after asking her where she was."

Biting my lip to stop the tears isn't working, so I clench my hands at my sides, my nails digging into my skin.

"I did ask her where she was that day. I asked her because she was supposed to be at the dinner at our house that night, and she didn't show up on time. She was exiting her apartment building at the time."

That's when I look at Helia and see him patiently looking at me.

Waiting.

But what startles me is the deep, ominous look in his eyes. He looks like he knows what I am about to say, though he won't be able to guess it.

"Track records show that. Testimonies by everyone show that. Everything points to me." I suck in a shaky breath, catching Helia look to the side. "Would you believe it was me, if you were to see those records?"

Helia looks back at me, his jaw ticking.

And I know the minute the look in his eyes changes.

An empty laugh trickles out of me, another tear dripping down my cheek.

Helia's eyes track its movement down my face.

"It was my father who leaked her location. He didn't want us in his life. He wanted a child-free life, to climb to the top. Having us, having daughters, was a big expense for someone who wanted to run up the ladder in society, to fit in the Elites, to be living lavishly. We set him back."

My fingers grasp at the edge of my black zipped-up jumper, and my knees weaken.

"I ran from one station to another, one private investigator to another, using my own savings to find her location, to find where she was, because she was and is the first and only important person in my life." I swallow thickly.

Energy starts to leave my body, but I continue.

"Aurora is my sister, the one person I tried to protect from our father." My voice trembles. "I was severely bullied in school. I wear long sleeves, long jeans, black tights, covering every part of my skin. I cover it, so Aurora could wear dresses."

Helia's eyebrows twist into a frown.

"I have put myself forward in our father's eyes so she could stay in the dark and live her life. I have dealt with losing myself so she could build her own life. I have hidden my scars, my struggles, my fears, and my dreams so she could live her own, Helia." I flash a shaky smile at him.

"I know I have ruined people's lives for the sake of our father, for his approval, and I accept my mistakes. I accept that I made bad decisions, too. I was too far gone, but I would never hurt Aurora or anyone so severely that they can't sleep at night. I have given back and tried begging for forgiveness."

My lower lip trembles, and Helia reaches out with his hand but drops it.

Something about that makes my heart clench painfully.

"I was the one who was ecstatic when we found a signal to her phone, and I sent special forces to pick her up. I was there feeding her, sitting outside her door all night long in case she couldn't sleep, knowing she hated the sight of me for leaving her alone in school, for letting her be alone in this life. But I tried to shield her as best as I could." My heads drops forward in shame.

"I tried as much as a sixteen-year-old could, but it wasn't enough. With a father and mother like ours, it's not possible to do much." My hand covers my eyes as tears fall out.

Lifting my head, I watch him through teary eyes.

"Ambrose," Helia starts, but I shake my head.

Unzipping my jumper, I drop it to the floor, leaving me in only my black bra.

Helia's eyes fall on my arms, my stomach, and they harden.

Taking off my leggings, I let them drop to the floor, my underwear the only thing left on me.

His eyes drop to my legs, and his jaw clenches just as his knuckles turn white.

Red ugly marks that are barely healed, faint scars that failed to heal properly cover my body.

"I didn't bother getting laser removal. What answer would I give if rumours of these were to leak?"

A chill passes through the house, and I shiver, but I stand still as Helia's unwavering eyes trace my body. They go over each scar, assessing each one carefully.

Then he speaks. "I will kill every single person who has

put their hands on you."

"No, you won't. This ends here, Helia. Me and you. Whatever this was. Whatever this is, it should stop. Not only will it destroy you; it will destroy me, too. It will leave us in the ashes of who we are, of what we want. I wish I could say I hate you, but I don't. Not anymore—"

"Stop saying that!" Helia bursts out.

His hands settle on my cheeks.

"I believe you. I'll believe you forever. I'll fucking kill every single person who has hurt you, who has left a mark on your body." His eyes drop lower to my body, where every single part feels ugly.

He starts breathing faster, as if trying to control his emotions.

I have never cried in front of anyone before, yet here I am, falling into a deep hole no one can save me from.

I'm falling into the abyss.

The abyss that is Helia.

Hands grab the back of my neck and pull me into an embrace. Helia's face settles in the crook of my neck, his hold tight and secure. My own hands go around him, burying my face into his chest, and I choke back a sob.

"Stop pushing me away. Stop trying to make me leave, because that won't happen. You have a hook in me, Ambrose. You keep reeling me back to you, every single time." His muffled voice makes my heart quiver in need. "Tell me, just once, that you want me, that you feel as deeply for me."

Instead of answering, I lift my head and grab hold of his

chin, pulling him lower until his lips mould to mine.

Helia's kiss turns desperate and harsh within seconds. He picks me up, my legs wrapping around his waist as he walks, then I am placed onto a cold counter with only underwear and a bra on. The cold makes goosebumps rise on my skin.

Pulling away, Helia runs his hand on my thighs, over the burn and cut marks, his eyes watching where his hands glide.

Then he raises his head and instantly melts.

"Every part of you is beautiful, Ambrose, even ones that you keep tucked away, even ones that you want to burn so no one sees your weakness, even the part that weeps for love."

A small smile touches my lips. Helia's eyes drop to it, placing a soft kiss on my lips.

"Let me help you. Let me quieten the monsters in your head and those venomous voices."

Placing me on the floor, Helia grabs my hand and walks into the hallway. We pass the staircase on the right, past the two doors on my left, and walk into an open space.

A gasp leaves past my lips.

"A pool room?"

Letting go of my hand, Helia removes his hoodie, throwing it onto the black marble floor.

The front and right walls are all glass. A deep forest is the only thing I can see, though it's nighttime, so I can't see much.

The pool is a sea green colour, and clear ripples flow in the water. It covers the entire room, with five chairs placed on my right in front of the pool. A ladder goes down into the water just to the left of it.

"This… Do you swim often?" I turn towards Helia, only for me to choke.

He's standing only in black boxers. His ripped abs are on full display. Tattoos are scattered all over his chest. The muscles in his legs and strong thighs make my mouth water. He runs a hand through his hair, and the tendons in his biceps flex, making me blink. A tattoo of a serpent goes around his forearm. Lightning circles around the other arm, with small stars near his wrist. Another spider is detailed on his shoulder blade. He looks like a powerhouse, all muscles, who could very much break your neck off if he were to punch you.

He walks over to me, where I am still standing with my mouth hanging open, with a smirk on his wicked face.

"Close your mouth, Ambrose." He nudges my chin with his bent finger, making me snap it shut.

I narrow my eyes on him. "Something funny?"

Helia's laugh echoes around the pool room, his eyes squinting ever so slightly as he throws his head back, the veins in his neck popping.

"No, nothing is funny." He shakes his head with a smile.

A mischievous glint shines in his eyes, then the next second, I am being thrown into the pool. My scream echoes around the room.

"Helia!"

We both drop into the water with a massive splash. When I open my eyes underwater, I swim away from him, catching him watching me with a big smile on his face as we both swim to the surface.

He runs a hand through his hair, mimicking me.

"You are so dead," I lunge towards him, wanting to push him underwater, but he disappears. When I turn around, Helia is there, his arms around my waist as he lifts me and throws me back into the water.

My screams follow.

I shake out of his hold and try again.

And I get pushed under the water.

And again.

And again.

Until I am a laughing mess.

Our loud laughs fill the room, my spirit feeling lighter, my heart wanting to burst out of me. Happiness feels like an achievable emotion to me when I look at Helia. He didn't walk away from me; he accepted me.

It's all I ever wanted.

I stay in the pool against the edge of it, taking a breather when I spot Helia swim closer to me. He stops right in front of me. His eyes filled with intent. Fiery intent. And suddenly the water feels too warm. The room feels too hot.

My ears ring as he cages me in with his arms on the back of the pool.

"Are you happy, Ambrose?"

I nod wordlessly. Apparently, words aren't even a thing to me.

"Words. I want to hear it." His hand holds my waist, the gesture feeling more than nice, more than friends, just more.

"Yes," I breathlessly whisper.

My eyes can't stray from his.

"Good. Now let me appreciate you." He places a kiss on my shoulder, eliciting a shudder from me.

"Let me show you that I am the endgame for you. It's me where everything stops, and it's me where your search for happiness ends." A kiss to my chest, down the valley of my breasts.

Helia grabs me by my hips before lifting me out of the water and setting me on the edge, my legs still in the pool. He looks up at me desperately, his eyes heated and his touch wandering all over my body.

He pulls my knees apart and pushes at my stomach, making me lie down. I comply.

Helia pulls my underwear down my legs and throws it somewhere, but all I can see is the ceiling.

"Fuck." That guttural word makes my insides quiver.

"You look so mouth-watering, I am practically salivating for you, Emerald."

Curiosity gets the better of me, so I get on my elbows and look down at him.

He is looking in between my legs, at my pussy, like he wants to devour it whole.

His eyes snap to me.

"No one else is allowed to touch you, or even think about tasting you, other than me, or I swear to God, Ambrose, there will be bodies all over this city." Somehow, his threat doesn't feel unrealistic. With this dangerous glint in his eyes and the carnal desire he approaches me with every time, it doesn't feel normal. It feels devilish, raw, and dark.

There is always this animalistic look to Helia, like he will destroy everything with no care for anyone in his path.

And he has that possessive look on his face right now as his breath fans my pussy.

His lips finally descend on me, and a loud moan releases from my lips.

He moves away, and I see him rise out of the water.

Water cascades down his model-like body. Those broad shoulders cast a shadow above me, the veins in his arms popping out from the force he uses to pull his body up. Black hair falls on his forehead, droplets dripping from it onto his face.

Fuck me.

That's mine.

Helia is and will be mine.

He stands above me like a monster, grabbing me by my waist and throwing me over his shoulder.

"Helia! Where are you taking me?"

He doesn't answer, just continues walking up the stairs.

I can't see anything properly from being upside down, but then I am thrown onto something warm, soft, and bouncy.

Shaking my head to rid the dizziness, I realise I am in his room, but I don't look for long before I am turned around, my ass up.

"On all fours," Helia commands.

"You can't order me around li—"

He grabs my waist and pulls me up, forcing me onto all fours.

My bra is taken off.

"You could have done it nice—"

"Do you want it nicely, Ambrose?" A hand wraps around my throat. "You want me to press kisses all over your body and give you sweet praises?" Another hand sneaks out to grasp my breasts, roughly grabbing and pulling and pinching my nipples till they feel tender to touch, and I hiss at the pleasurable pain.

"Or do you want it hard and fast? Do you want to be fucked and owned? You want control taken from you?"

I open my mouth, then shut it.

"Speak, or I will leave this very second."

I glare at him over my shoulder. After all that teasing, he will leave? Just like that?

"What is it going to be?" He raises a brow, his naked muscled body behind me.

"I want you to fuck me, Helia."

A smirk appears on his face. Helia wraps his hand around my hair, once, twice, then pulls, making my head snap back and my back arch. His hand goes around me till it dips into my pussy, and I gasp, my body jerking in hot pleasure before it's gone.

"Good girl," he murmurs in my ear; like me being wet for him was all it took for him to be pleased with me.

Then he pushes into me.

We both groan the minute he does.

I feel stretched. Full.

Complete.

A minute later, Helia fucks me. He goes hard and fast, just like he promised, and he fucks like a goddamn monster. Just like I imagined. He dominates me, hitting a deep sweet spot inside me. My pleasure soars high until soon I am collapsing, coming hard.

My screams and his name echoing all around the room.

"Helia!"

"Fuck, baby," he grits out, continuing to rut me until he finds his own release.

But he doesn't stop after that. He flips me around, his mouth latching onto a breast, and he starts fucking me again. My body is limp, but he rips another orgasm from me.

And again, as he places me on his table, fucking me against it.

Instead of burn marks and cuts, all I see are hickeys left all over my body.

Like love letters written to me from him. Each one imprinted on me.

I am lying limply, out of energy, as Helia settles in his tub behind me.

He starts to clean me up, washing me as my head rests

back against his chest.

"You know, I've never let anyone take care of me like this before," I murmur, moving my hand through the water, watching it ripple.

"Really?" he murmurs, his chin on my shoulder as he raises my other arm and runs a loofah over it.

My voice turns quiet. "Yes, it was always me, and only me. My parents were too busy, and I didn't have a friend to look after me on my bad days." I'm not ashamed, but it's weird admitting something so personal to him.

"Do you have friends now?"

There is a moment of silence from me.

Then I shake my head.

"Have you always looked after yourself when you were sick?"

I nod, my eyes trained on the water in front of me as Helia moves the loofah to my back.

"Is that why you do yoga after a long day?"

I freeze in the tub.

My blood runs cold, as does the water.

No one knows that.

I've done it with my doors closed.

I've never—

"Yes." My voice is scratchy and small.

The full force of betrayal hits me deep in the heart.

"Do you enjoy baking things?" Helia's questions continue, simple questions that don't take time to think.

Right now, everything has been lit by flames.

No.

It can't be.

I won't believe it.

But what good will denial do?

Helia is …my stalker?

He's watched me for months.

Terrified me to the point I wanted my own death?

He's the one who has sent me letters?

Killed men who were after my hand in marriage?

Helia killed? With his own hands?

He did all this?

What else did he do?

Suddenly, the man who I was going to consider my lover doesn't feel like it anymore.

And it feels like I just broke through the water, realising it was all an illusion.

"Do you know that I feel what others call love for you?" Helia murmurs against my neck.

My mouth doesn't want to open to answer.

It can't.

I'm stuck. Paralyzed.

I slept with a cold-blooded serial killer.

With my own stalker.

And I've fallen in love with him, too.

33

AMBROSE

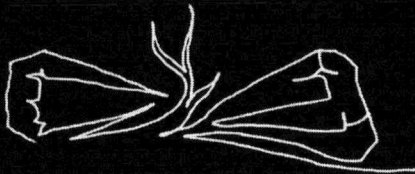

I'm hiding.

In my bedroom.

I haven't gone to work. I asked for leave for a few days, and I'm waiting. I'm biding my time, not knowing how exactly I would go about this.

Not only am I ignoring Helia, but I left that same morning, silently, without telling him. He has been calling, he's been messaging, and I've only replied with one-word answers.

I've been giving him the cold shoulder. It hurt to put myself out there in front of him, to reveal such a crucial part of me, to show my weakness, and yet he betrayed me?

When was he going to tell me?

Doesn't he realise that what he did has weighed heavy on me?

I keep refreshing my email, waiting for the hackers to

get back to me.

Time is ticking. I need to know if the stalker in the pictures is actually Helia.

Why was my stalker there the day I saw Remo leave our house? The day my father was murdered?

"Ambrose! Get out of that room now!"

A bang startles me. I glance at the wooden door, dread settling deep within me.

"How much longer will it take you to get ready for this ring appointment?"

My mother had picked the very next day for me to grab the groom's ring. She didn't wait. Not for a single second to ask me, to give me time. No. She wants this done fast to get rid of me, to secure herself.

I used to feel bad for Mum, for what she has been through, but now... now I see that while she may have had depressive episodes, she has bounced right back to her normal self and has not for one second shown any remorse, love, or affection to either of her daughters.

"Coming!" I rush out, leaving my laptop, then we head to the jewellers in Knightsbridge.

"How about this one?" Mum points to a simple band with diamonds encrusted all around it.

"It is a very good choice, ma'am. It's one-of-a-kind and very unique."

I glance around the private room, feeling caged.

Trapped.

Everything is slipping out of my grip.

And I am sitting here being controlled by one of my parents. Again.

I decided I was going to change, didn't I? I was moving in the right direction, but now I am right back to square one.

The dim lighting of the private room weighs heavy on my eyes, the murmurs of the sales assistant and my mother bounce off the shiny walls. The small hum of the air conditioner ringing in my ears doesn't help either. It's making me feel dizzy.

I blink, trying to rid the fuzziness from my brain, but it doesn't work.

"Mum," I whisper, shaking my head, but she doesn't listen.

I slept with my stalker.

Helia.

He didn't tell me.

My marriage is being arranged without my consent.

"What size do you think he may be, Ambrose?"

This isn't right.

"Do you think he will suit this?"

"Where is your mind these days?"

"Don't worry about her. She didn't get a good sleep last night. You can package this one for us."

My ears start to ring.

I want to scream. I want to cry. I want nothing to do with anything.

I don't want the company.

I don't want the money. The clothes.

Nothing.

Please.

I just want peace. Silence.

Please.

"Excuse me." My throat scratches. I get up from the sofa and walk out of the room and out of the shop.

I take the driver with me and go right home, into my bedroom once more.

What do I do?

Another wave of dizziness hits me.

That's when it hits me that I didn't eat all day yesterday, nor today, and it's already four in the afternoon. As I am about to turn to go to the living room, a loud thud makes my ears perk up.

He's here.

I spin around and find my stalker—or, rather, Helia—standing in my room.

He wears combat boots, black cargo pants, and a black hoodie, and stands tall and unmoving in the middle of my balcony as the curtains flare aggressively.

My words climb up my throat and so does my scream, but I shut it down.

He takes a long step inside, moving the curtains out of his way, then another step, and my heart rate spikes.

"Seems like someone missed me." He tilts his head. The faint sunset behind him casts him in shadow and makes him look all the more threatening.

"It's you," I breathe out, my hands starting to shake at

my sides.

A huff of a laugh leaves him when he looks all around my tidy room.

Nothing is out of place. Thankfully, my laptop is shut. So he can't see what I was working on.

I don't want him to know about it until he tells me the truth.

"Yes, me, little sin." He takes another step towards me, and fear scratches at my throat like nails on a chalkboard.

"No," I whisper, willing for courage to fill me. "It's Emerald, isn't it?"

He stops in his tracks.

This time, I take the step towards him.

"Isn't it?" I repeat.

His jaw tics.

A laugh trickles out of me. A mocking laugh.

"Had fun playing with me… Helia?"

I take hold of his hood and throw it off.

There he stands.

"You—"

He doesn't move, doesn't has the intention to.

His, it's so fucking haunting. He doesn't look like a CEO or a friend of Remo. He looks like a killer. His eyes hold this empty, yet psychotic look in them, and I realise I never even knew Helia. This man in front of me isn't him.

He's not Helia. This isn't who I thought Helia was.

"You not only tormented me in my workplace, not only took everything from me, but you did that when I was in my own home too, in the security of my bedroom," I chant it all with a gasp. "You took, took, and took and still you weren't satisfied?"

He shakes his head, his hair falling into his eyes. "No, Ambrose—"

"You lost the right to call me that the moment you decided to use two faces to haunt me! You made me believe the Madden sisters sent you. You made me believe someone wanted my death. You made me believe I should just wish for death. You want know what's ironic? I have finally given up. I don't care anymore." I sigh.

"What?" His brows crinkle. "No, you are supposed to always fight, Ambrose. You can hit me, punch me, throw insults, and I will take it, but please don't give up on yourself." His voice sounds so pained, so broken, that it almost makes me feel bad for him.

"So what? So you could get my company and go on with your life? Be free of the problem you have?" I push him, I shove him, and he lets me.

Angry tears burn my eyes.

"Was seducing me and making me fall into your trap part of this whole big plan of yours? Was it? To bring me to my knees? You wanted me to bend to your will, and you accomplished that." I sob.

"How fucking dare you!" I scream, slapping him across the face with such force his head whips to the side. "I trusted you. I told you about my deepest secrets, but you are going to use that against me. I made a mistake with you," I whisper, my own heartbreak dripping into my voice.

"No, I would never do that. You *own* me, Emerald," Helia whispers. "You are all I think about. You have bewitched me the moment I saw you. The moment Remo asked me to look after you so you didn't get your company back. And I did. I hated you at first, but not anymore. There is no hate for you left in me. You've ruined me."

I shake my head. He uses his words wisely. He knows his way around words.

He's lying.

"If we had never met, it would have saved us all this mess." I grit out.

"Once upon a time, I loved looking into your eyes, now? All I find is deception." I whisper.

How do I hold myself back when I had loved someone for the first time in my life and he did this to me?

"You don't believe me, but trust me—"

"Trust you?" I gasp in disbelief.

"Baby, please." He grabs my hands.

I try to shake his hold off, but he doesn't let me. He pulls me to him, making me crash against his chest, then leans down, letting his forehead rest against mine. I shut my eyes.

Tears. Tears and more tears.

"I'm tired," I find myself whispering. "I'm tired of everything,"

"I know, baby." He runs a big, soothing hand down my cheek, wiping away my traitorous tears. "I will ruin everyone who's brought tears to your eyes."

I open my eyes and look up at him. At the deep depths of his green eyes.

"What if it was you?" My voice travels across the silence in the room, and the wind outside howls as if it's screaming my pain.

"Then I will take any punishment you give me."

I reel back.

"Then I want you gone. I want you to leave me alone. I don't want to look at your face."

"That, I won't do. That's one thing I can't grant." He looks around my room, then grabs my wrist and pulls me towards the bed.

"What are you doing? Let go." I try to shake my wrist out of his hold.

He lifts me and places me on the bed, then takes his shoes off and gets under the covers with me, his front to my back. I go to turn around, but he doesn't let me.

"Stay still, Ambrose."

"What do you think you are doing?"

He places his head into the crook of my neck, wrapping an arm around my waist and the other under my head.

"Sleep, rest. Ambrose. You need it. I'll be gone by the time you wake up."

"I said I don't want to lay with you."

He places a hand on my mouth, shutting me up.

Silence.

Helia's steady breathing sweeps softly across my ear. My heart doesn't feel like it's intact anymore.

People like me don't get happy endings.

People like Helia don't love.

The moonlight spills into my room. The curtains have stopped flaring, and are softly humming to the tune of the wind outside. There is silence.

I can feel Helia's racing heart.

The warmth from his hand on my stomach burns my skin. It settles on the small gap between my sports bra and my leggings. The soft rhythm of his breathing slowly lulls me to sleep, all fight leaving me.

"Who made you lose your fight, Ambrose?" Helia's voice is the softest it has ever been.

"Why would I tell you?" I mumble.

His hand leaves my mouth and I sigh.

"Who hurt you, Ambrose? Who made you hate your body?" His voice is the same tone, same softness, but I know he feels anything but calm.

"The Madden sisters." Why hide it when I know tomorrow holds nothing but loss and failure?

I swallow, the memories so haunting that I find myself grabbing Helia's arm on my stomach.

He will get this from me, but tomorrow, that will all be gone.

I will resign. I will fight this case myself, and I will throw him out of my life.

Helia listens to it all until I finish describing everything that happened to me. I tell him about how mistreated I was, how Dad then forced me to steel myself to anyone who belittled me, humiliating them.

Helia doesn't respond at all, but I keep speaking, wanting to get this burden off my chest.

Once I am done, I still, my eyes drooping.

"I'm proud of you for being so strong all this time, for giving back to the people you hurt," he says.

That's also a lie. I know it.

And I fall into slumber.

It's been a cold world for me.

And I feel warmth seep into my heart for the first time.

Even if I know this won't last.

He will be gone.

He won't ever be mine, nor me his.

This isn't a love story.

Helia created such a dark deception for me, and I fell for it. Now, we both are heading towards the wreckage that will rip us apart.

34

HELIA

"Can you repeat the names?"

I grind my teeth, knowing Remo will be holding this over me, but I will take it knowing I am going to be leaving not one but hundreds of funerals for Ambrose at this point.

I gave her a couple of days to come to terms with what we had done when we slept together, but I didn't expect her to lash out and be angry at the small information I let slip so she could figure out a part of me.

Not because I was a coward, but I feared she would walk the other way, and I would rather not use crude ways to keep her.

Remo advised me against it.

It's crazy how fast Remo accepted my new mission, but I think what Aurora saw in that sleepover night has also made an impact on Remo. She definitely told him. It's exactly what I wanted, and it played right into my hands.

After all, I was the one who'd orchestrated it all; the idea and the very reason Ambrose was invited to the Cainn mansion for the first time that night.

She doesn't know what I am doing to keep us together, what I am doing to keep her life together, and yet she still speaks of giving up.

Clearly, I left some loose ends.

It's time I clear those up.

"The Madden sisters. They need to go."

Remo raises his brows at the names.

"I'm sure you know who they are. Do you have a plan in motion to keep this under wraps? You don't think Ambrose will walk away once she finds out? She isn't as forgiving as Aurora."

I laugh, shaking my head. "There will be no one else for me like this. There is no second Ambrose."

"That's also correct." He drops his fist on the table and taps his finger. The moment it hits the third tap, he will have a solution.

After all, isn't this how we climbed to the top?

"Celebration party of Lanon's new role as deputy leader in the Labour party?"

I nod at the location of the party.

Five minutes pass by and another tap on the desk from Remo.

Two minutes and the final tape echoes.

Remo looks right at me, our eyes clash, and we both

smile.

***

He's here with his wife.

"Target secured."

Both Remo and I lift the champagne cups to our lips as we watch Mr Fox Madden, the very legend of the famous pharmaceutical in Britain.

The celebration party is held on the highest floor of the Shard. There are politicians present all around, the Labour party members, shareholders of Madden Pharmaceutical, and its investors. Of course Remo made it here. Didn't he build half of these people in here? Money in their parties, acquiring islands, most wanted art pieces for the party members and the billions Remo has put into their elections will of course have them on his side. His investments in them are all worth it because here he stands, among the elites, the most prized people in the country, and despite their power and position, he is by far the most powerful.

Remo is the monster of the business world.

We wait until Fox is free, then Remo approaches him. He's tall with white cropped hair, a good figure for his mid-sixties, a significant number of wrinkles on his face, and a little fluffy moustache. Kind of reminds me of Mace Torre, Ambrose's father. Poor him. He left very early.

Thanks to yours truly.

Remo starts to murmur in his ear, Fox smiles and laughs,

then Remo lets a small laugh slip, knowing how much he is deceiving him.

I let him do all the talking, knowing he is telling him that he should stay long here, that this party is going to be the talk of the town. Buttering him up in simple terms so that he gets wasted.

The new glass in Remo's hand? It is drugged.

Remo hands him the glass, and Fox downs it all in one go. Remo nods and walks back towards me, standing in the shadows.

"Done. Get the fuck out of here now."

I hit Remo on his head, making his head snap to me in a glare.

"Sometimes you just gotta relax, man." I wink at him, his glare hardens.

"Have a drink, go home, and let Aurora bake something sweet for you. She puts enough drugs in those to make you like her."

Remo grabs the front of my shirt as he sneers down at me. "Don't you fucking say that you like her now after the shit you pulled," he snarls, then lets me go.

"Get the fuck out of here before I punch you and ruin that pretty face."

"So you think I'm pretty?"

"Helia!"

"I'm going. Aurora might make you sleep in the living room tonight if you stay this grumpy, though."

He lunges for me, but I rush away, my laughter booming

down the hallway as I make my way towards the elevator.

I disable the signal on my phone, then put on a balaclava, my hoodie, black jeans, and boots, and I am on my way to the apartment the sisters share. They couldn't go out tonight due to a stomach flu they all got.

What a pity that theirs drink from their regular cafe had some extreme ingredients in them.

I walk past security, easily climbing up the residential tower owned by Fox Madden himself. As I reach their apartment door, I pull out my phone and disable the cameras, then drop a message to Remo to let him know I am here.

Taking out a duplicate of their key card, I swipe it, and it clicks open.

The apartment is cloaked in darkness when I softly make my way inside. From what I know, there are three bedrooms, so I need to gather them all in one.

As soon as I enter through the first bedroom, I take out a white cloth and dip it in the chloroform bottle before walking up to the bed and pressing it against the woman's mouth.

She jerks awake. Her eyes snap to me, panicked, and she thrashes in her bed, her nails scratching my gloved hand, but I press harder and wait. A second goes by. Her eyes roll to the back of her head, and she goes limp.

I repeat the process for the others, then carry them into one room. They are already wearing tank tops and shorts, so I don't need to go the extra length to change them into something else.

I didn't want to undress them. I'm not going to do that

to Ambrose.

She will kill me if she saw me look at another woman's body.

A chuckle escapes me just thinking of her placing her hands on her hips and lifting her brow at me, silently demanding for me to explain myself.

My cute little tigress.

Placing a chair in front of the three tied up sisters, I wait. I've gathered all the things already.

After twenty minutes or so, they will be awake.

My phone pings, and I take it out to see a message from Ambrose. I sit up straight.

Emerald: Seriously? Another note? Why can't you leave me alone?

Attached with this message is a picture of the note I left her that said: *You sleep pretty.*

Me: You do. It's not a lie.

Emerald: *middle finger emoji*

A laugh booms out of me, making one of the ladies jerk.

Me: I'll take anything you give me. Even tonight when I will be there to have my fill of you.

Emerald: I will have my doors locked.

Me: That won't keep me out.

A grunt pulls me out of my little bubble, and I see the sisters wake up. The minute they all do, their eyes widen. Their muffled screams alert the others of their presence, and they shake and scream.

But their lips are taped. Their ankles are tied to the legs of the chair. Their hands are bound behind them.

"Shh, these screams might make me take out your vocals before I even do anything."

That shuts them up real quick.

"I will be super quick, since my girl is waiting for me." I get up, rotating the heating device in my hand.

"You hurt something precious to me, and now I just need to take a little revenge. Just with the same principles, because we don't discriminate around here." I lift the burning hair straightener in my hand, and their eyes widen.

"You hurt people, and I despise people like you. People who use their power and their money to do whatever you please."

I get in the middle one's face. Layla Madden, the power-house of this trio. I lift her chin with the burning end of the iron. Her scream pierces the silence, her eyes scrunching shut.

"You hurt Ambrose. You made her hate herself, and that's more than enough reason to get rid of you. I originally thought it was just a case of light bullying, but then I saw the marks, the burns, and the cuts, and it made my blood fucking boil." I press harder, hearing the skin burn.

Her other sisters are throwing a fit, screaming and thrashing in their chairs at me.

"Silence!" I shout.

They quieten, but their whimpers continue.

And I begin, with their arms, then their legs, burning, cutting them open, and keeping them alive and conscious through this pain. This is exactly what Ambrose felt when they did this to her. I continue for three hours until their bodies are no longer holding them up.

I grab a knife and slice their wrists, their ankles, and then slide one clean cut across their necks, enough to kill them but not enough for their heads to roll off. Once done, I set down my knife and take a step back.

I take out my phone and dial a number.

"Come and clean this shit. I got somewhere to be."

I will reactivate the cameras tomorrow morning.

Now, I need to be with Ambrose. Once the news hits, she will realise what I did for her.

I rush towards Remo's home, running past Aurora, who opens the door for me. I walk to my bedroom in the house and change into a simple black t-shirt and black jeans and then head back out. It would have taken me too long if I went to my own house, and I want to make it before she is asleep.

As soon as I am in her back garden, I see that she is in

her final steps of yoga, so I quickly look around and climb up her balcony. As soon as my shoes hit the floor, her head snaps to me.

She rises and puts her yoga mat away.

"Not even trying to hide yourself now. Good one." She sighs and walks away from me towards the toilet.

I rush to her and grab her wrist, spinning her around, pulling her against my chest.

"Didn't you miss me today?"

She fights me to get me to let her go, but it won't work.

Dipping my head down, I look into her scorching hot eyes. "I will work hard at asking for forgiveness from you, Ambrose."

"If you know I am mad at you, then why are you still holding me? Don't you know you repulse me now?" Her eyes narrow, making me smile.

There's my little emerald.

"Be mad at me from my embrace. Be mad at me while I kiss you."

Then I kiss her. She fights it at first, but then she melts into the kiss.

She kisses me harsher and bites my lip, bursting my lip open, then sucks the blood, making me moan. I lift her off the ground, and her legs wrap around me as I walk us towards her bathroom. I let her go, and she stands in front of me. I remove her sports bra, take off her leggings, then take off my clothes, and we stand naked in front of each other.

My eyes take in my fill of her, her perky breasts, her

335

long legs, perfectly manicured nails, and her blond hair that cascades down her back. With every breath she takes, her breasts bounce softly. I also see the marks all over her body, but they don't faze me nor bother me.

I also see the faint hickeys I left around her breasts and on her neck.

I reach out, softly running a finger over the fading marks.

"You look good with my marks on you."

She slaps my hand away and walks to the shower. My eyes stay trained on her ass.

And I follow.

As soon as the shower turns on, and I step in behind her, I snake an arm around her waist and pull her to me.

"Now that you have given me every inch of yourself, I can't let you go, Ambrose. It never was only physical with you. My raw emotions were dripping for you to take your fill." I murmur.

The bathroom starts to steam up.

"It was me admitting you in my life, knowing how much danger I would be in if I were to say in London longer than two years, yet here I am, making the impossible possible for you. Here I am laying myself bare for you. Take everything from me, Ambrose, but please forgive me, baby."

I place a kiss on her shoulder.

"Please forgive, Ambrose," I murmur. "Do you forgive me?"

She shakes her head. But it doesn't matter. She will.

I place kisses all over her body, on any inch of skin I can

reach, to let her know that I'm sorry if I hurt her. I won't fuck her but being close with her brings me immense peace and I can't let that go.

After the shower, I wrap her in a towel, then myself, I turn her towards the mirror and grab a comb.

And I comb her hair.

"Tell me what that little attitude was about earlier. Hmm?"

She scowls at me through the mirror. "Do you expect me to be nice and sweet to you?"

I smile with a shake of my head. "No, I like you just the way you are, hard edges, two-edged knife, and a little minx."

Her scowl slowly melts at my words while her hands grab hold of the edge of the counter in front of us.

"You are perfect for me." I place another kiss on her shoulder.

"Why do you keep kissing me there?" She surprises me.

I look at her through the mirror and grin.

"Because you close your eyes for a mere second when I do that, and I love that look on your face."

She instantly scowls again. I grab her chin and turn her around. She crosses her arms.

"Stop it," she grits out.

"Stop what?" I smile.

"Sweet talking your way through. It won't work." Pushing my shoulder, she walks out.

"It won't? You sure?" I ask, following her.

She doesn't answer as she walks into her walk-in closet.

"No. You hurt me, Helia. How could I recover from that?" Her voice quivers ever so slightly, making my heart ache.

"I know, and I'm sorry, baby. I shouldn't have kept two faces, but once I did, I couldn't stop. You intrigued me in a way no one else ever has. How could a woman who looks so strong and confident look so fragile? How could she make my heart burn yet ache at the same time?"

She turns around as soon as those words leave my lips. "A woman you should have left alone." Her eyes turn sad. They dim as she takes a shaky breath in.

I grab her cheeks in my hands and kiss her on her lips.

"I'm sorry. I'm sorry. I'm sorry."

She shakes her head and steps out of my hold. "It won't work. Please. Stop." She turns me around and changes before she throws my clothes at my face.

She walks out, and I quickly dress and follow her.

She's lying on her bed, facing the balcony.

My emerald looks sad.

I climb in behind her and hug her from behind her, pulling her closer to me.

"I'll fix it. I'll fix us. I promise."

35

AMBROSE

"Ambrose!" Helia's loud voice booms through the living room.

Mom glances up from her breakfast and scowls. "Who is that maniac shouting this early in the morning?"

Abandoning my food, I head to the front door and step out into the bright early morning. The sun is blazing down, burning my skin through my clothes. It feels wrong to feel the rays of the sun when London is all about gloomy clouds and rain.

Helia stands under the sun, fuming, with crazed eyes and a heaving chest, his suit jacket crumpled at his feet as if he threw it in a fit. His sleeves are messily rolled up to his elbows, and his hair is unruly.

He shakes papers in front of my face. "What the fuck is this?"

Helia left in the morning, just as I expected. I emailed

him that same morning asking for leave for a week, and now, a week later, I have sent him a resignation letter.

He's holding it in his hand right now.

His eyes look so angry I would think he might light me on fire just with that look alone.

"My resignation letter?" Indifference paints my face.

Funnily enough, there was no one watching me do yoga for the past week, there was no feeling of being watched, no one disturbing my peace anymore.

And yet, I felt empty.

"Why?" He steps closer, but I take a step to the left and walk down the steps, standing away from him.

He follows me.

"Why did you resign?" He stands in front of me again, panic clear in his voice, his eyes searching mine for answers that he won't find.

"I don't want the job anymore." I shrug.

He blinks. His mouth opens, then closes.

"Was it because of me?" Anguish laces his voice.

I finally look at him, actually look at him. "What does it matter anymore? I have stopped fighting, and you got what you want. Aren't you happy you won?"

He shakes his head frantically. He drops the papers and reaches for my hands, but I step back. He takes one more step closer to me and cradles my face, but I look the side.

I ignore the skip of my heart at his touch. I ignore my foolish organ calling out to him, wanting to be back in his warm, secure arms.

"Look at me, baby, please," he begs.

Helia begs. I never expected someone like him to beg like this, to ask me to look at him. With his power, his brutal energy and strength, he could force me to do so, but he isn't. He needs to know he fucked up and killed whatever I felt sizzling between us.

That's what he wanted, wasn't it?

With his lies, his manipulating ways, he got what he wanted in the end.

I can't allow myself to weaken at the new nickname he has chosen for me now.

I won't allow him to win the final battle.

I take a step back and out of his hold, and his hands drop to his side.

"Leave, Helia. I have places to go." With that, I turn around and head back into my house, awaiting an email that I should be receiving this week.

That email is my only hope now.

"Ambrose! Come back, baby. Please! You can't walk away from me like this! Ambrose, listen to me!" Helia shouts from behind me, but I shut the door, my heart aching at his voice calling out to me.

Why now?

"Ambrose, please!" He cries out.

Why couldn't he have been more open with me?

"Ambrose!" He screams, his voice so pained.

I know we hated each other, but now I feel something much more. Something that has me almost destroying myself for a mere moment in his arms. For just one last kiss. For one last touch from him.

Because I'm addicted. To him. To his eyes. To his hold. To everything that reminds me of him.

"This dress is beautiful, isn't it?"

I blankly look at the figure-hugging golden dress. It has full sleeves and a sweetheart neckline. It reaches the floor, embellished with beautifully encrusted yellow diamonds, and with each movement of mine, I can hear the dazzling diamonds clink.

Why does it feel like I am cheating on Helia?

"You will have every head turning." Mom smiles at me, her eyes moving over the glittering dress in awe.

She's pushing her dreams onto me.

"Mum, please. I don't want this. What good will it do—" My head whips to the side with a crazy burn.

She slapped me.

I look back at her, and she's still smiling, her eyes wide, looking around the boutique.

"You will stay quiet, and you will—"

The bells ring above the door at the entrance.

My whole being freezes as I watch a figure walk straight at us.

Not a figure. Helia. In a black suit.

And he looks livid. His eyes are trained on my mother, and with each step he takes, my heart buzzes with excitement. He's here.

But then the hope shatters, knowing all I did was push him away from me.

Why would he come here to save me? To help me?

I open my mouth, but before I can get any words out, I watch the scene play out in front of me in slow motion.

Mum turns around, and that same second, Helia grabs her neck and pins her up against the wall. Her legs lift off the ground as he bares his teeth at her, his eyes murderous, his hold tightening until her face turns red.

The sales assistants all freeze in their place, fearing for their own lives as they watch this play out.

Thankfully, there are no other customers. Mum booked it for me in advance.

"Helia," I whisper, my eyes wide.

"You touched her. You raised your hand against your own daughter?!" Helia screams in her face, but she just shakes her head. "Do you know what I do to people who harm the woman I love?"

Everything stops.

He loves … me? Ambrose?

It cannot be. I heard wrong. I know I did.

"I don't let them live a second longer."

No. He will kill her. In broad daylight.

"Helia, stop." I rush towards them, pulling his arm, but he isn't listening.

His eyes are trained on my mother, who is slowly turning blue from the sheer force of one of his hands pinning her to the wall.

Sweat breaks out on the back of my neck.

He won't listen. He's not in his right mind.

I need to do something. Fast.

I look around the boutique, trying to find something, anything to stop him, but what?

"Ow!" I instantly bend down low, my hand rubbing over my knee, acting like I hurt myself.

Helia's head snaps to me. He lets go of Mum instantly and rushes to me. Grabbing hold of my face, he looks panicked between my face and my knee with me on the floor.

"Are you okay? What happened?"

Fuck. I can't let myself get this weak.

"I hurt myself, my leg," I murmur, pointing to my knee, watching my mother out of the corner of my eye gasping for air, holding her neck.

I shouldn't have helped her, but I did.

"It's okay, I'll fix it." Sliding an arm under my knees and shoulder, he lifts me off the ground, making me yelp. I wrap my arms around his neck and freak out when he starts to walk out the door.

"Helia! My dress, I haven't paid for it!"

"They can add it to my tab," he snaps.

I gasp, looking back at the employees who are rushing towards my mother, who is glaring at me.

"It's a two-million-pound dress, Helia," I protest.

He stops in the middle of the road, glancing down at me with such intensity it makes my stomach burn in desire.

He has looked at me like that when I was on my knees for him with his cock in my mouth.

With possessiveness.

"That's nothing to me, Ambrose."

An hour later, I am in a gold diamond dress in Helia's home, on his sofa, when I should be angry and running away at the first chance I get.

Why am I so weak for this man?

He betrayed me.

How will he feel when he finds out that I am building a case against him and it's only a matter of time before it is officially announced? I was going to drop it until he revealed the part of himself he kept tucked away.

I hear footsteps behind me then here he is, holding a first aid kit. Lifting my legs on the couch, I wrap my arms around my knees and look away from him.

"Let me see your leg."

I continue to look away from him, at the small dresser pushed against his far-right wall.

Was he born here?

"Ambrose, let me see your knee."

I don't know anything about him before he came to Glamorous.

"Ambrose, this is the last time. Let me see your knee."

He will hate me again. It's only a matter of time.

That thought fills my eyes with tears.

I want that, don't I? Then why does everything in me ache at the thought?

A shout leaves me when I am lifted off the sofa, then placed back down in Helia's lap, my legs stretched over on the sofa.

"Look at me." He turns my chin towards him, but I look away. "Fine, your anger is justified. Just let me look at where you hurt yourself, that's all. I'll leave you alone after."

I don't move. My heart is burning up in flames and all that will remain are ashes.

Helia lifts my dress himself, bunching the expensive dress like a flimsy little gown at my thighs. When he sees no injury on my knee, he sighs.

I see his head drop back on the sofa from my peripheral vision.

"You drive me crazy," he murmurs, running his big warm hands on my legs, raising goosebumps. My body temperature skyrockets.

"You did that to protect your mother? Why?"

I climb off his lap and give him my back. "Give me a change of clothes," I murmur, watching the door, spotting something fly right past the window wall of the living room.

Within a couple of minutes, I am changed into black sweatpants that I had to roll a couple of times and a big t-shirt that engulfs me and makes me feel like I am small.

I walk out of the small bedroom next to the poolroom, passing the staircase to the front door. As soon as I am out, a wave of fresh air hits me.

A glittering orange sunset covers the entire sky, as if the sun was a couple of miles away from the Earth and it lit everything on fire. The tall trees are each touched with a speck of gold, and the sight reminds me of Helia's eyes when he smiles at me.

Helia stands with his back to me with Blaze on his shoulder. He looks over at me with a small smile and nods for me to follow him.

I don't move for a couple of minutes and watch his figure retreating into the forest, but then realise that it will get dark soon. I don't know anything around here, and Helia is my best bet.

I could stay in the house, but somehow, being with Helia feels safer than being alone in a big glass mansion in the middle of the woods.

So I quickly catch up to him. Twigs break under our feet, and we have to push branches out of our faces, making flies and some grasshoppers taking flight. Amongst the chaos of taking a walk in the forest, a certain calmness washes over me.

It feels like I was on fire my whole life and being in Helia's silent presence threw ice cold water on me, dimming my madness.

"I was eleven years old when I got this scar on my eye." Helia voice travels back to me. He doesn't turn around, and Blaze doesn't caw either.

He's sharing a part of himself with me today.

Why does that make me want to cry?

347

"Me and my sister… We were homeless for a couple of years. Our mother abandoned us, and we barely scraped by. We weren't able to pay rent, due to us being too young to work, so we got kicked out of our house and lived inside an abandoned warehouse."

There is not a single ounce of emotion in his voice, but when I glance at his hands, they are in his trouser pockets, clenched into fists.

"My sister used to disappear for days sometimes. Maybe one day or maybe a whole month. She used to take drugs and often passed out. I didn't know then, but it's not hard to put the pieces together now."

There is a pause, leaves rustle, and a quiet chirp of a bird hits my ears.

"She brought her boyfriend back one day."

I see him swallow and another pause follows.

"They got drunk together at the warehouse with me beside them. He saw me and decided my eyes were something to possess, something he wanted. His excuse for wanting to carve out my eye? That he gave us food and money, and that made us his possessions."

How could a child understand how fucked up that is? How did he survive being on streets?

Just thinking about a younger Helia, bleeding, crying, and unable to go anywhere makes me want to bawl my eyes out.

"I was bleeding for days on those winter nights, feeling every burn, every ripped open skin around my eye, fearing

I would lose sight in this eye, or worse, lose it altogether. It's crazy how I never once feared for my life while being homeless, but those days were the worst. He made me feel like I was beneath him, as did every single man in London, but he also thought he had the right to do as he pleased."

Tears well up in my eyes as I imagine Helia bleeding on the streets, his skin ripped open around his eye, fearing for his life.

Oh Lord.

"Aren't we all slaves to our desires? Why do some feel like they have the right to act upon their sick imaginations and some don't?" Helia stops just as the sound of water fills the silence. Like a fountain or a waterfall.

"The only difference is they think money can hide their sick mentalities," he says quietly.

I come to a stop right next to Helia, and when I glance down, my mouth drops open with a loud gasp.

There is a waterfall to the left, a big drop to the ground, and a beautiful sunset right in front of me. A couple of birds take flight, and here, life feels simple.

Everything feels like it can be accomplished.

Reaching my hand out, I grab Helia's hand without looking at him and give it a small squeeze before letting it go.

I can't give him too much hope.

"Blaze, have anything to say to make Ambrose forgive me?"

Blaze caws loudly and shoots up to the sky. My eyes follow him with a smile, watching him do hoops and caw happily.

"I hope the presents I sent to your home aren't too small."

I don't reply, emotions choking me.

"Would you at least look at me? I can't bear to not have your eyes on me."

I lose all resolve and finally slide my gaze from the waterfall beneath me to Helia's emerald eyes.

And they take my breath away.

So does his smile.

His jet-black hair has never looked more beautiful. Even now, just seeing him in front of me, I feel my heart throb in need of him.

I should hate him and push him away, but can I truly move past it?

He says he loves me but to the extent of killing people for me?

What does one call that?

Such dangerous love?

Madness?

The little presents Helia was talking about?

They are diamond necklaces, earrings, and bracelets. All in silver and green emerald diamond set in green velvet boxes. With not a single note. I huff at how arrogant he is to assume I will know who these are from straight away.

"Can you place these in my room, please?" I ask the maid on my way to my bedroom.

The next morning, a small bouquet of white roses arrives, and at first, I think it's something small enough to throw in the trash. I don't keep any of that around the house, but then I see it.

Small diamonds placed right in the middle of the twelve roses. When looked closely, they are each possibly worth over twenty grand each. I would know, I have requested a set with these diamonds this for Aurora once.

Again. No note.

Helia: Did you like this one?

Me: You think my value is just £240k?

That resulted in something even bigger delivered to my home.

"Who is this person who keeps sending you all these gifts? Have I met him or her?"

I don't answer my mother as I open the black velvet box and gasp.

A key. Not just any key.

An emerald-coloured Ferrari LaFerrari. Parked outside my home.

Helia: Do you like this?

I can't even reply to this because within just a couple of days, he has sent millions of pounds worth of gifts to my home, taking it seriously when I said he can never win me. But if he keeps spending money on me like this, it will make him go broke at this point.

Me: Stop it. It's too much.

Helia: Do you forgive me then?

Me: No. Nothing was worth my forgiveness.

Helia: What do you want? Me on my knees?

Me: No.

Helia: Tell me what you want, and I will make it happen.

I have no reply to that. I wish to forget everything, to erase myself and live as I felt in the moment at the waterfall near his home. I felt free. Free from the responsibilities. Does that mean I feel at home and free when I'm with Helia?

That when he is with me, no one can ever harm as they always did?

"Ambrose, what happened to the Madden sisters?"

"What?" My head snaps up when I walk into the living room.

"What is the news saying?" She turns the volume up.

"Recently reported is the death of the three daughters of Fox Madden, the owner of Madden Pharmaceuticals, one of Britain's richest man. He is now grieving the loss of his three daughters. This case is being investigated by officials. Initial reports confirm that the murder took place the night Hayes Lanon was appointed the deputy leader of Labour party. Now onto the heist that has been successfully carried out in the art gallery of London…"

My ears start to ring.

What has Helia done?

36

AMBROSE

"You can go right in. He is waiting for you." I nod at Remo's assistant and walk past her towards his office.

As soon as I turn the door handle, I know I will not be leaving without my whole world shifting. This conversation will wreck me and destroy everything I have known. Just how much will I be able to handle?

It's time I pick myself back up and take back the reins of my life. To stop everything spiralling out of my control and take action.

I won't be sitting in my room being depressed when I have so much money, power, and resources at the tip of my fingers to do as I please in life.

The door shuts behind me, and Remo stands up from his seat, buttoning his suit jacket.

"Ms Ambrose, please sit down." He motions to the chair in front of him, and I take my seat.

He watches every single movement of mine, quite like Helia.

"Can I help you with anything?" He lifts a brow, running a finger along his jaw, quietly watching me.

"Yes. In fact, you are the only one that can help me." I lift my chin up high.

"Right."

I nod with a smile. There is something about today that feels right. Like I finally understand everything and nothing can make me fall again.

"How long have you known Helia?"

Remo doesn't answer for a second, something a lot like amusement twisting in his eyes.

"Why? Finally interested?"

"Well?" I lift a brow, waiting.

"For about a decade or so." He shrugs, but when you are so close to people you cover murder for, you know exactly how, when, and where you have met them. You remember every detail as to always stay ahead of them in case anything goes wrong. So for him to act so casually, my suspicions have turned out to be correct.

"Right. I will ask you one more question, and I want the truth. The complete truth. No lies. No deception."

Remo's lip quirks up.

"Helia has done some questionable things, and I have been in the midst of them, or sometimes the cause. Unintentionally. How long have these 'things' been going on for?"

Remo doesn't answer. In fact, he doesn't even look to be

in a mood to answer.

"What 'things' Ms Ambrose?"

I slam a hand on the table, leaning forward. "Murders, Mr Cainn. Murders."

Remo looks me dead in the eye for a moment, then he throws his back with a taunting laugh.

"I cannot believe it. With the number of bodies I had to clear up, you were bound to find out," he continues, looking me directly in the eyes. "Helia is a murderer. Yes. And I hide them. We have never boasted of being clean businessmen, as other people do. No one at the top is a sweet, innocent angel. Every single one of them has made a deal with the devil. Is that what you wanted to hear?"

I blink.

"Everywhere you walked, Helia followed in the shadows and left bodies behind him. You only have to look back and see the bloodied path he has created for you. Helia... doesn't know how to deal with emotions like a normal person, as you have no doubt gathered." Remo gets out of his seat and walks around the table.

"He is unhinged, too carefree, but he isn't stupid nor someone to take lightly. Helia's obsession with you began as soon as he saw you the first time. He argued with me. He gave me, Remo Cainn, an ultimatum. You are not something he will lose or easily let go of." Remo leans down, grabs the arms of my chair, and narrows his eyes. My words climb up my throat and lodge there.

"You are his obsession. A very dark, very twisted obsession. If you are here to find a way to get rid of him, it's best not to linger in that delusion. It won't be happening. If you are here to confirm what has been going, especially with the recent news of the Madden sisters, then yes, your suspicions are correct."

Pushing my chair back, so he has to release me, I get up, crossing my arms.

"I have suspected it for a while but didn't want to believe. But then I realised that if my father could fake his persona in front of the media and still be a monster behind closed doors and sell his daughter? Anything could happen, honestly." I shrug.

It's hard to maintain contact with such a powerful figure like Remo, but I'm going to stay in my place and not back down.

"How did it happen? How did you pull off the Madden sisters? I'm sure you are aware of their father and what position he holds in society."

Remo nods, looking to the side as if to hide a smirk. "Of course I do. Just as you know my position in society, Ms Ambrose. Because of Helia, I know exactly how and where Fox Madden has been smuggling lab-made diamonds into the UK. It brings in billions of dollars but at what cost? All it took was one meeting and a little video evidence, and it shut him up."

Remo moves away from me towards the floor to ceiling window of his office wall.

"Everyone loves money to the point they will even sacrifice their own children in this city. It's disgusting because they gamble lives for money, not even seeking justice, but at the end of the day, we all are power-hungry humans." Remo looks over his shoulder at me, his black hair slicked and not a single strand out of place as he stands at the top of the city he owns.

"Someone is willing to protect you in this city, in this country, this world, so be grateful. Especially since that someone is Helia. If it were up to me, after finding out about what happened to Aurora, I would have dug your grave long ago."

My heart stops.

His words pierce a wound in my heart, but I keep my mouth shut.

"Thank you."

I turn around to leave when he stops me.

"One more thing. Don't think Helia doesn't know about this marriage of yours with Erik Kellias. He's keeping quiet about it to help you come to terms with everything. He not only has been bothering me and Aurora about what to do with you and how to approach about his feelings without scaring you off, but he has also been trying to put you in my and Aurora's good graces, to save your relationship with her, because in his words 'my emerald looks very sad these days.' That motherfucker is getting too sappy for his own good."

My heart pangs inside me. I lift my hand to soothe it, but it doesn't work.

Nor does it work when I am in my kitchen, waiting for Mum to come home, to tell her that I am going to publicly announce that I am breaking off my engagement with Erik Kellias. It has to be done.

Remo's words keep repeating in my mind while I wait in the quiet kitchen.

My emerald looks very sad these days.

I look sad, he said. *My* emerald, he called me.

My eyes drop to my hand where I am wearing one of his gifted rings on my middle finger. It's a silver band with small rectangle emerald-cut diamonds all around it. It looks gorgeous against my slightly pale complexion.

I run my hand through my golden hair, a smile touching at my lips, recalling how Helia noticed when I only cut just two inches off my hair.

"You won't let me go, right?"

My head snaps to my left, where the door of the kitchen is. Helia stands there with a grin on his face, dressed in an all-black suit, hands in his trouser pockets as he leans against the doorway, his black hair falling into his eyes.

"What?" I whisper, slowly standing up from the stool.

He rests his head on the doorframe, the sharp edges to his face more prominent, dangerous, and haunting.

"I love you. You know that, right?"

My hands grab hold of my blue wide-legged jeans. I suddenly feel hot under the long-sleeved jumper I have on.

"Do you love me, Emerald?"

I open my mouth, but no words come out.

Helia pouts in front of me. I look down at the floor.

"I've done so much for you, laid the world at your feet."

I gasp when his voice comes from behind me. I turn around and see him standing there, looking through my fridge.

I look back to where he was, and he isn't there anymore. What…?

"I gave you a part of me as you gave me a part of you. I know you never gave anyone that privilege, so I gave you something in return." He straightens and looks at me.

His eyes…they are filled with love.

For me.

"There will be no one after you for me. Never was before you either. Do you believe me?"

I nod, biting my lip as tears start to gather in my eyes. I do.

I do so much to the point I believe I can look past his sins and mine.

He made mistakes, and so did I.

"I will love you obsessively." Helia's right next to me now, grabbing my hand and lifting it to his lips.

"Believe me, still?"

I nod, a smile spreading on my lips.

"Love me?" he pleads, his eyes waiting.

Yes. Yes.

Yes, I love you.

I open my mouth to say just that when I blink, and he vanishes.

He's not here.

It was just a hallucination, but I need to tell him.

I do.

Rushing towards the kitchen door, I walk through the hallway and bump into someone I didn't see coming.

"Where are you rushing to?"

Mother.

I step back. She walks into the kitchen and grabs a fresh glass of water from the fridge.

This is my chance.

I need to set everything right. I need to do this.

I can figure out about my company later. Figure out everything else later.

I just need to tell Helia how I feel.

"Mum. I sent my written statement about breaking off the engagement with Erik. I'm not marrying him."

Mum's head snaps to me. "What did you say?" she grits out.

"You heard me. You force me once more? I will throw you out of this house. Enough from you. I had enough from you. You get yourself together, or I will not be so gracious anymore." I walk up to her and bend down to her height.

"Raise your hand at me once more, and I promise you I will put you in jail for life. Don't underestimate me. You don't know who I am, it seems. Go ask your friends, your colleagues, anyone in your tea party, and they will know exactly what I have done. And I will not hesitate to do any of it to you."

She opens her mouth, probably to scream at me.

"Shut up!" I snap.

Her mouth shuts.

"Not a single word out of your mouth, Leyla Torre. You have lost everyone in your life." I step back, not trusting her to not attack me as I move away and walk back up to my bedroom to grab my car keys.

As soon as I am in my bedroom, I release a sigh. It feels as if the bricks that were weighing down my heart have finally fallen.

My laptop pings, and my eyes snap to it, the subject of the email freezing my world.

Result of the hard drive. Successful.

My hands lift to my lips.

They did it. They retrieved the footage.

As soon as I open the email with the retrieved footage, I sit down and watch it.

The first starts off on the day two figures walk into our house: Remo and Helia. I look at the date and see it's the date… my father died.

The clip switches, and I see inside the office. Remo threatens Dad. Dad shouts and screams, but Remo stays silent until he grabs hold of his throat and gets in his face to say something that makes Dad's eyes widen. The clip switches to Helia standing in the hallway with his gun raised as he shoots at every single guard that rushes towards him.

My heart bleeds in heartbreak inside of me. It shouldn't be feeling, bleeding, or calling out for Helia.

It's a bloodbath, blood everywhere, as I had seen that day.

Remo starts to hit and beat Dad up, forcing him to sign a document that Helia takes and walks out with a manic smile and bloodied hands and face.

Remo shoots Dad, and he falls limp to the pool of his own blood.

My hands lift to my lips as I see the driveway footage of me and Mum walking up to Remo, who whispers something in my ear and walks away. They were both wearing black clothes, so I couldn't have seen the blood.

My eyes lift to the corner of the house and see Helia standing there.

The picture I saw!

It was Helia.

And the rest of the clips are ones that had been deleted. All of Helia standing outside my home every night for the next month. It continues until recently.

My hands shake.

The document he signed.

It was the papers to put Glamorous in Helia's name, under Remo's control.

It was all orchestrated, as I expected.

I saw the own murder of my father.

And I don't feel a single ounce of remorse.

No one knows it was committed by Remo Cainn.

I have been able to uncover a dirty secret of Remo and it's in my hands.

I could ruin everyone with this one tape.

What do I do?

I get off the chair, running my hands through my hair, trying to think through what I should do.

I love Helia.

I love whatever he is, however he is.

But this… what do I do with this information?

It could get my company back. But I don't think Helia would be willing to give it to me if he is here only for this company.

I sit down at my desk again and type up a report, asking a reporter to investigate the document that was been signed by my father. I copy it, ready to send it to the lawyer who has been preparing my case for this company.

But I can't attach the file.

I should delete it. But then how will I get my company back?

Remo won't give it up, he isn't that generous, except to Aurora. And I doubt Helia would give it to me. He won't. Not when it's the only thing keeping him away from the police knocking on his door. It could help him explain where he has been if they were to question his presence.

It solves all his problems. That's why he has been so tight-lipped about it.

But this company, it's mine. It has been my mission and my motivation for most of my life.

I love working for it, I love everything I do.
But… I can't betray Helia like that.
I don't know what to do.
My company is a part of me.

37

AMBROSE

"Ambrose!" My door slams open, making me jump in my chair.

Mum comes, fuming into my room. She looks crazed, like nothing can stop her from getting what she wants.

Well, I will be damned if that happens under my roof.

This house is in my name, not hers. I let her get away with too much, wanting some kind of motherly love, but I am past it. Waiting for that to happen is like waiting an eternity for what was never written for you.

"What are you doing on that laptop? You think you can order me about without consequence?" she screams.

I get up from my chair and stand in front of her. "Yes. I can. Get out of my room."

She glares at me. "No. You are my daughter. I gave birth to you, and I will not have you disrespect me like this." She pushes at my shoulder, making me stumble a step.

"Don't touch me," I grit out, clenching my hands into fists. I don't want to harm her, but I'm not opposed to it.

Not anymore.

Whatever I had left for her, any kind of remorse, emotion, it has all evaporated into thin air.

She has lost the only daughter, the only family, she had left.

"I will touch you, hit you as I please. Who are you to stop me?" she screams.

I shut my eyes and take a deep breath, then sink onto the edge of my bed, rubbing my forehead.

"What the fuck is this? Is this the man—Is that Aurora's husband?"

My head snaps up when I see Mum watching the footage replaying on my laptop. I lunge towards her as I see her switch to the email tab. I go to push her when she turns and shoves me with such strength that I stumble back a couple of steps.

No. No.

No.

"Don't touch that!" I scream. I go to her again and push her away from the laptop.

No, please don't tell me she sent the email.

No.

If Helia sees this, he will kill me.

I was supposed to tell him I love.

I *chose* him above everything.

This cannot be.

367

"You sent the email!" I scream, turning to my mother.

There's a smug expression on her face.

"What have you done?!" I scream, getting into her face, but all she does is glare at me.

"You thought to control me? You don't know me at all then, dear daughter." She tuts and shakes her head as if disciplining a small child.

What has she done?

What has she actually done?!

"You don't know what you just did! Do you have any idea what will happen now? Do you have any idea about—" My voice breaks as tears gather in my eyes and fall to the floor.

I drop to the ground, crying.

I can't undo this.

This cannot be happening.

No.

I will lose everything now.

Remo will know I sent it.

Helia will think I sent it.

They will all hate me.

Especially Aurora for getting her husband sent to jail.

Everything is over.

"You just ruined my fucking life!" I scream, shaking and punching the floor.

"Noo!!" I cry out as I watch her smash my laptop against the edge of the desk, effectively taking away everything.

"That should teach you a lesson." She turns and walks

out.

I get off the floor to rush to her. All I see right now is her torment and punishment.

I will not let her live after destroying my life within seconds.

I twist the knob and find it locked.

I twist and shake the door but nothing.

"Stay in the room until you learn what respecting your mother is." Her voice trails off on the other side, and my heart drops to the ground.

How will I tell Helia that I didn't do it?

I can't climb down the balcony; there is nothing to hold on to.

I start to breathe faster, my chest heaving as I look for my phone all around the room. I flip the bed covers, throw my desk drawers open, wrench my bed out of place, but nothing. Everything is turned upside-down in my room, but I can't find my phone.

She took it.

My fucking mother took it.

Every minute that goes by, I can feel my life being set aflame.

I can feel my heart stutter, its beat no longer working properly.

Helia.

I need to tell him.

It wasn't me.

It wasn't me.

I don't know what I was thinking, typing up the email.

I was never going to include the clip. I was going to delete it.

I don't want to lose you. I wasn't—

I drop to the floor, my hand in my hair.

Helia will hate me once he finds out.

He will hate me.

38

HELIA

My office door slams open, and a fuming Remo walks in.

"What now?" I sigh, only for me to freeze in place when Remo throws papers at my desk.

"Ambrose retrieved the CCTV footage of Mace's murder and released it to the press." He slams his hand on the table.

What!?

"You're mistaken, Remo. How could—"

"She did! And you should realise now that keeping her alive all this time was for nothing! I told you time and time again that she is a liability, ready to destroy us; a time ticking bomb that will take advantage of everything to turn it in her favour."

Getting up from my desk, I grab the papers, looking over headlines upon headlines from different tabloids, all reporting on the murder of Mace Torre.

I hid myself. I worked years and years to get to where I am today.

I was hiding from government officials; I was building a small life here and thought to spend it with her. And to see this?

"I don't believe—"

"Fucking believe it, Helia! Stop this madness right this second and look at the facts. I had the IP address tracked, and it was released just half an hour ago from the Torre mansion, Ambrose's laptop. Look at the reports if you don't believe it, or do your own research." Remo walks up to me and gets in my face, brows twisted and a frown on his face, and yet his eyes blaze like never before.

He doesn't realise that something feels off, but it definitely is my heart chipping away with every word that is coming out of his mouth.

"You fix this, Helia. You fucked up, so you take care of it. I want her gone. There is no place for her here anymore. Rip her out of your heart, destroy her until there is nothing left. I don't want to see her walking around ever again." Remo's nostrils flare, his gaze unwavering. He makes sure his words have made it into my head, then he leaves.

And I am left in a mess I never thought would happen.

I've never failed.

Whatever was softening my heart for Ambrose is slowly burning up in flames inside of me. My heart takes a different turn with my eyes stuck to the papers in front of me.

There are photos of me in the Torre mansion, and my hands start to shake.

How fucking dare she take what I gave her and use it against me?

I was going to give her the world. Even burn it and destroy it for her.

It hurts.

It fucking hurts to see what she has done.

She made me believe she never needed anything when all this time she was going to use it against me?

She never changed.

I will make sure that she burns the way she burnt my world around me and left me in the ashes of everything I built. I will break her to the point she will be begging at my feet for mercy, but I will have none left in my heart.

Without wasting another minute, I rush out of the office building and don't bother changing as I speed towards the Torre mansion. On the way, I ran IP tracking and indeed, Ambrose is the one that leaked the footage. As soon as I arrive, I stride towards the back and climb up the walls and onto her balcony.

It's time you face the hell I am about to deliver, dear Ambrose.

I grab hold of the annoying curtains and pull, throwing them to the floor with a crash.

My eyes fix on the huddled figure against the bed.

She jumps up. Her eyes are red, and a part of me wants to ask her what is wrong, but I smash it down.

She destroyed me.

"Helia…" Her voice is weak, but there is no going back now.

"How fucking dare you?" I walk up to her, grabbing her neck in a tight hold as I lift her off the ground.

She gasps, her hands clamping around my arms with her legs thrashing under me.

"No! You've got it w-wrong!"

I lean forward, and her perfume surrounds me. I can't help but feel pathetic for ever falling for this wicked woman.

"I should have fucking known you would turn out to be like this. You're disgusting, do you know that?"

She shakes her head, her red-rimmed eyes flooding with tears.

"P-Please," she sobs with difficult gasps.

My heart pinches in pain at seeing her hurt because of me, so I throw her to the floor.

She drops with a loud thud, gasping, rubbing her throat.

Snapping her head to me, she rushes over to me on her knees, grabbing hold of my hands. Her hair is a mess, her clothes wrinkled, her hands freezing, and her body trembling. She doesn't look like herself.

"Believe me, Helia. I didn't do it." She shakes her head. Her speech is slow but strong enough to get her message across.

"You lost the chance to ever beg when you decided to ruin my life for your selfish reasons. How could you be so cruel to destroy me like this after all that has happened between us?" I shake my hand out of her hold and step back before bending down and grabbing hold of her hair. "Did you want to see me in pain?"

She sobs, shaking her head, the motion restricted by my hold on her.

"Did you create all this drama to get your back company? You wanted it so badly you decided the only way was to reveal me like this?"

She continues shaking her head, but what is there to deny anymore?

My eyes scan her face, over the marks, the new and old tears, the smeared lipstick, the red eyes, and the shakiness in her body.

And I break with her. I feel with her.

My lip trembles as I speak. "Why did you have to destroy us, Ambrose?"

She shuts her eyes, sobbing and crying.

"Helia, I didn't do it. It wasn't me. It was Mum. I didn't have anything to do with it."

I let her go, push her away from me, but stay in my hunched position.

I take out the knife from my back pocket and try not to show how my hand trembles.

"Let's say I believe you…"

Her eyes are on me. Waiting.

"How did you get the footage then, Ambrose? You surely had to go looking for it, didn't you? The email that was written? That sounded exactly like you. I have been reading your emails for months."

She looks away from me, and it gives me my answer.

I grab her throat, twisting the knife so it points right at the jugular vein on her neck.

Her eyes snap to me.

But she doesn't look away.

My own hand trembles.

What have you done, Ambrose?

"Given your history, I should have known better."

39

HELIA

Pushing my arm away, she tries to hug me, but I don't let her.

It hurts.

Fuck, it aches.

"I gave you everything I had," I grit out, feeling my heart hardening inside of me. Or whatever is left of it.

Tightening my hand around the knife, I dig it into her skin slowly. Her sobs fill the room, my own breaths falling in short pants.

The shaking doesn't stop.

I can't do it.

The minute I see a drop of blood, my hand fails.

She shudders and whispers, "Helia, I lo—"

The door bursts open, and people in black uniforms flood the room, filling it with the crackles of the walkie-talkie and masked faces. One after the other, special forces surround me with guns raised.

"Drop your weapon," the one in front of me warns.

"I didn't do it…" Ambrose's voice trails off, and I glance at her. Her eyes roll to the back of her head, her body falling into my arms, unconscious.

"Him! It was him!" Leysa Torre walks inside, pointing her finger at me, and my heart shatters to the floor.

My eyes trace the red puddle around Ambrose. She must have fallen onto something sharp. I look around the room and spot her smashed laptop. Her bedroom is in complete disarray, and her doorknob is almost broken off. Everything is out of place in this bedroom that belongs to the most tidy woman. The signs of struggle are all around the bedroom. I recall her slurred speech and the shakiness in her body.

As realisation sets in, my heart freezes in my body, not working anymore.

"Drop your weapons. This is your last warning," the muffled command comes, but my eyes don't move from Ambrose's prone figure on the floor.

She… didn't do it.

"The footage showed him killing my husband…" I don't hear anything that comes out of Leysa's mouth after that sentence.

I fucked up.

I fucked up so bad to the point I hurt the only woman who loved me. Who cherished me.

Without wasting another second, I move towards Ambrose with a heavy heart, only for arms to force me back.

They don't let me move.

"Let me fucking go!" I thrash against their hold, my eyes on Ambrose.

"Ambrose!" I scream, willing for her to get up.

I'm sorry, baby. I'm so sorry.

"Ambrose, get up!" I plead, thrashing, trying to get out of the hold of the four people on me, but my emotions aren't letting me focus on anything other than Ambrose.

"Ambrose, I'm sorry, please get up," I beg. "I'll do anything, but please get up for me. I'm so sorry!"

"Stop moving." A muffled voice comes from my left, and that makes me rage.

Using my elbow, I hit one of them in their stomach. Their bulletproof vests barely let them feel anything, but I still try. I hit, kick, punch, and do everything to make them let go of me.

But it doesn't matter. More and more officers pile into the bedroom, holding me back and keeping me in place.

I hear the faint sound of a helicopter circling the mansion, and more special forces appear on the balcony. They have surrounded the mansion, but I cannot allow them to hurt Ambrose, to use her against me.

"Ambrose! Ambrose! Wake up, I believe you. I'm sorry!"

The knife lodged inside me keeps twisting. I did this to myself and to her.

I ruined what we had.

What was gifted to me.

"I'm sorry for not believing—"

A punch cuts off my sentence, sending me flying back.

"Shut up!" the officer in front of me barks, but my eyes don't move from Ambrose's unconscious form.

"Ambrose—"

Another punch is thrown at my face. This time I can feel blood dripping down my chin.

"He helped kill my husband." Leysa is crying in the corner of the room.

"You think I will let you live peacefully after this?" I give her a lopsided smile. She tried to destroy everything in Ambrose's life and mine.

She looks up at me, crying, screaming like a toddler, and kicking at the officer consoling her and taking her away.

"Every single one of you is dead." I look them all in the eye. They don't react, not knowing what is awaiting them. Death is too easy for keeping me from Ambrose.

I will kill each person they care about first before I move onto them, forcing them to watch everyone they value meet death.

A kick throws me to the floor, and handcuffs wrap around my wrists. I scream and keep screaming at her, but she doesn't wake up.

Did I ruin the only thing that I wanted desperately in my life?

The only thing that made me feel like a living, breathing man?

We were wrong for each other, we were on opposite

ends, and in the end, I have been put on my knees for her.

The officers force me to walk towards the door, but I keep looking back at Ambrose, at the officer tapping her cheek.

"Don't fucking touch her! I will kill you and skin you alive!" I shout at him. "Ambrose!" I roar one last time, wanting her to just look at me. One time. Just one time.

I see her eyes flutter, but the officers force me to walk away, and I don't get to see if she saw me pleading for her forgiveness.

She doesn't get to hear me tell her I believe her and love her.

As they drag me away, my eyes burn with tears that I will turn into knives for every single officer on duty here today.

When I am taken outside, my hair ruffles with the helicopter so low, the buzzing of its blades above me, cars upon cars of MI5 crowd the driveway. An array of reporters is outside the gates, taking pictures, and I make a note to tell Remo to erase all articles of this case.

I look back at the second floor of the mansion, knowing Ambrose is unconscious, and I have done that.

I tore us apart.

40

AMBROSE

When people speak of love, they talk about the sweetness of it. They talk about the flourishing of emotions and the way their lives have never been better.

If someone were to ask me what love meant for me, I would describe Helia. I would describe his darkness, his rough yet soft touch, his emerald eyes that hold such emotions that it wrenches out my own. His smiles bring warmth to my heart. I would talk about the small acts of kindness towards me despite his rough nature and everything he has given me.

I have lost my all to him.

I lost my soul, my heart, and my mind to Helia.

And I don't ever want to have anything back.

Not because I think he deserves it, but because I know he will guard it all from the monsters of this world.

Even if he were to hate me now, if he doesn't care and

despises me, I know deep down, he would still keep everything I have given him safe.

I have lost my heart in this game of deception.

As soon as my eyes crack open, the first thing that floods my mind is Helia's name and the hatred I saw in his eyes.

The heart monitor goes crazy when I lift my hand to my mouth, tears instantly filling my eyes. I have lost the battle against my mother, against fate.

"Ambrose?" My eyes snap to the side and see my mother.

"Who are you, and why are you here?"

Her face converts into a frown, her eyes going to the other side of my bed towards Aurora.

"What—" Mum starts.

"Why are you still here after destroying my life? What right do you have to be in this room right now?" I continue, my hands clenching at the blanket on me in the hospital bed.

"Ambrose." I shake my head at Aurora, and her eyes bounce between Mum and me.

"No, Aurora, she's ruined us before anyone else ever did. She gave us scars first, and Dad abused us while she did nothing to help." I look away from my mother and fixed my gaze on the white ceiling.

Murmurs of the hospital and the noises of the machines slowly take over my mind, and I cannot help but feel the need to walk out of this hospital to wherever Helia is to tell him it wasn't me. I want to drag my mother to his feet and force her to apologise to him for destroying his life.

"Mother, could you please leave?" Aurora's soft voice travels across the room.

"Why would I leave? I am her mother. I have done everything to save you both. I have done so much, and yet this is how you treat me? After your father's death, I have worked hard every day to help you live a comfortable life," Mum says, her eyes switching between me and Aurora, not able to understand what she did wrong.

I let out a mocking laugh.

"That's the thing, though. You *thought* you worked hard. You *thought* you did everything to save us and keep us safe, but if you just walked out of this bubble you created for yourself, you would see how much it was hurting us," I say, keeping my eyes on the ceiling.

"You abused me. You raised your hand against me, the daughter you supposedly wanted to protect. You pushed away Aurora because you couldn't handle the grief from the loss of your husband. Mind you, he was just as abusive, mentally and physically."

Mum frowns, her lips twisting as she shakes her head, like she's denying everything coming out of my mouth.

"Didn't you? Are you going to deny it as well?"

She opens her mouth but shuts it.

"I hate you." I spit out, turning away from her.

My eyes fall on Aurora, who has been looking at me this whole time.

Her hand grasps mine in a soft hold, her eyes watery as

she gives me a shaky smile.

"It's okay, Ambrose." She squeezes my hand. "It's okay to let her go. She hurt you too much. Put yourself first. You deserve happiness too."

A tear drops onto my hand, and I squeeze back. "I'm sorry, Aurora."

She shakes her head, silencing me. "It's in the past. Please, recover so we can bring Helia back. You need to heal to fight for him." She raises her brows, waiting for me to agree.

"You need to know that I didn't do it, Aurora. I didn't release those clips."

She brings my hand up to her lips, kissing it as tears drip down her cheeks.

"I know, I believe you. Helia told me about you a lot when you weren't around. He was the one warming my heart to you, Ambrose. He was the one who has been pushing me to give our relationship a go, the one to urge me to invite you over and help you connect with me again. He has done so much for you without you realising. It's only fair I help you guys now."

The heart monitor takes a dip before it rises at an incredible rate.

"What?"

She nods, a wide smile spreading on her face as she sits down at the chair next to my bed and goes into full detail about exactly how involved Helia has been in my life.

I didn't even realise Mum left until a nurse walks in and

checks on my injured foot and my vitals. She tells me I am good to go, but not put pressure on my feet for a week to allow it to heal. And I'll have to regularly change the small bandage around my neck where the knife pierced the skin.

When I am in my bedroom again—it's clean now—my eyes move over every surface. Not a single thing is out of place. Aurora is in the bathroom, running me a warm bath, and all I can think about right now is Helia in jail.

He left thinking I hated him and did this to him when he poured so much of himself into me.

I need to tell him before it's too late.

Instead of fighting my case for my company and using this as an advantage to get it back, I will be fighting for him instead.

The thing is that he had more than enough time to plunge that knife inside of me. He could have done without a second thought, but he didn't. I saw him hesitate. I saw his eyes well up with tears, and I saw the love for me fight through the anger and betrayal.

I need to hear it from him that he doesn't despise me.

I won't be able to live with myself if he did.

"It's done. Ready to go in?" Aurora walks out of the bathroom, a messy bun on her head, a pastel-pink coloured sweater on top of a white skirt, and flats on her feet.

She smiles at me as I try to get up, rushing to me and helping me limp to the bathroom.

"I'll leave you to change and get in. If you need help, just give me a shout. I will be right outside."

I nod, biting my lip, and watch her walk away.

How can I keep crying when, once upon a time, I never once shed a tear?

The only person who has brought every single light back into my life isn't even here to witness it. The one person who actually bothered to get to know me, to fight against me and keep me on my toes, isn't here to even see that I love him with all my heart.

It feels like my love for him is as easy as water falling from a cup. Simple. Fast.

I don't care about his past. All I want is him.

So before I fell asleep that night, I decided to set everything right in the morning.

The next two days, Aurora sleeps with me on my bed. Remo drops by a couple of times, not bothering to walk inside the house at all. Aurora stays here and takes care of me, and I watch her the whole time.

I was supposed to do that for her. To get her trust and love back, and instead, I am in need of her.

Mum hasn't visited. I don't know of her whereabouts yet. The maids around the house still work, security detail still switch their schedules.

Everything feels and looks normal.

Except it's not.

It's the third day when I sit down in front of Aurora's laptop and take a deep breath for what I am about to search. My heart ticks inside me like a bomb, waiting for me to type and see destruction all over the press.

I haven't been out of the house, so I haven't been bombarded by the paparazzi or questioned about this whole situation. As soon as I type in Helia's name, I hold my breath.

But…

There is nothing.

I type his whole name, and still… nothing.

Then I type my name, then Remo's, then Aurora's. I try Glamorous magazine, and the only articles that have been published are about the internal management of Glamorous changing, but that was old news. Many people were applying for the new job opportunities, since Helia had just fired most managerial staff.

Who did this when Helia is in jail?

"Ambrose? Do you want to have dinner with me today? Downstairs?" I look up from the laptop and see Aurora in the doorway.

She wears a simple cream tank top with wide-legged cream trousers and slippers on her feet. I'm wearing black leggings, a sports bra, and white socks. The heat is really getting to us. Though a chilly air is still among us.

"Yeah."

As I walk into the dining room, my steps falter.

"Sorry, I didn't get to tell you. I hope it's okay he joins. He can leave if you want," Aurora says quietly.

I shake my head and continue towards the dining table.

Remo looks at me with a calculating gaze, watching my every move as he has always done, not uttering a single word even when Aurora sits beside him and the maids start to bring food out.

"I made all this for you since it's my last night here. I hope you like it." Aurora grins at me, and I smile back, eagerly looking over the dishes.

"There is garlic bread, lamb chops, Caesar salad, roasted potatoes, and hand-squeezed orange juice. That's Remo's favourite." She glances over at him with twinkling eyes, and he looks down at her.

I catch the smallest, most miniscule smile on his lips. As if the minute she looked at him, everything inside him melted.

"Okay, let's start before it gets cold." We all dig in, but I keep looking over at Remo, wondering if he did it.

How else would all the articles disappear?

"Out with it," I say.

Remo raises a brow. "Out with...?" He motions with his hand at me.

I drop my spoon that second, not wanting to miss this chance, especially since Aurora is with us currently.

"Did you have those articles erased?"

He continues to eat. "Yes."

"Did you remove Helia's and my name from them?"

"Yes."

"You paid them or bought the publishing news outlets out?"

"Paid."

"How?"

"The reporter you sent it to is part of Gustav Media, and

I happen to know the Chief Executive and he warned me, it put me in a tight spot but I managed to remove it all. Helia's software also helped."

"Why?"

This time, he looks up, a smirk taking over his face.

No answer.

Fine. I don't care about his reasons. He's saved me a lot of trouble.

"Is he… on trial?"

They both nod at me.

Would he even want to meet me?

"You should visit." Remo's face darkens, like it's killing him to say so.

"I don't think I should," I murmur, taking a sip of water, forcing down the thorns stuck in my throat.

"Ambrose," Remo grits out.

I look at Aurora, but she only shrugs.

"Remo?" I copy him, making Aurora laugh silently.

"Just go. If you don't go, I will kidnap you and take you there myself."

My eyebrows shoot up at his threat that doesn't feel like a threat at all.

"Why? Is something wrong? A reason you are practically forcing me to go?"

Remo looks to the side, his jaw ticking. "You will see."

I swallow at Aurora's calm demeanour.

Why are they acting like this?

Two days later, I am getting ready to go visit Helia when

my mother shows up.

"What are you doing here? Why did security even let you in?"

"Ambrose, listen to me, please," Mum begs, but I shake my head. "If your sister's husband cares about you and that good-for-nothing guy, if you think these people around you care about you, then you should think again. I have lived amongst these people. I have been in your position, Ambrose. You need me."

I sigh, rubbing my temple.

"Listen to me, dear. Remo never does anything unless it benefits him. Ask him, if he could remove the email I sent through to news channels, why hasn't he gotten that guy out of jail by now?"

My body tenses when her words poke through my mind.

"You said I destroyed your life, but those around you are doing a much better job than me. I tried to help you by arranging a marriage to someone powerful. You could save money, have your name around the elite circle, then divorce him if it's terrible. You are smart. You could—"

"How little do you think of me, Mum?"

She opens her mouth, but I raise my hand.

"You don't think I could become what I want to without the help of a man? Without marriage? What have I been doing all these years? Sitting around and shopping with my daddy's money? No. I earned that money. I got us this mansion. I got us the money you spend, and every single penny that flows in and out of the Torre mansion. I am the brain behind Glamorous's success. So why do you think I would struggle without a male figure in my life? Leave. I don't want to hear any more of your nonsense. Get out," I grit out.

"That's it? You will cut ties with me just like that?" She raises a brow, arrogance still dripping from her mouth.

"Get the fuck out, Leysa." I drop the familial sentiment just as I am dropping her.

She turns and walks away. I ensure she has left the property, then I remove her from the entry list, block her cards, block her phone number, and order a service to remove her belongings from the house. I have no more forgiveness left to give her. She'll get nothing more from me.

Instead of heading towards my original destination, I take a detour and go to Cainn enterprises. I step out at the tall black tower amongst the city of London, with the powerhouse of London working at the top of it.

Forget the monarchy in Britain, the man who has funded and backed most recent politicians is Remo, and now I realise Helia has been hidden in the shadows of his success. They work hand in hand, together; one cannot exist without the other.

So the question prods in my mind again.

Why didn't Remo help Helia by releasing him from prison yet?

"You can go in there."

I nod at Remo's assistant with a polite smile and walk inside, ready to face him once more.

"Are you actually working on releasing Helia?" I snap.

Remo laughs. "Good morning to you, too, Ms Torre."

I narrow my eyes at him. "Are you?"

"It's a hard job. It will take time." He shrugs, but I don't believe him.

I truly don't.

"I find that very hard to believe, brother-in-law."

His eyes snap to me, dark, menacing, a threat in them because of the tone of my voice.

"On my way here, I called the prison of London, asking about any updates in the process of appeal for Helia Nashwood. Only to hear that there has been no appeal. There hasn't been a single demand for release or any lawyers visiting him."

Remo's eyes darken.

"Tell me, Remo. Why the fuck haven't you asked for an appeal?"

41

AMBROSE

"Careful how you talk to me, Ambrose. Threats won't work well with me," he grits out.

His voice is the only clear indication that he is feeling threatened by me. His hands rest casually on the table, his body relaxed, and not a single muscle in his face moves or tics.

"If you think, for one second, that I will sit back and watch you leave him in there, you are mistaken." I point a finger at him. "You need to bail him out. The appeal needs to be done right this second." I slam a hand on the table, my voice dropping low.

Remo raises a brow, joining his hands on the table. "Do you know what I could do to you? I could have you killed and gone." A small muscle in his jaw twitches. That's all I need to see to know he is fuming.

A smirk travels across my lips. "Your wife will love

handing you the divorce papers if you carry through with that threat."

Remo stills, his unwavering eyes fixed on me.

A second ticks by.

Then another.

And I know the victory here is mine.

His love for Aurora won't allow him to harm me in any way, not when we have been growing closer again, and one small mistake from him could have Aurora suspicious. She isn't dumb, nor is she a mindless fool.

She may be forgiving, but not when it comes to those she loves.

Grabbing my bag, I turn around, happiness a piercing light in the darkness I was drowning in.

"Two days."

I look over my shoulder at his hardened face and smile.

"That's right."

I flick my hair over my shoulder and make my way outside.

"Miss Ambrose."

My head snaps up, and I rise from the waiting room chair. My trembling hands become harder to hide with each step I take closer to the visiting room.

With my heart in my throat, the only thing I can think

about is Helia's hate and his raging fury. How could I ever ask for forgiveness for something I didn't do?

The tall, muscled guard holds the door open, and I nod at him on my way in.

I hold my breath.

For a second.

Two.

Three.

Until I am seated in the grey plastic chair.

The clear glass in front of me keeps me separated from Helia's wrath, and his handcuffs restrain him from reaching for me.

Tears gather in my eyes, but I blink them away. Now is not the time for me to get emotional. I have to set records straight with him. I need to clear up this misunderstanding and build a happily ever after for myself.

The lock turns and the door on the other side opens. My mouth opens with a small gasp as Helia walks in.

His hands are cuffed, but he is as handsome as ever, even in his prisoner uniform of grey trousers and shirt, showing off his muscles, with his tattoos peeking out. His hair falls into his eyes, unkempt and unruly.

My hand flies to my mouth, and the minute he raises his head and his eyes align with mine, my world tilts and explodes.

Those emerald diamonds collide with my own, and I forget how to breathe.

I remember how I fell in love with him and how far I

could go for him.

He couldn't have been bailed out due to the evidence against him, but we need him out before our trial. Remo will be pivotal in getting Helia out.

"Helia." The whisper falls from my lips.

I watch him settle into the seat in front of me. He doesn't speak, nor does he look me in the eye longer than a second before he looks away.

The door shuts behind me, and we are cloaked in silence.

My lower lip trembles, but I bite it, holding myself together.

"Helia," I try again, my voice croaking.

He looks up for a second at me, and it feels as if I've been holding my breath, just waiting for him to look at me.

He doesn't speak.

No jokes.

No remarks.

"What are you doing?" I snap.

He blinks, the tendons in his neck flexing.

"How dare you leave me like this?" I continue, speaking in the only way I know. "How dare you not believe me? How could you not trust me, Helia?" My hands shake in my lap. "Was our love this weak?"

I keep looking between his eyes, trying to find anything, but I come up empty. His jaw tics as he stares at me, his eyes so intense I feel them cut through me.

"Mum left. I kicked her out before she could do anything more. I've sent police after her for a domestic violence case and have her locked up. Aurora helped me. She stayed over at my house and looked after me. Remo even came a couple of times. Everything happened. Everything settled."

My voice drops to a whisper. "Except you."

I look at my lap, at my pale, trembling hands. The prisons need to do a better job of keeping the temperature warm.

"You left. You didn't trust me enough. You found me guilty of a crime I never committed. I know I wrote that email, but I wasn't thinking. Mum had just said some things to me that really hurt me. I was losing you because you hid yourself from me. I didn't have Aurora. I didn't have my company. I was lost, running out of options, and still... I didn't send it. I couldn't."

When I lift my eyes, I find a rush of emotions in his. Like an angry storm waiting to strike destruction.

"Ambrose." His strong voice echoes around the room. "Won't you ask me?"

He lifts a brow and leans forward, resting his arms on the small separator between us.

"Won't you ask me if I have lost?" he says.

"Lost what?" I frown.

He inhales, his brows dipping, and he looks the very exact image of a lover admitting defeat in front of his love.

"My heart." He leans back in his chair, runs a hand through his hair, and looks to the side before looking at me again.

And then a curved smile touches his lips.

"I fucked up. With the only woman in my life I'd be

398

willing to go to these lengths for." He chuckles to himself, shaking his head.

"I don't understand, Helia." Why isn't he asking for proof? Why isn't he blaming me?

"You, Ambrose, took everything from me. How could you make me love you so much that even when hate took over me for a second, I still couldn't hurt you? I couldn't handle seeing you in pain because of me."

My heart thunders inside of me. It flutters and races with each word coming out of his mouth.

"It's not my first time in here. Stop stressing, Emerald. When I get out, I will claim you, a ring around your finger, the biggest diamond you want, the most expensive wedding gown, the biggest wedding hall. I will give it all to you all. We both collided in a way that the universe could be laughing at us right now. Two of the most unlikely people have fallen in love. How does that work?" He raises his brows with a smile.

"Helia." I scramble closer to the divider between us. "You... Even if you fell into the ocean, I would find you. Even if you drown me with you, I would accept death if it meant loving you till my last breath. Never doubt me. Never doubt my love for you." I place a hand against the glass, and he raises his own, placing it against mine.

"You will rise to the top, Ambrose. You will be right among the people who have always thought of you as little. You will rule this kingdom. I promise to get you there." He tilts his head, his eyes following a lone tear falling down my cheek. "Don't cry, baby."

I start laughing, wiping the tear away.

"When I get out—"

"Promise you will?"

Helia stops, a smirk pulling at his lips, and he looks more handsome than ever. "Your love is a spell. You have me hooked on you; you have me dancing to your tune. Nothing will keep me away from you. Okay?" He dips his chin. "Okay, Ambrose?"

I give a jerky nod. "O-Okay."

He smiles. "Good girl. Now go back to work. I will be out soon. There is only so long they can keep me in here."

I frown. "What do you mean?"

"Remo didn't tell you?"

I shake my head.

"The prison governor practically eats from Remo's hand."

My mouth drops open while Helia's laugh booms through the room.

"You will need a long paper for me to name the people who bow to Remo. Crazy world we live in."

"The elite circles… the ones Dad wanted to get into," I whisper, my eyes wide.

Helia helped Remo rise to the top of this circle.

"How does one get into this circle?"

Helia chuckles, and a cold shiver touches me at the empty sound.

"You get on Remo's good side or you have an insane

amount of money. You can also make dirty deals with Remo, which provides you with more power through his connections, hence the private parties every so often. It's a circle full of people hiding their dirty work."

"You can't be saying this here," I look around for cameras.

"Any and all video footage of me in here will be removed by me personally. It's also currently being monitored by Remo's men. Don't worry."

I take in a shuddering breath, not realising a side of London existed like this, but then again, why wouldn't it?

"Are there any deals you or Remo have made with people that are outrageous?"

Helia lifts an amused brow at me. "What do you want to hear?" He crosses his arms, sitting back into the seat like being in a jail cell doesn't bother him at all.

And here I was, worried sick about this man.

"Remo's random purchases of some private islands? Me getting yachts? Or me erasing murders from the eye of public and Remo making deals with many people who end up owing him favours?"

I instantly look around, glancing up at the cameras in the room and trying to see the guard outside the door behind him.

Helia's empty laugh snatches my attention back.

"Not a single soul can touch me in here or ruin me. They will need more than a big army and a helicopter to keep me in here."

I have a very, very bad feeling while looking into the dark forest of Helia's eyes, knowing that I am his obsession. He's wrapped around me like a tangled web of yarn.

The only way out is through death for me and him.

42

AMBROSE

I researched more about what Helia told me, and it seems the previous circle of elite are dead, and all these mysterious deaths couldn't be looked too deeply into because their families wanted privacy and also due to insufficient evidence.

No one batted an eye because they were killed a couple of years apart and in different ways. These deaths looked like they were suicides, accidents, and even natural deaths, and yet my gut tells me Helia and Remo have been building an empire very, very carefully for years.

And no one caught on, and if they did, Helia and Remo would be on top of them.

To have the head mayor of London and even secretary of state to be a slave to Remo, for some politicians to want into the Elite circle, it was bound for my father to want this 'investment' from Remo. It was his only way to truly get an in to the group.

The five main family names in the elite circle are: Cainn, Anta, Lonan, Gustav, and Dame. The Dames have a loose link to the underworld, similar to the mafia, though I cannot be certain.

Remo may not be in the mafia, but this elite circle hides crimes, illegal diamond smuggling, money laundering, prostitution, and so much that I may not even be touching the tip of the iceberg.

As everything fell into place, I found that an appeal had been made for Helia and he was getting out today, three days after my visit to him.

I'm anxiously waiting for him to walk out the doors; I keep pacing, walking in the circles. I've practically burned a hole in the ground.

Chewing on my lip, I constantly look over at the front gates of the prison. It's foreboding, with tall concrete walls extending for miles on either side, topped by rolls of barbed wire.

The creak of the door snatches my attention.

Helia steps out with an all-black outfit just as the sun bursts out from behind a cloud and shines down on him. It highlights his stupidly perfect face and the tattoos peeking out from under his t-shirt.

I sprint towards him.

I jump into his arms, and he spins me around.

The smile on my face is the widest it has ever been.

"I never want to spend another day apart from you," He-

404

lia grumbles, his face in the crook of my neck.

I tighten my arms around his neck.

"I missed you," I mumble.

It feels like I've taken a hit of my drug of choice. Helia has pumped strength back into my body just by hugging me. Knowing he doesn't hate me feels better than any high.

I lean back, my hair falling to one side as Helia holds me up.

I kiss him.

I kiss him a second longer.

This is the end of this torture for me.

"Live with me so I can keep breathing. Move in with me so I can keep living," Helia says against my lips.

My face lights up, and Helia tucks a strand of hair behind my ear, cupping my cheek.

"Say yes. Please say yes," he pleads.

"I will. You know I will. Where else will I go?" I hug him once more, finding home in his arms.

"You said it was impossible for you to live in London longer than two years, though," I murmur with Helia carrying me to the green Ferrari he gifted me.

"I have left a trail of bodies with each step you took. You think some cameras will keep me away from you? You think anyone could stop me?"

I have faith in his words.

As we drive at a hundred miles per hour through the rich thick forest, I know that Helia will stop at nothing to keep me. He will destroy the sun if needed and pluck every star from the sky if I wanted to live in the dark.

Helia is my impossible wish coming true.

Despite him being an obsessive monster within the Elite circle, I won't walk away from him.

43

HELIA

Pressing on the gas pedal, the speed of my car pushes me against the seat as I race after Remo's midnight Bugatti Chiron on the open streets of London.

A dark smile touches my lips. I grip the steering wheel harder, switching lanes from to the left, avoiding a car as he does the same from two cars in front of me. By the end of the day, he will have a shattered Bugatti due to his stupid decision of keeping me locked up for longer than we had decided.

A laugh spills out of me when I notice him narrowly missing a white BMW trying to switch lanes from left to middle.

My heart pounds. I watch the speedometer rise the longer I follow him, and as when as we reach an empty roundabout, he swerves in front of me, smoke rising from his back tyres. I swing my steering wheel to the right, too, pulling up the handbrake as I follow closer than ever when he takes the third exit.

"You are so fucking done today."

He wanted to drive himself, knowing I was coming the second I left that fucking jail. I was coming to find him as soon as I dropped Ambrose off at her house, telling her I would be back soon.

My visit to Remo is long overdue.

Taking a deep breath, I press the gas pedal harder and reach the back of his Bugatti. He switches lanes to the left, and I follow, then moves to the middle. I chase right behind.

As soon as an empty plot of land comes into view, Remo takes the turn and starts to swerve, turning at a one-eighty angle, making me slam my brakes.

Fucker.

The dust rises from his drift, and as it fizzes out, we both are left facing each other, a crazy smile on my face and a deep frown on his.

Exiting his car with one polished shoe in front of the other, Remo rips off his jacket and throws his tie to the floor. Opening my door, he pulls me out, but I land a punch to his face before he has the chance to.

And a second.

And a third. Remo pulls me up, punches me twice and jumps high, slamming his shoe into my chest. I stagger back.

"You fucking psycho!" Remo grits out, panting, watching me run my hand over my lower lip, blood painting my skin.

"Psycho? You shouldn't have left me locked in there. Big mistake. Big fucking mistake."

Remo runs a hand through his hair, mirroring the colour of his Bugatti.

"We decided I would be in there for two days, max. And what did you do?" I stalk towards him, grabbing at his shirt.

"Fuck off." He steps back, keeping his frozen eyes locked on me.

"You knew the blame would fall on you. You knew this would come out the minute Ambrose uncovered it. No matter who sent it to the media, it was bound to happen." He points his finger in my face.

I admit, we planned this part long ago, but why the fuck had he kept me in there for long?

"Is this your petty revenge for when I told Aurora about you?"

He doesn't move a single muscle, but the small tic of his jaw reveals it all for me.

I didn't think he would be so childish about his revenge and take it when I needed to be there for Ambrose.

"You know when to strike, don't you?" I laugh, shaking my head. I need to constantly watch my back with him.

You can never, and I mean never, predict Remo.

Even within our carefully laid plans, he switches at the last minute without telling me, and I have to readjust because he doesn't know how to keep to the script.

"Go talk to your prison governor friend and fuck off out

of here before I blow up your Bugatti," I snap.

Remo's jaw tics twice this time, and a flicker of amusement rises in me.

Actually, that isn't a bad idea.

He can afford more than one, anyway.

"Or maybe I can ask Aurora about what you were doing while you refused to get me out. What will she say when she finds out that you were just being a petty little bitch?"

This time, Remo's lip twitches as if he finds something humorous.

"What?" Confusion fills me like a poison.

Remo's tight shoulders relax, and the fury drains from him.

"What will you tell her?" He takes a step towards me this time, looking down at the ground. "That we killed her father? That I didn't take out her sister's lover? That you couldn't cover your tracks? Or that her husband is a murderer?" A loud laugh booms out of him, and he throws his head back. "Oh, she knows. She knew the minute she saw me drenched in blood from head to toe, not a single speck of clean skin." He looks back at me, daggers in his glare.

"No, that is old news now," I counter. "How will you tell her about the little secrets you know about her friend? Don't have anything to say about Ruel Fargos?"

His eyes spark in anger.

A beat of silence passes between us. The longer he is silent, the bigger my victory.

"I think you should pay us a visit for dinner. I'll tell Aurora to invite you over for dinner in two days."

"Will she make the dinner herself? I just love her food."

Remo sharply turns back, making me burst out laughing. "Helia."

"Tell her I want mashed potatoes. I'm really craving them. Prison food isn't—"

"Get in your car," he interrupts.

"Maybe even some of her special—"

Remo pulls out his gun and aims it at me, making me shut up.

"All right, mister. I'm going. I want to see how this dinner will end."

I climb into my car, and before Remo can get in his car, I slam on my gas and smash the back of his Bugatti. Because fuck him. His sharp eyes turn to me, but I salute him with two fingers and a smile and reverse out.

Oh, what fun this dinner will be.

"I know you are here," I hear Ambrose call out from her bedroom.

She's watering her plants in a lounge set, hair down and curled in waves.

"About time you showed up, I was going to climb into bed and act dead till you freaked out for taking so long," she mumbles.

A laugh spills out of me. "I got us an invite to dinner at the Cainn mansion in two days."

Ambrose straightens, her face now my moon during the darkest nights. "Really?"

I walk closer to her, cupping her cheek and letting my lips trail over my cheeks all the way down to her neck, where I feather her with small kisses. Her hands dive into my hair and hold the back of my neck.

"Yes. Though you may see some fights happen because I love pissing Remo off."

Ambrose's laugh feeds my dying heart like a miracle medicine.

"You love pissing everyone off, but Remo seems to—oh…"

I suck at her pulse, and her hands fist my hair tighter.

"What did you do that… will piss Remo off?"

I let her go and grab her cream-coloured lounge top and take it off, my breath catching when I see she isn't wearing a bra.

Her soft pink peaks are a magnet for my lips.

"Stop talking about another man while I'm trying to seduce you, Ambrose."

Her hand cups my chin and lifts my face, but I'm not willing to let go of the heavenly sight of her full tits in front of me.

When my eyes collide with the melted chocolate in hers, my heart skips a beat.

The way she looks at me? I know she will be ready to

fight any battle for me the way I would for her.

"I love you," she whispers, almost shyly.

Her lashes flutter when I don't respond, and she glances away before looking back at me, unaware of the storm she has created inside of me. It's twisting harder and harder, ready to wreck everything in its destruction.

"Again. Say it again."

She smiles. "I love you."

Another skip of a beat.

"Again."

Her smile widens and stars dance in her eyes. "I love you, Helia."

My head falls back with a smile.

"I love you too, baby. I love you. I love you. I love you." I press kisses all over her face, neck, chest, then her lips.

"Now take off your trousers. I need to be home, and that's inside of you."

With her trousers off, her legs hooked around my waist, I unzip my own jeans and stand still.

"Loving you feels just like hating you. It's strong, it's fierce, it's intense, and it's me and you." I slam into her, stealing her breath.

"I hate you and want to strangle you all the same, just with me inside of you."

Ambrose slams a hand on my shoulder, her eyes snapping to mine. "Are you going to actually fuck me or chatter like a teenager in love?"

My grip turns punishing on her thighs. "This is why I

hate you."

A soft smile touches her lips. It vanishes when I start fucking her, driving her up the wall, my cock deep inside her tight pussy.

Riding the high with her is like conquering the world with this crazy woman in my arms.

"Do I look fine? It's not too much, right?" Ambrose says, a small pinch between her eyebrows as we stand in front of Remo's front door.

She's wearing a sky-blue dress that is pinched at her waist and held up by thin straps on her shoulders. She clutches a white purse in her hand and wears gold jewellery and white heels.

The dress is sleeveless. That alone has me weak in the heart.

"You look like you should take your clothes off." I wink at her.

"Helia!" She slaps me on the arm just as the door opens. "Helia."

We both turn towards the door to see Kamari, her curly hair big and frizzy in the heat today.

"I may find some nests in that hair. How many birds do you have in there?" I ask.

Ambrose pushes me away as she walks in front of Kamari, who greets her with a polite smile while glaring daggers at me over her shoulder.

"Ambrose, Aurora is waiting for you in the dining room. Go in."

"Thank you. You look beautiful today," Ambrose says.

"I think someone didn't understand that being rude gets you kicked out," Kamari comments as I walk past her.

"I was just making an observation about your hair."

Kamari smiles tightly. "Sure. I suggest turning around and walking back the way you came."

"Careful there. I might think you are jealous of my personality." I grin at her.

She sighs and shakes her head. "Just get inside, Helia. You are like an annoying child." She walks past me. Of course she would think that.

The dining room is an open plan of the kitchen and dining room combined, but what really captures my attention are the open sliding doors and the table outside in the garden. It's decked out with sunflowers in the middle of the white tablecloth.

And everyone is wearing shades of blue and white.

Even Remo. His navy-blue dress shirt is tucked into white trousers. He's wearing fucking sunglasses as he taps away on his phone.

Aurora is greeting Ambrose, looking very pregnant in her white dress that reaches her calves and white strappy heels. Her hair is down and curled.

My gaze scans the extensive garden, and I spot Ruel

talking on his phone, under the tall, old tree that is shading the table. He's wearing sky-blue trousers, a white t-shirt and sunglasses.

Was I supposed to wear sunglasses, too? What's with this new trend?

I walk towards Aurora to greet her but catch Remo looking straight at me. I grin.

I raise my eyebrows playfully at him.

"Helia, thank you for coming. It's a nice summer day, isn't it?"

I nod, keeping an eye on Remo, who is walking over to me.

"Remo, Helia is here," she says.

"I can see that," he grumbles, keeping his eyes on me.

"Oh, hey," Ruel says, then walks over to grab a glass of water.

"Why are you both looking at Ruel like that?" Aurora whispers.

I look at her, then at Remo, then back at her.

"Ask Remo." I walk away towards Ambrose and drop into the seat next to her.

"It's beautiful, isn't it?" she says.

I nod, silently watching Aurora and Remo talking in hushed tones while Kamari drops into the chair next to Ruel, who places his arm on the back of her chair.

Remo walks over and sits down next to Ruel, and Aurora sits down next to me. Then servers start bringing food out.

"I cooked everything, guys. Compliments only, or else

the door is right there," Aurora announces, looking pointedly at me.

"No complaints from me." I raise my hands.

"Keep a leash on your man, Ambrose," Aurora teases, and Ambrose laughs from next to me.

"I don't need to. He's got attachment issues." She gives me a side eye.

"That's for sure," Remo grumbles into his glass.

"Right. Ruel, how is football going?" I ask instead.

Remo's eyes burn holes in the side of my face.

"Good. Got a game again in Monaco soon, so getting ready for that, attending the F1 race there, too. Great couple of weeks coming up."

Everyone starts to dig into their food. Platters with little sandwiches, fruit, cheese boards, and so much more get set on the table.

"Dinner looks a little different today, I thought it would be night time," Ruel says with a smile on his lips.

"Okay, Ruel, we need to have a best friends day now. You stole the words out of my mouth," I say.

"Stop it, the weather was too good to pass up on having lunch," Aurora argues with a sigh.

Everyone around the table laughs, except for the grumpy motherfucker called Remo. I swear this man has never laughed in his life.

"Were you born here, Ruel?" I ask.

"Yes, all thirty-three years of my life."

I watch Remo slowly start to smirk at my attempts to

irritate him. Now *that* is something out of ordinary.

"Something funny, Mr Cainn?" I ask.

He shakes his head. "Nothing,"

"You—"

"We should play a game after this! Truth or dare. It will be fun," Aurora interrupts, casting a brief glance at Remo.

His smirk grows all the while he keeps looking at me.

When I look back at Aurora, I see her eyes flick to Ruel for a second.

He told her.

He fucking told her.

Of course he did.

Remo never loses.

Never mind that then. I will find other ways to harass him.

The dinner continues, and I stay quiet. Every time I look at Ambrose, she's got a big, genuine smile on her face, and that is all that matters to me in the end.

I will die protecting that smile.

I will kill while protecting that smile.

No deception ever felt darker than one I had with her, but it turned more real and more dangerous than ever.

It will never end.

44

AMBROSE

A few months later

"I have a surprise for you."

"My eyes are closed. Don't worry. Bring it on." I laugh.

Helia's surprises are always a little weird.

Helia and I have spent the past three months trying to figure out how to work and live between two places. I am not ready to give up the Torre mansion, and with Mum out of the picture, it's only me living there, but Helia wants me to move in with him.

While I can keep the Torre mansion and still live with him, his home is too far away for me to travel back and forth every day into Central London. I have also been waiting for the right moment to ask him what we will do about the working conditions between us. I still want ownership of Glamorous, but Helia needs it to hide his cash for two years, and while it's nearly a year since he has been sitting at the top, I don't know what he will do in twelve months.

We really need to sit down to discuss it, but the past three months have felt like a fever dream, like a dark fairytale. We still fight. We disagree hard. Then we end up fucking it out. That's one thing I love about us, because it gets intense, Helia grabs my throat and kisses the soul out of me.

Helia doesn't love softly. He has more harsher sides to him than soft, though he has never made me feel anything but loved. Whenever I stay over at his house, he wakes me up with breakfast. I often walk out of the bedroom and find him shirtless, cooking for me, with Blaze zipping through the house, full of energy.

We run together through the forest near his home all the way to the cliff edge, where the small waterfall flushes out my worries, and Blaze has the time of his life shooting through the sky while we both catch our breath.

Sometimes, Helia joins me while I do yoga at the end of the day. His wandering hands always end the practise early, because he can't keep his hands to himself and fucks me right then and there.

Life feels like life.

Like it's worth living.

During the past few months, I haven't had any thoughts of not wanting to live. I haven't for one second thought I'm unlovable, and Helia has been there to support me on days I've felt down.

"You know, I want to come over today. I was thinking we could—"

"No." Helia stops me.

I frown, my eyes still shut. "Why? You have been saying no for the past couple of weeks."

"I told you; I am renovating some parts of the house, and it's not safe for you to visit. I'm not even staying there at the moment."

That doesn't make sense.

"You can open your eyes now."

The moment I do, I spot Blaze sitting on his shoulder in my driveway, tilting his cute head at me. Helia is wearing a black windbreaker with its hood on and black trousers. We both came back from the office a couple of minutes ago, but he told me not to go inside yet because he had a surprise.

With autumn now here, the skies are darker. Brown and orange leaves are scattered across wet pavements, and the sharp wind pierces my skin.

"What's this?" I take the white paper he offers me, scanning the words.

When I finally register what this is, the paper shakes in my hand, and my breath falls in short, quick puffs.

"Helia... this..."

His eyes crinkle in the corner, his lips lifting in a smirk.

The emerald of his eyes glows as he watches tears form in my eyes. My knees weaken, and I drop to my knees, my hand in front of my mouth, eyes still on him.

"You gave me Glamorous?"

He drops to his hunches in front of me, his hands finding my cheeks, eyes trailing down my cheeks, following the tears.

"Don't cry. Your makeup will get ruined."

A laugh spills out of me. Placing the papers next to me on the pavement, I launch myself into his arms.

"Thank you," I mumble into his neck, my heart racing.

"How will you hide your cash?" I lean back.

"I found myself another target. I couldn't do this to you anymore. I want you to live out your dreams and not think I am using you for your company either."

I shake my head. I trust him.

"Will you move after the next year is over?" I ask quietly.

Helia's eyes feel magnetic the longer I look into them. I have found the closest colour of his eyes is an actual emerald. He has gifted me many emeralds now, and it has become my favourite precious stone.

"I may need to move every once in a while, but I will always come back," he confesses, his eyebrows falling, his voice quiet.

"I'll follow you. You know I will."

He looks up at the sky as a thunder clap rumbles above us, then the faint smell of rain fills my lungs.

"I know you will. To hide my actual work, I will need to move around sometimes. We can travel around, visit any country you want—"

I kiss him.

The first drops of rain fall on us, and the wind ruffles my hair. I lean back and stand up, and Helia follows.

The next couple of droplets fall, and Helia turns to look for Blaze while I watch him.

He walks down the driveway, jogging towards the gate, where Blaze sits on top. Blaze shoots off and goes straight for the roof of the mansion, and Helia sighs, shaking his head as if tired of a child misbehaving.

If we were to have children, Helia will protect him or her just like he protects me.

I watch him walk back to me with a grin on his face, the rain drenching us both. He shakes his head to shake the rain out of his hair but to no avail. The rain comes down harder, and I smile at him.

He walks up to me, and I see my whole future with him.

I see him with me as we kiss at the altar. I see him with our kids. I see him with me as we travel; him hugging me whenever I feel down, and I see myself giving him my all.

Reaching me, Helia grabs my hand and retrieves the papers from the ground, then walks me inside our home. And I follow him, as I will for the rest of my life.

It's you and me, Helia.

EPILOGUE

AMBROSE

❝She looks just like you," I comment.

Aurora smiles at Lavinia, who yawns with her eyes closed.

"She's got our nose, don't you think?" she asks, and I nod.

"She does. Oh my God. She does!" Aurora laughs.

She gave birth just three weeks ago. I didn't want to bombard her with me being there, but I did visit after her delivery, gifting her flowers, and today I brought many little hampers with baby clothes, cute bottles, little bows, and dresses for her.

"I got her really cute little dresses. I will be her favourite aunt, I know it already."

Aurora lifts a brow, then looks over at Kamari, who rolls her eyes.

"I already took the title, thank you," Kamari counters

playfully.

I shrug.

"She can tell who her favourite aunt is, can't you?" I softly rub a finger on Lavinia's cheek.

She twist, a small frown on her face that kind of, sort of looks like a smile.

"See? She smiled at me!"

Kamari rushes over from where she was standing behind me.

"Come on, Lavinia. I got you different flavoured foods. Don't you think you should say it's me?"

The poor girl doesn't even know what's happening with Kamari and me arguing over who her favourite aunt is.

I really like Kamari. She was there for Aurora when I wasn't, and I don't take that lightly. I will forever cherish her for supporting for my little sister. She has given a lot to Aurora and vice versa. Their friendship is truly heartwarming.

"I have to go now, but if you need anything, let me know, okay?" I get up and kiss Aurora on the cheek, then Lavinia, departing after a hug from Kamari.

I head downstairs and see Remo making his way towards the staircase with Venezia behind him, holding some files in her hand.

"Venezia," I say with a smile.

She looks up at me and smiles, too.

"Hi, leaving already?"

I hug her and nod.

"Yes, I have some work to get done before tomorrow's board meeting. It's getting hectic."

Remo nods at me and walks past me.

"Don't mind him. He has been on edge since Aurora gave birth. He cares a lot, and seeing him as a father and husband really set some bars high for me." Her eyes soften, making me smirk.

"Why? Have someone in mind?"

She bursts out laughing. "I have no time right now. I just turned twenty and want so many things from life. I am so grateful for my brother to have given me this new life, away from what I had in Edinburgh, and I love it. He isn't overbearing, giving me my personal space and wanting the best for me. Aurora, she's been my rock in this, there for me when I felt down. Those two have been my angels."

Tears pool in her eyes, and she fiddles with the papers in her hand.

"Focus on yourself. You are doing amazing Venezia. The right man will find you in the most unexpected place."

She nods, wiping away the tears and giving me a tight hug. "Won't keep you now. Go ahead. I want to meet Lavinia, too."

I nod and walk out, finding Helia talking to one of the guards to my left. When he spots me, he walks over, winking at me. I blush like a teenager in love, but I wouldn't have it any other way.

"What do you say? Want one for yourself?" He grins.

I huff, shaking my head. I lift my left hand in front of

him and wiggle my fingers in front of his face. "With no rings? I don't think so."

He frowns for just a moment. "Right." He chuckles, opening the passenger door of his Porsche for me, then walks around and climbs behind the wheel.

Once we are on the road, Helia's hand drops to my thigh. But that's no surprise; he does that quite often. When his hand climbs higher, my heart rate spikes.

"What are you doing?" I breathlessly mutter.

He removes his hand instantly. When I look over, he seems to be smiling like it was some kind of joke. I shake my head. It seems the sleepless nights have been getting to me. Working for this board meeting is creating dark circles under my eyes, but it's only a couple of days away.

They will be impressed, I am sure.

Since Helia resigned from Glamorous, he has taken over another smaller magazine business. It isn't a direct rival of Glamorous because it's smaller, but it works for him.

Twenty minutes into the ride, I realise we aren't going to the Torre mansion but to his house. I settle into the seat for the hour-long drive. When we emerge through the thick trees and arrive in front of his house, my heart jumps out of my chest at what is in front of me.

I hastily climb out of the car, my mouth dropping open at the mansion in front of me.

"You made it bigger?"

Helia walks towards the front door with me following behind.

He has extended the house with another level on top.

"Is this what you have been doing?"

"Yes."

"Why?"

"So you can live with me. You love it here, but one bed-room isn't enough for both of us. You need a bigger closet, a bigger bathroom, another couple of rooms, and an eleva-tor."

He takes me on a tour me around the new floor of the house, pointing out the elevator to the left of me, in front of the staircase.

"But why?"

He doesn't answer and keeps walking until we reach the rooftop with clear glass railings.

The wind is a little stronger up here, it being November doesn't help.

"Helia, why?" I blink, then blink again.

A plane flies right over us through the cloudy sky, emit-ting green smoke and leaving behind a cloudy shape of a green heart. Before me, Helia kneels on one knee, white flower petals under him, decorating the ground. There are two tall lamps on either side of me, emitting a soft golden hue with a white cloth connecting them.

"Helia." I take a step closer, and another, and another, until I am in front of him.

And this bastard is smirking.

"So you can have babies with me now."

I burst out laughing.

"That's not how you ask." I slap his shoulder, making him chuckle.

"I have lost my everything to you, Ambrose. Everything I hated, everything I despise, feels a lot sweeter and a lot more bearable with you by my side. I have found myself wanting to give you everything I own, to lay myself at your feet, to hand you the knife if killing me is what you want. It's impossible to think of a future without you. Whether you want it or not, you are stuck with me. There is no me without you, my emerald."

Drop by drop, tears fall down my cheeks, my heart throbbing with only one word.

Helia.

Helia.

"Will you marry me?"

I nod.

Helia takes the ring out of the box, one I didn't even notice, and slides it on my finger. An emerald diamond stone is surrounded by smaller circle-cut diamonds; there has been nothing more perfect for me.

Helia stands up, grabs my face, and gives me a kiss that seals our fate.

When he pulls away, we both are breathing heavily as rain pours down above us once more, as if in celebration of us becoming one.

I softly run my hands all over his face, over the scar across his eye, over his midnight hair, his nose, his cheeks, and his lips.

"I also kind of bought you an emerald mine."

"A mine?"

He nods cheekily.

"An actual mine?"

"But for emeralds," he murmurs against my lips.

"This was why you extended the house, right? So you can fill it with babies?"

He shrugs with a proud smile.

A laugh spills out of me, and Helia watches me with a grin under the rain.

The End

REVIEW

If you liked reading about Ambrose and Helia's story, I would love for you to drop a small review on Darkest Deception's Amazon page. Couple of words is more than enough to help an author. It also helps readers find their next favourite book of the year .

ACKNOWLEDGEMENTS

Helia and Ambrose have been with me for over 2 years now and I am brimming with excitement to have shared them with you all. Making this book come true is all due to my bestest friends that pushed me more than anyone to publish Helia's book, she quite literally almost even bullied me honestly. Helia caught her eye and it was done for her. I also want to thank my editors, my BETA readers and ARC readers who helped me shape this book into its best possible form.

ABOUT THE AUTHOR

Akwaah K is an author living somewhere in the UK while trying to finish a degree and write all the same. From bookstore trips when any inconvenience happens, to writing about soft morally grey characters just to see them fall in love. When not writing, an iced drink and a shopping trip heals it all for her.

ALSO BY AKWAAH K

STANDALONE:

Tangle Of Obsession

DECEPTION SERIES:

Sweetest Deception
Bitter Deception
Darkest Deception

Made in the USA
Columbia, SC
09 June 2025